T... ....Hall

Me.. the ph..... ....olings: unconvention..., ...ce.. ....ermined to make a difference in the world.

Raised at Haberstock Hall, Anne, Thea, Thomasia and Rebecca know that they have the means and the knowledge to help those less fortunate than themselves. Each with their own mission, they won't be dictated by the patriarchal confines placed on them. But is the world ready for the sisters to make their mark?

Generous in spirit and heart, can these women find men who will be their advocates rather than adversaries?

Meet the men worthy of these kindhearted women in:

Anne and Ferris's story
Lord Tresham's Tempting Rival

Thea and Edward's story
Saving Her Mysterious Soldier

Thomasia and Shaw's story
Miss Peverett's Scandalous Secret

All available now

And look out for Rebecca's story
Coming soon!

Author Note

Thomasia and Shaw's story is about being your authentic self even when society and opportunity reject who that self is. It is a struggle that was just as relevant in the 1850s as it is today. For Thomasia, the fight is both internal and external. Internally, she is conflicted about who she is supposed to be: A mother? A woman with passion? A woman hungry to love and be loved? And what of the girl she used to be, who loved dancing and parties? Is all of that to be sacrificed in order to be a mother? Externally, society has rejected her. Being a popular debutante was one thing, but being an unwed mother is not tolerated. Society defines her as a fallen woman, while the young lordling who got her pregnant is untouched by the scandal.

Thomasia refuses to accept society's verdict, committing herself to fighting for the girls who are likely to come after her and who will have fewer resources than she for dealing with their situations. For Thomasia, authenticity is tied to social justice. For Shaw, being true to himself, and true to his heart, means opportunities he's spent his adulthood cultivating will be lost to him just as he's on the cusp of achieving them. Are his ideals and his heart worth the sacrifice of other dreams? This is a question we face today in the twenty-first century as well.

I hope you enjoy Thomasia and Shaw's story,

Bronwyn

BRONWYN SCOTT

Miss Peverett's Secret Scandal

ISBN-13: 978-1-335-40780-1

Miss Peverett's Secret Scandal

For questions and comments about the quality of this book, please contact us at CustomerService@Harlequin.com.

Harlequin Enterprises ULC
22 Adelaide St. West, 41st Floor
Toronto, Ontario M5H 4E3, Canada
www.Harlequin.com

Printed in U.S.A.

Recycling programs for this product may not exist in your area.

Bronwyn Scott is a communications instructor at Pierce College and the proud mother of three wonderful children—one boy and two girls. When she's not teaching or writing, she enjoys playing the piano, traveling—especially to Florence, Italy—and studying history and foreign languages. Readers can stay in touch via Facebook at Facebook.com/bronwynwrites, or on her blog, bronwynswriting.blogspot.com. She loves to hear from readers.

Books by Bronwyn Scott

Harlequin Historical

Scandal at the Midsummer Ball
"The Debutante's Awakening"
Scandal at the Christmas Ball
"Dancing with the Duke's Heir"

The Peveretts of Haberstock Hall

Lord Tresham's Tempting Rival
Saving Her Mysterious Soldier
Miss Peverett's Secret Scandal

The Rebellious Sisterhood

Portrait of a Forbidden Love
Revealing the True Miss Stansfield
A Wager to Tempt the Runaway

The Cornish Dukes

The Secrets of Lord Lynford
The Passions of Lord Trevethow
The Temptations of Lord Tintagel
The Confessions of the Duke of Newlyn

Visit the Author Profile page
at Harlequin.com for more titles.

For the three girls in my life:
Catie, Brony and Rachel. The things that
matter are always worth fighting for.
The only person who gets to define you is you.
Choose to be your authentic self.

Chapter One

November 1855, Haberstock Hall, Hertfordshire

She was likely the only person in England who was looking forward to winter. Thomasia Peverett pressed her forehead against the windowpane of Haberstock Hall's music room and peered out into the gathering dusk, hoping to catch sight of snowflakes this early in the season. It was certainly cold enough. If she had her way it would snow indefinitely from now until May, although such weather was improbable. This part of Hertfordshire wasn't known for acquiring long-lasting accumulations of snow. That was too bad.

Snow was insulating. Scientifically, it kept the heat in. Socially, it kept people out. It was the latter she was banking on. Snow froze roads, and when it melted the muddy sludge left behind continued to make roads impassable.

Thomasia closed her eyes and wished for snowdrifts as tall as a man, drifts that would keep the world out a while longer.

'Come and sit by the fire, Tommie,' her sister Becca coaxed from the rug set before the hearth, where she was entertaining little Effie-Claire with a rattle and a stuffed bunny.

Effie-Claire gurgled in delight and Thomasia turned towards the sound of her baby daughter's laughter, unable to resist a smile despite her contemplative mood. She moved to the fire, taking a seat on the floor and tucking her skirts about her.

'I don't remember you liking winter so much when we were up in York last year.' Becca gave her a quizzing look as Effie-Claire crawled to her.

Thomasia let the sweet baby weight of the infant settle in her lap before answering. 'Last year was different.'

Last winter she'd been six months into a difficult pregnancy that had begun poorly and continued with much worry. By the middle of January she'd been confined to the security of her aunt's home, not even allowed the freedom of the garden for fear she might slip on the ice and do herself or the babe an unrecoverable injury.

For a girl who loved the outdoors and socialising with people, last winter had seemed interminable. But that girl was no more. She was a mother now, a mother bear in hibernation, fierce and defensive on behalf of her cub. Winter was no longer a prison, but protection for herself and her daughter. The coming winter meant she was safe at home, at Haberstock Hall, amongst her family, surrounded by love, snow and unnavigable roads that kept people at home and the world at bay.

Winter was not a season of curiosity, but spring was. Spring was the season of going abroad, of exploring the world, of seeking out the changes that had occurred while the world had lain dormant, seeing what had been wrought beneath winter's white blanket. Spring burgeoned with babies and beginnings. Spring was innocent. Winter was wise and wary.

Thomasia breathed in the soft baby scent of her little daughter, a reminder that to be wise and wary was better than being wild and reckless, although it had been wildness and recklessness that had brought Effie-Claire into her life.

Effie-Claire gripped her bodice with pudgy fingers, trying to pull herself up.

Becca laughed. 'She'll be walking soon, and then we'll really be on our toes.'

Thomasia frowned and dismissed the idea. 'She's not even a year old. It's too early for her to walk.'

It was all going so fast. Soon Effie-Claire would be too old to breastfeed, too old to sleep beside her in bed. An Effie-Claire who walked wouldn't be a baby so much as a toddler and Thomasia was already missing the baby.

'Mother always claims Anne walked early.' Becca held out her hands to Effie-Claire. 'I could make her a little walking contraption to help her along.' Becca was always inventing things.

Thomasia shook her head against the idea. 'Whenever she walks it will be soon enough.'

How was it that a year ago Effie-Claire hadn't even been born and now that little scrap of a baby, born a few weeks early, was nearly walking? Talking wouldn't be far behind, and questions would follow.

Thomasia pushed the thought away. There would be

time to contemplate answers to those questions. Surely she had a few years yet before Effie-Claire realised she was different from other children, or other children realised it for her. Children could be unintentionally cruel that way. Effie-Claire must never know her father didn't want her, didn't want *them*.

She glanced anxiously towards the window, as if expecting to see a face from the past at the panes. It was for the best that he'd walked away from them. She could appreciate that in hindsight. But such a thing would wound a child. She didn't want such hurt in Effie-Claire's life.

'He's not out there,' Becca offered quietly from the floor.

'I know.' But it was an old fear—one that had plagued her for months when she'd carried Effie-Claire. That Anthony would change his mind again and come to claim her baby in order to satisfy his great-aunt's will and she would be able to do nothing about it.

Once, she would have swooned at the thought of marriage to Lord Anthony Halston, but that had been before she knew the truth of him, even if that truth had come too late to save her. Someone else had married him this past summer, thank goodness. That marriage had made it possible for her to feel safe enough to return from York. They were beyond one another now. He need not darken her door again. His presence need not remind her of her foolishness and she would not give him the chance. She would do all in her power to ensure that their paths never crossed. Out of sight was out of mind. She, who had once loved the thrill of Town, would live out her life in a quiet village and be thankful. It was a penance she was happy to pay if it kept Effie-Claire safe.

The music room door opened, startling her with a draught from the corridor. 'Girls, you're not dressed for dinner yet,' her mother scolded with a smile, sweeping up her beloved granddaughter in her arms. 'We have guests tonight, don't forget. Mr Rawdon and his sister are coming.'

'Tonight? But the weather… Isn't it too cold to be out visiting?' Thomasia protested. She'd hoped their guests would stay at home and send their regrets. If she had a choice, she'd choose to spend the evening before the fire, playing with Effie-Claire.

'Mr Rawdon and Miss Susannah are good people. You will enjoy their company if you give them a chance. Seeing others will be healthy for you, Thomasia.' Her mother firmly shut down the protest for what it was—a chance to prolong her retreat. She never could put anything past her mother. 'You can't hide away here for ever.'

Thomasia disagreed. She *could* hide here, and she would for as long as possible—which meant until spring. She had no desire to cut that time short, although such seclusion wasn't easy. She was a social creature by nature. She'd become a recluse, a veritable hermit, by necessity.

'Mr Rawdon is our MP, Tommie. Even Thea and Anne think he's quite progressive,' Becca offered in support of their mother.

'Quite progressive for a man, you mean.' Thomasia shot her sister a look that said *You're supposed to be on my side*. Men were only progressive to a point—that point being when their grip on power was threatened.

Some men would agree to progressive politics in theory, but in practice they were hard-pressed to act on those beliefs when the time came. She'd met a few 'progressive' politicians in York and found them lacking.

'You could persuade him to your cause, Tommie,' Becca wheedled gently, dangling the one carrot besides Effie-Claire that could tempt Thomasia to act.

Thomasia would do anything for her daughter, or for The Cause—that cause being the advocacy for and the protection of women's rights when it came to health-care and their children.

Aunt Claire, Effie's namesake, with whom she and Rebecca had lived in York, had introduced her to The Cause early on in her pregnancy, when she'd been inclined towards self-pity. She'd been sick, depressed and entirely despondent, but Aunt Claire had had little sympathy for her self-pity.

'If the world frustrates you, Thomasia, do something about it,' she'd said. 'The world wants you to think you're alone. You're not. There are other women who want what you want: equality, protection, recognition before the law.'

And Aunt Claire had introduced her to those women, taking her to a meeting of those like-minded females in Coffee Yard Close. They'd welcomed her, pregnant belly and all. Thomasia had not looked back since.

The work of educating herself and educating others about the subtle and not so subtle suppression that kept women in a subservient position had been the antidote she'd needed. She missed that work now that she was home. She still kept up on the goings-on from the Coffee Yard group, but it wasn't the same as being there and being actively involved by talking to others about The Cause.

When she'd left York, earlier that autumn, the ladies had been just beginning to rally support against an attempt to overturn the 1845 Bastardy Act, which allowed unmarried mothers to petition for an affiliation order that would require the father of her child to pay maintenance. The attempt to repeal the Act was being engineered by a Lord Stanton, and would be introduced at the upcoming Parliamentary session in January. Thomasia smiled to herself, an idea taking shape. Perhaps there *was* something she could do. Perhaps Mr Rawdon might have his uses after all?

Becca caught her expression. 'You're already thinking of ways to persuade our Mr Rawdon—I knew it,' she crowed.

Thomasia rose from the floor and shook out her skirts. 'Well, I can at least survey the terrain. The Cause doesn't have so many allies that we can ignore the potential for more.'

An MP would be a coup for The Cause. They'd made inroads using newspapers to promote their agenda with the general public, but they had yet to gain a strong toehold with actual members of Parliament—proof to Thomasia that male openness to progressive politics stopped when action was needed.

Catherine Peverett glanced between her two daughters. 'Just be polite, Thomasia. We *like* Mr Rawdon, and I'd rather not have the best company within miles scared off before the cheese course. Besides, one catches more flies with honey than with vinegar, as the saying goes.'

Thomasia dropped a kiss on her mother's cheek as

she headed for the door. 'I know, Mother. I'll be good. I promise.' She lifted Effie-Claire from her mother's arms. 'I'll drop this little darling off in the nursery before I change.'

Effie-Claire, of course, need not worry about dinner and politics with guests. She'd be tucked away with a maid. The Rawdons would leave none the wiser regarding her existence for the time being. But Thomasia was well aware that such a strategy was a temporary one only. When spring came and it was time to be out and about there'd be no more hiding. By then, both she and The Cause would be out in the open. It would be nice to go armed if Mr Rawdon could be persuaded.

Suddenly dinner was shaping up to be more interesting. The thrill of having a purpose outside of Effie-Claire began to hum in her veins, like a little piece of herself coming back to life.

Armed with a newfound sense of usefulness, Thomasia dressed carefully for dinner, selecting a gown of green silk taffeta trimmed with red velvet ribbon. The gown was fashionable, but discreet enough for the country, with a bateau neckline instead of one that plunged. A fitted bodice formed a V at the waist and sported velvet paisley-patterned buttons for decoration, while the skirt was full and plain, devoid of the ostentatious trims and ruffles one might see in London.

Thomasia twisted and turned in front of the cheval mirror that stood in the corner of her room, critical of her appearance from all angles now that the maid had stepped out for a moment. It had been eight months since Effie-Claire's birth, and she still wasn't sure she had her figure back or would ever get it back. Despite the returned flatness of her stomach, there was a decid-edly new flare to her hips that suggested she'd not see nineteen inches again—something the slight snugness of her gown attested to at the waist and across the bust.

At least she didn't *feel* full. She'd fed Effie-Claire before she dressed, but to her critical eye she could see the womanly fullness of her breasts. Gone was the high, girlish pertness that had once defined her silhouette. It was worth it, though, to breastfeed Effie-Claire.

'Oh, miss, you look a treat!' Her mother's maid returned—sent, no doubt, to hurry her along under the guise of offering help. 'That green becomes you…sets off your dark hair, it does. Can I help with your hair? Perhaps do it up in a twist?'

'Yes, that would be lovely.' Thomasia took a final look in the mirror. 'Do you think we should lace the corset tighter?' Old habits died hard, even when she knew better. Restrictive clothes, even if she could get into them, weren't healthy for the body, and they were one of the subtle ways in which women were oppressed. Still, she secretly did like how she looked, although she hated to admit it. 'Perhaps we could squeeze out an-other inch or two?'

'Absolutely not, miss,' the maid scolded. 'Twenty-one inches is perfectly respectable, and you've had a child. You look wonderful. Now, come and sit. I've promised your mother I'll have you downstairs at half past six without delay.'

Thomasia managed to delay anyway, despite hav-ing new motivation for charming the dinner guests. It had been a long time since she'd kept company. She worried they'd take one look at her and guess her secret. Was there something about her that would give it away? She fussed over wearing a red or green velvet ribbon at her throat, so that by the time she finally descended to the music room, where her family liked to receive guests when the party was small, everyone was already assembled.

Her mother and Becca sat on the settee. A pretty young woman, who she guessed was Susannah Rawdon, sat perched adjacent on a chair, leaning forward, intent on whatever Becca was saying.

Her father stood at the mantel of the fireplace, tall and straight-backed, engrossed in conversation with the man who must be Mr Rawdon. His back was to her, but there was plenty to study even without seeing his face: the set of broad shoulders beneath a dark brown jacket, his significant height, topping her father by three inches, and his russet hair, a stark contrast to her father's greyer shades. He was, in fact, a veritable autumn flame set against the greys and whites of oncoming winter. He was a spark, a fire, and something unbidden in her answered to him, before he even turned around.

The new MP was handsome.

Handsome. The word made her cringe. What was wrong with her? She'd promised herself no more recklessness, no more acting on intuition. She was a mother now. She had a child to protect. It couldn't be any other way.

'Ah, Thomasia, there you are!' Her father had spied her and gestured for her to join them at the fireplace. 'This is my youngest, Rawdon. Now you have met all my girls.'

'Miss Thomasia, I am sincerely charmed.'

He bowed over her hand as if they were in a London drawing room, his touch sending a warm jolt of awareness up her arm. When he raised his gaze to hers she was met with striking blue eyes the vivid cerulean of a summer sky, and a pair of cheekbones set high and sharp against the lines of a long, masculine jaw.

He had at once the look of a rugged sportsman and the elegance of a gentleman, the perfect cross between Town and country. For a moment Thomasia was rendered speechless. Against her will, he'd set her pulse to racing. That was another thing she'd promised herself after the debacle with Anthony—that she was beyond such superficial appeal as physical attractions, that she'd learned her lesson. But before her stood a man who was both Adonis and Apollo, a man who she knew would be good at everything he did, indoors and out. No, he would be better than good. He would be *excellent*. He was likely as dangerous to men as he was to women—sucking secrets from the unsuspecting with all that easy charm, whether it was over a shooting match or a musical soiree.

Such a man would not be easily persuaded to The Cause. He had too much to lose. But Thomasia liked a challenge.

She felt Becca coming to stand beside her in encouragement and solidarity. Becca's arm slipped through hers in support.

'Don't say anything foolish, Mr Rawdon,' Becca laughed. 'Like *You've saved the best for last*, or *She's the prettiest one of the bunch*, because I *am* still in the room.'

Rawdon laughed—a warm, genuine sound, as if they were all old friends. 'I wouldn't dream of it, Miss Rebecca.'

His blue eyes crinkled at the edges and Thomasia wondered just how much help her usually stalwart sister would be against such a good-looking onslaught of charm. Still, there should be *some* safety in numbers...

But within moments she found herself alone with Rawdon. Becca had rejoined Susannah, and her mother had pulled her father aside to confer with him on something. That left her with Rawdon and fifteen minutes before dinner would be served. Fifteen minutes to meet charm with charm and strike a blow for The Cause. The situation would be ideal if only he was less handsome and her pulse less rapid. As it stood now, the caution she'd developed over the last year and a half counselled her to retreat, while the woman in her who was committed to The Cause told her to push on, that this was too good an opportunity to waste, and the woman in her who insisted on admiring a handsome man agreed.

She plunged in with a smile and a tried-and-true strategy learned in London's ballrooms. 'I'm told you are our new MP. How do you find Parliament thus far?' No man could resist the chance to talk about himself. The trick was to use it to one's benefit.

He gave a smile and a shake of his head. 'Tedious, stultifying, yet at times exhilarating. Sometimes I imagine Parliament is like an enormous ship, setting out to sea: cumbersome to start, with tugs straining under the tonnage as they haul it to the open water, but once underway it's unstoppable as it reaches full speed. It's an engine of change, Miss Thomasia, perhaps the best one we have.'

Whatever she'd expected for an answer, it hadn't been that, and she found herself unarmed against such passionate honesty. This was going poorly. She didn't *want* to like him, didn't want to have anything in common with him.

'Why, Mr Rawdon, you may have missed your calling. I don't know if I've ever heard Parliament described in such poetic terms.' She favoured him with a smile, aware that he'd unknowingly given her an opportunity to advance The Cause. 'You speak of change… What sort of change?'

It was a vital question. His political agenda would tell her much about the man. How far did his progressivism go? Perhaps his answer would help her like him less, make him less attractive. Thanks to Anthony, she knew all too well that handsome faces could hide ugly things.

He was ready with his answer. 'Expansion of the railways, Miss Peverett, and with them an expansion in education—particularly for the poor. Railways will bring the country closer to the city. Not only that, they will bring the *world* closer. And all people, regardless of their social status, will need an education to navigate that new world, from foundlings to lordlings.'

Did he truly mean that? It was a laudable sentiment and it spoke well of Rawdon's intellect. Few understood the consequences advancements like railway expansion would have on the lives of ordinary people. Before she'd met the Coffee Yard ladies she, herself, had not given any thought about the railways beyond the transportation benefits they provided. But now she knew better.

She decided to test him. 'And women? Are they included in your definition of "all people regardless of social status"?' She was sure this was where he would fail, she was certain of it.

He met her question evenly, with only a slight tightening of his jaw. He'd clearly not liked being challenged, or, more particularly, he hadn't liked his *word* being challenged.

'When I say I seek change, Miss Peverett, I mean I seek change for everyone. As much change as I can manage before my views become unpopular.'

'And when they do? What happens then?' Thomasia pressed. 'It's one thing to want change, it's another thing to actually vote for it.'

His blue gaze rested firmly on her in a long considering glance that she felt to her toes. 'Yes, Miss Peverett, it certainly is.'

She would have liked to pursue that line of questioning, but Rawdon was saved from her interrogation by the announcement of dinner. If she had offended him he gave no sign of it. Instead, he offered her his arm, and another sharp sting of awareness crackled through her, intense and definitive. She was acutely alert to the solid muscle that met her touch beneath his sleeve, to the male scent of him. It was all winter spice, with a top note of cedar, a base note of patchouli and a hint of something—sandalwood, perhaps—in between. He smelled of comfort and strength.

His voice came low and private at her ear. 'There is much that needs fixing in England, and I mean to fix it for as long as I can.'

There was, indeed, Thomasia thought. Starting with its men. She slid him a coy look. What would he think of that? He might think a little differently about change then. Men usually did.

Chapter Two

Ah, so Thomasia Peverett was a 'new woman'—one of the women who were beginning to publicly attempt to equal the social pitch between men and women. She was also a woman of surprising depths.

Shaw held her chair for her before making his way to his seat across the table from her. He'd truly enjoyed their discussion and been reluctant to have it interrupted. And he thought the feeling mutual.

That was yet another surprise. In his experience, outside a select few, women weren't interested in detailed political discussions. *Screw more, talk less.* That was what Cecile, his last lover, a rather ambitious Society widow, had said on more than one occasion. *When a woman has a man like you in her bed, she doesn't want to hear about the Poor Laws.*

Nor had that woman wanted to be reminded of his lowly antecedents. She'd only cared who he was now—a self-made man of wealth and property. But Thomasia Peverett seemed different—once he got over that stunning face with its tawny lioness eyes and that mouth with its sensual bow.

If a man got past the intoxicating mixture of youth-
fulness and lushness that was Thomasia Peverett, he'd
realise she had a mind to go with the body. And what a
mind it was—although not every man would appreciate
it. She'd not hesitated in mining his political beliefs or
challenging them. He quickly chided himself for judging a book by its taffeta-and-velvet cover and assuming there was nothing but blank pages within. He was
sorry to be summoned to dinner, where he'd have to
share Thomasia Peverett with everyone else.

The meal did offset some of that disappointment.
It was a delicious affair of well-prepared roast beef,
greens and rosemary potatoes, accompanied by an exquisite red wine courtesy of Dr Peverett's new in-laws,
the Treshams—a connection Shaw whole-heartedly
approved of. He liked Dr Lord Ferris Tresham, Anne's
new husband, and had made it a habit to consult him
on healthcare legislation when Parliament was in session. Tresham might be the second son of the Duke of
Cowden, but he had a heart for the people, evidenced by
his commitment to creating mobile medical clinics that
brought healthcare to London's worst neighbourhoods.
It was a cause Shaw himself was eager to get behind.

Shaw reached for his wine glass as he scanned the
table, reminding himself with whom he dined. Despite
their appearances of being a gentry-class country family, the Peveretts now had powerful connections through
two of their daughters' recent marriages. Last summer,
a year after Anne had married Lord Tresham, the oldest, Thea, had married the Earl of Wychavon.

Shaw's gaze rested on Thomasia as it finished its
circuit of the table. With her elegant, polished looks

and quick mind, it was easy to imagine her at a London supper, dressed in silk, charming every gentleman in the room. For a man in his position—an MP in need of a wife—that consideration was worth lingering on.

If the sharpness of her tongue could be transformed into a blunter instrument she'd be the perfect hostess for someone like him—a man who hoped his star was rising. A more avaricious man would see, too, the benefits of her connections. A country gentleman might inherit family associations with a duke and an earl. For himself, however, he would be happy enough with a good hostess and someone with whom he shared mutual affection. What would she be happy with? Would such an arrangement suit Thomasia Peverett?

It begged the question: with two of her sisters so well situated, would she go to London this spring and seek an arrangement similar to theirs? Surely, with her sisters' connections as a social entrée, Thomasia Peverett would be able to move in high circles and meet a certain sort of gentleman—a gentleman with a title. But would she be interested in such a man for that reason alone? For what that man had instead of who he was? It seemed to be a trend with London's women. An up-and-coming MP, with an ambitious political career and an estate in Hertfordshire he'd had the audacity to purchase instead of inherit, and who hadn't a hope of inheriting a title, couldn't compete with an incompetent earl. Cecile had been quick to point that out. He knew she'd done him a favour, but her rapid abandonment of him for the buffoon who was the Earl of Southwick still stung.

'Mr Rawdon, would you like more wine?'

Thomasia's enquiry intruded on his drifting specula-
tions and he wondered what he'd missed in the interim.

'Wine? Yes, please. It's excellent. My compliments,
Peverett.' He nodded towards Thomasia's father briefly
before returning his attention to her. 'I was wondering, Miss Thomasia, if you and your sister plan to go
to London this spring?'

Susannah leaned forward in her eagerness. 'It would
be marvellous fun! You could stay with us. Shaw could
take us to the theatre, to balls, driving in the park...'

Shaw interrupted with a laugh. 'When I'm not working, dear sister.' He gave a broad smile, and nudged his
sister affectionately. 'Susannah forgets that I have re-
sponsibilities beyond her social calendar when we're
in Town.'

But apparently Susannah's enthusiasm was not
contagious. He didn't miss the subtle down-sweep of
Thomasia's gaze. The offer had clearly discomfited her.

She shook her head. 'That is kind of you to offer, but
I am not one for Town. Haberstock is as far as I venture.'

'It will be London's loss.' Shaw offered a nod in her
direction. 'Do let us know, though, if you change your
mind.' He turned his attention to Rebecca. 'You are
welcome on your own merits, Miss Rebecca, if you
wish to come. I know Susannah would like the company of a friend.'

The other Miss Peverett was politely noncommittal
as well, and the conversation moved on—but not his curiosity. His curiosity remained fixed on Thomasia Peverett. She was a woman made for London in both looks
and situation. Certainly she was old enough for Town.
Most girls who meant to try their luck on the Marriage

Mart went at eighteen. How old was Thomasia? Was she Susannah's age? Older? Younger?

He admitted it was hard to tell. There was a timeless quality to her that made it difficult to know. She lacked the naïve immaturity of a dewy-eyed debutante, and yet there was still a freshness to her that spoke of youth.

Shaw did a quick set of calculations in his head. If her oldest sister, Thea, was in her late twenties, and her next oldest sister, Anne, in her mid-twenties—he knew both girls had married well, but rather late by London standards—and if Rebecca was also older than Thomasia, Rebecca would be around twenty-two or -three... which placed Thomasia at twenty. Could that be right? Her mannerisms and her polish made her appear older, but the calculation certainly made her much younger than himself. He was a geriatric thirty-two by comparison— perhaps twelve years her senior.

Shaw took another swallow of wine, careful not to stare. He knew many men older than himself who took brides younger than Thomasia, but the idea of mature men preying on young girls barely out of their teens had always sat poorly with him—in part because he knew the reasons behind it, many of which struck him as socially corrupt, and in part because he'd always imagined marriage as a partnership of equals. It wasn't the most commonly held sentiment on marriage. His mother and stepfather had managed and it seemed the Peveretts had, too. He hoped to manage it himself someday.

Catherine Peverett rose, signalling the end of the meal and the removal of the women to the music room, leaving him and the doctor to a post-dinner brandy.

'We won't be long,' Dr Peverett assured his wife.

'Take all the time you wish.'

She smiled, but Shaw wasn't fooled. This would be a short drink. That suited him fine. He enjoyed Peverett's company, but tonight he wanted another chance to converse with Thomasia and perhaps to gain insight into why a woman so perfect for London Society would decide to stay in Haberstock. She was a conundrum, and he admitted to being intrigued.

Twenty minutes later, Shaw and Dr Peverett made their way to the music room, where the ladies had set up a table for cards. There was the initial polite flurry of settling on partners. An attempt was made to draw Thomasia into the game but she quickly demurred, offering to play the piano instead.

'You must have music,' she insisted when her sister tried to press her into partnering Susannah.

She took up a spot on the piano bench and began riffling through sheet music while Dr Peverett, who liked a game of cards, clapped him on the back.

'Shall we play against the girls, Rawdon?'

Out of the corner of his eye Shaw could see Catherine Peverett, obviously prepared to play the good hostess and sit the game out, although he knew she liked cards as much as her husband and was equally skilled.

'I've a better idea. Why don't you and your wife take on the girls?' Shaw suggested. 'Susannah has been wanting to try her skill against the two of you for months now.' If he wanted a chance to continue his conversation with Thomasia, he wouldn't get a better opportunity. 'I'll assist with the music.' He grinned, to assure his hosts he would not be bored, and wandered over to the piano before Dr Peverett could protest.

At the piano, he lifted the lid for Thomasia and smiled. 'I hope you weren't trying to avoid me,' he joked. 'If so it didn't work.'

'I see that.'

Thomasia's attention remained focused on sorting out the music. Her response not quite off-putting, but neither was it as welcoming as it had been before dinner.

'Did you not want to play cards?' She raised a slim dark brow to indicate the table where the others had gathered.

'Not when I can talk to you.' It was a rather bold line, even if it was honest, but she struck him as a bold woman, her reticence over going to London notwithstanding. And that boldness was part of her riddle. 'Not when I can continue our pre-dinner conversation.' It was something he very much wished to do.

She arched a dark brow and offered him a cryptic, 'Hmm...'

What had changed for her between dinner and now? Had he said something to offend her over the meal? He wasn't a vain man, but he was not used to having such little effect on a woman. Usually women were interested in conversation even if they weren't interested in a titleless marriage, and there were plenty who were interested in something between the two.

Shaw dropped his voice. '*Do* you mind? Honestly? I did not think you were indifferent to our conversation earlier. I apologise if I misunderstood.' He would gladly retreat to spectate at the card game rather than impose his company upon her if it was truly unwanted. Perhaps she'd been seeking solitude in her choice to play the piano this evening.

Her hands had stilled on the pages of music, and her tawny eyes, wide and expressive when they met his, had taken on the shade of rich port in the lamplight.

'No, I don't mind.' She patted the space beside her on the bench, her tone approaching some of her earlier friendliness. 'I suppose you'd best make yourself useful turning pages. I trust you do read music, Mr Rawdon?'

'Is that a challenge, Miss Thomasia?' He slid onto the bench beside her in answer. He did read music, but he read people better. She was relenting, softening—or perhaps she was merely resigning herself to continuing their conversation…resigning herself to *him*? Why?

She looked at the music before her, a Schumann piece, and discarded it, selecting the piece beneath it.

Shaw furrowed his brow as she began to play. 'You'll play Clara Schumann, but you won't play a piece by her husband, Robert?'

She shook her head, but kept her gaze fixed on the pages before her as she delivered a succinct but scathing opinion of Robert Schumann. 'His wife is a modern living genius at the piano, bringing up seven children and being in general overlooked, while he slowly goes mad from the consequences of a "playful" young adulthood, leaving her to fend for herself and their large brood.'

'Ouch.' Shaw winced. Schumann had spent the last year and a half in an asylum on the Continent, and it was tacitly assumed that he would never leave alive. It was also tacitly assumed that his ill health was due to syphilis.

Thomasia shot him a look. 'He's put her at risk, you know, through no fault of her own except to have married the lout.'

Shaw turned the page. 'I hope that will not be the

case.' What else could he say? He was not used to discussing syphilis with well-bred young ladies—or discussing it at all. He braced himself, because it was clear Thomasia had more to say if the accelerated tempo of the piece she played was an indicator.

'A man contracts a deadly contagious disease that risks his wife's health, without her consent or awareness, and all anyone can say is that his youth was "rather playful".' Her hands came down hard on a chord and drew glances from the card table. She immediately corrected herself and softened the volume, her voice falling to a whispered hiss beneath the music. 'If that doesn't suggest a woman is nothing but a man's chattel, I don't know what does. She can't even protect her own body—can't even legally deny a sick man access to that body if he's her husband.'

Shaw turned another page and said nothing for a moment, but his mind was whirling. What a bold virago Thomasia Peverett was. 'Once again, I am surprised you eschew London, where you might find other women who think as you do. I believe you'd enjoy the political salons if nothing else. I would be happy to introduce you to some friends of mine—women like yourself.' He was thinking of Mrs Barbara Bodichon and Mrs Elizabeth Rayner-Parkes, both very progressive women who were working for women's equality. They actively recruited young women to their cause. He had no doubt they would adore Thomasia.

'London is not for me.' She concluded the lied with a firmness to match her words and moved into another tune.

'How do you know? Have you been?' She'd not

been in London for her sister's wedding to the Earl of
Wychavon—he knew that much.

'I went to Town for Anne and Ferris's wedding. I did
not find it to my liking.'

There was a certain finality to her tone, but he wasn't
ready to leave the subject alone. 'You didn't like it?' he
probed. Susannah loved the Season. He couldn't imagine Thomasia Peverett not revelling in all its entertainments and opportunities. Who did she exercise her sharp
mind upon in Haberstock? Surely the conversation to be
found in London alone was worth the journey?

Rawdon was exercising her patience—with herself
and with him. She was annoyed with herself for the attraction she felt, annoyed that a handsome, intelligent
man had come to dinner, and even more annoyed that
she found him engaging. And she was irrationally annoyed with his long gazes and his insightful questions.
He was trying to solve her as if she were a puzzle. She
was *not* available for solving—not even for The Cause.

'No, I did not enjoy London.'

She managed to skewer him with a sideways glance
while still executing the piece flawlessly. She meant the
glance to be withering, so that he wouldn't see through
the lie. She'd loved London—all of it. The balls and
parties, the Venetian breakfasts and boating picnics,
and the shopping—oh, the shopping had been divine.
She'd loved afternoons at Gunter's, eating ices from
a carriage, surrounded on all sides by gallant young
gentlemen...

Only not all of them had been gallant in the end.
She'd not understood that until it was too late.

'What didn't you like?'

Mr Rawdon's voice was low, his gaze steady, inviting her confidence. Her stare had not squelched the conversation, it had only fostered more. Short answers normally discouraged a man, but in this case the more terse her answers, the more insistent he became. She was happy to talk about legislation, but she was not pleased to talk about herself. Surely he was astute enough to have taken the hint and yet he'd deliberately chosen not to.

She stopped playing and shifted to face him squarely. If he would not cease until he had the truth of it, she would give it to him bluntly. 'I didn't care for any of it. The whole Season is subjugation dressed up in silk and satin and just as slippery. It's nothing more than putting a girl—a *girl*, mind you—who has no notion of herself, let alone of the world, in a pretty dress and showing her off to the highest bidders.'

And in the meanwhile, under the guise of romance, sharks lurked, waiting to destroy young women all for a lark or in the search of temporary pleasure.

Rawdon was studying her again with those blue eyes. 'Is that what happened to you, Miss Thomasia?'

She was quick to answer. 'No, of course not. My parents taught me to think for myself.'

There'd been no selling of daughters to the highest bidder—the Peveretts were above such ridiculousness. But that hadn't stopped the sharks from circling a pretty face, and neither had thinking for herself. She'd still managed to run headlong into disaster.

She crossed her arms over her chest in defiance, daring Rawdon to disagree with her, and immediately wished she hadn't. The motion reminded her that the evening grew late and it had been a while since Effie-Claire had been fed. The familiar tingle that preceded the flow of milk began, sure and unmistakable. She had only moments to effect a departure.

She rose abruptly from the bench. 'Mr Rawdon, please excuse me.'

His gentle hand on her arm stopped her. 'Please, don't rush off. You needn't worry that you've offended me—'

'I don't worry about it,' she interrupted. 'This does not concern you, Mr Rawdon. I must go.'

Effie-Claire would be needing her, and she needed Effie-Claire. The two of them—that was her world now. Effie-Claire and The Cause. She would never go to London again, no matter how tempting, just as she would never again allow herself to be drawn in by a man, no matter how tempting he was. And Shaw Rawdon *did* tempt a woman, with those broad shoulders, and those blue eyes that said *Trust me... Tell me your secrets*, and that smile that teased, that made her feel as if she'd known him for far longer than an evening.

Her first impression had been right. He *was* dangerous. And, despite her love of a challenge, the caution in her warned that it might be necessary to withdraw, his being an ally for The Cause notwithstanding.

Upstairs, Effie-Claire was fussing. Thomasia took her from the maid and felt the baby quiet as her milk let down. She rocked Effie-Claire gently as she fed. *This* was peace, here in this dark room, late at night, with Effie. She didn't need Gunter's ices and a wardrobe full of once-worn ball gowns and the insincere flattery of selfish young men. The girl who had liked such things was gone. By necessity and for the better.

But deep down inside, where a little piece of the girl she'd once been still lived, came an echo of the past. *It had been nice while it lasted.* She immediately felt guilty. She was a mother now. She shouldn't miss those silly, superficial things, and she certainly shouldn't want them now that there was Effie-Claire to think about.

Chapter Three

'Rawdon, are you listening?' Sir Phillip Maldon barked, demanding Shaw's attention.

Shaw felt guilty for his momentary lapse. In his defence, it was the only lapse he'd had in the entire hour Maldon had been prosing on about his recent trip north to hunt fox cubs with Lord Oliver. Shaw's meeting with Maldon had been intended to discuss positions for the upcoming session of Parliament, which would convene at the end of January, but most of the meeting had been dedicated to a discussion of Lord Oliver's stable and the fine hunting. Still, Shaw had been able to glean enough between the lines to know what was really at stake: votes and favours.

'We're to support Lord Oliver's bill in exchange for his support on our infrastructure legislation,' Shaw surmised.

It would be the first of many trades brokered and negotiated over the early winter, before Parliament even sat. It was how business was done. Without such trades, nothing would be accomplished. A group of men all with their own agendas was an obstinate bunch.

'Yes—and Lord Stanton's legislation as well.'

Maldon slipped in the mention and Shaw grimaced. He had no quarrel with Oliver's bill, but Stanton's sat poorly with him. Stanton wanted to repeal the 1845 Bastardy Act. He had hoped Maldon—his mentor, and the man who'd seen Shaw elected to one of the three seats Maldon controlled—would not be drawn into the debate over Stanton's bill. Shaw had wanted to be left to decide his vote on his own. This Act was personal to him, having spent the first eight years of his life as a bastard—the product of an affair between his mother and the lord of the manor's son when she'd served as an upstairs maid. Support such as the relief offered in the current Act would have made a difference to him and his mother. Stanton wanted to destroy that.

Maldon sighed impatiently, drumming his thick fingers on the polished surface of his desk. 'What is it, Rawdon?'

'I find Stanton's bill unpalatable,' Shaw answered honestly. 'How can a woman who has little chance of gainful employment to begin with be expected to bring up a child on her own without financial support?' he queried. 'If Stanton's repeal passes, men will be able to avoid all financial responsibility for their children. That hardly seems fair *or* right.'

Maldon fixed him with a paternal stare that bordered on patronising. 'That's your Unitarian friends talking, Rawdon. Mrs Bodichon and Mrs Rayner-Parkes are women who have no notion of what it takes to actually implement a working law that doesn't unravel the moral fabric of Society. That's the problem with women meddling in politics. They're all sentiment and ideas, but short on practicality.'

A vision of Thomasia Peverett on her mettle flashed through Shaw's mind. What would she say to the idea that her passion was a useless sentiment?

The older man leaned forward, steepling his hands on the desk. 'I've spent the better part of two weeks listening to Stanton up at Oliver's box, and it's not as unpalatable as you might think. It's all gone too far—starting with the 1839 Custody of Infants Act, with its notion that children are better off with their mothers, and extending to the 1845 Act that suggests fathers should pay for children they aren't even bringing up. Ambitious women will be pinning paternity on the richest bloke they can find.' He shook his head in distaste. 'We don't want to send a message that women can be paid to have children and bring them up on someone else's coin without bestirring themselves. It's akin to rewarding them for their misconduct.'

'*Their* misconduct? A woman does not make a child on her own.'

As if begetting a child is all a woman's fault when it occurs at an inopportune time.

Shaw could almost hear Thomasia Peverett's response as if she were in the room with them. His mother had felt the same way. Although she'd not been in a position to exercise those opinions, she'd certainly brought up her son on them. At times like these it was difficult to reconcile his personal beliefs with his political ambition.

Pick your battles, Rawdon, his conscience counselled. *You'll not convince Maldon otherwise today.*

'Surely the legislation won't get far,' Shaw said carefully. Perhaps it would never get out of committee. If so, it was useless to argue the legislation's content today or any other day. 'It will be met with public outcry if it does.'

The public was decidedly more liberal than Parliament these days. MPs who wanted to retain their seats had to keep that in mind. It was a deuced thin line to walk, pleasing one's conservative patron and the more liberal public, but not nearly as difficult as pleasing one's own conscience.

Maldon waved a hand to dismiss the public. 'The public is fickle, Rawdon. What they want one day is not what they want the next. We have to make them see that the sentiment of some laws is not always what is reproduced in the law itself. They need to be made to understand that the implication of the current Act actually leads to the very immorality the public thinks it's circumventing. It will achieve exactly what they wish to avoid. Make no mistake: Stanton is counting on us. Start lobbying your liberal friends, Mrs Bodichon and Mrs Rayner-Parkes. Get them to start seeing the purpose of the repeal.'

That meant more letters, acting against his conscience and asking his friends to do the same. He grimaced, and Maldon was quick to respond.

'If it's the workload you're worried about, hire a secretary, Rawdon. No one writes their own letters. For heaven's sake, hire two, if you must. This is an opportunity for you. Stanton is prepared to be very generous.' The man's keen eyes glittered as he dangled the proverbial carrot. 'He's interested in supporting your project for foundling schools.'

They both knew what that meant. Support from Stanton would see the project accomplished. His lack of support would easily sink Shaw's project before it even got out of committee. In politics there was a fine line between favours and threats, and there was always the greater good to consider. All those children who would benefit from an education. This Act was one piece of legislation. With luck, women's rights would survive without it, or Stanton's repeal might fail on its own merits. But the trade-off rankled.

He was still bothered by it as he started his journey home astride his big hunter, a bay gelding named Chiron. The rain and recent cold weather had resulted in frozen ruts, making the road into a collection of uneven bumps and depressions. It made for slow going, and for too much time in his head. He'd known politics would be like this, of course. He'd not gone into it with naïve intentions. But somehow he'd thought he'd be able to hold himself above the fray, that he'd not be caught in the web of favour-trading because he knew to beware of it. But that was proving not to be the case. Awareness was not the same as prevention.

Think of the generations of children you'll be helping... children who can grow up with a better education than you had. Where would you have been if your stepfather hadn't come along?

Alan Rawdon had been his saviour. The man had married his mother when Shaw was eight and had adopted him, given him his name and a start in life. His stepfather had seen to his education, sent him to school when he was old enough, and when he'd been ready for the world Alan Rawdon had offered either to buy him a commission in the army or to give him that money to use for purchasing a small share in a shipping venture.

Shaw had chosen the latter and begun building his wealth—the same wealth that had allowed him to buy Rosegate and become a man of property...a man eligible to hold an MP's seat. Not every bastard had an Alan Rawdon in his life, but they still needed an education. It was unjust to make a child pay for circumstances they hadn't created.

Then again, perhaps he was being too dramatic. Perhaps Stanton was right? And Maldon, too. Perhaps the repeal would discourage licentious behaviour at its root? Previous attempts to do so hadn't worked, but perhaps if he understood Stanton's proposal better it would appear differently to him.

He mentally added a close reading of Stanton's repeal to the growing list of things that needed his attention. Between Parliament, the estate and arrangements for Susannah's Season, he was feeling his time stretched thin. The sixty-five days between now and the opening of the Parliamentary session would hardly be enough—and that was without throwing Christmas festivities in there, too.

He flexed his right hand, already imagining it cramping from the amount of correspondence and report-writing he had to look forward to. Maldon was right about one thing: he did need a secretary.

Chiron lurched beneath him, and the big gelding's gait was unsteady as the horse nearly went down. 'Whoa, boy...' Shaw gathered the reins and quieted him. Assured the horse wouldn't bolt, he dismounted and looped the reins over his arm. He bent and inspected its hooves, hoping Chiron hadn't pulled up lame. Luck wasn't with him. He found a pebble lodged in the left front shoe.

He picked it out and flung it away, but the damage was already done. Chiron was limping, damn it all. It added to his foul mood. Shaw looked about, gauging his surroundings. He was still a few miles from home, but he was very close to Haberstock Hall. That made him feel better. He would call in there, borrow a horse to get him home and leave Chiron well tended until the gelding was sound enough to travel.

You might also have a chance to see Miss Thomasia, a little voice in his head nudged.

Perhaps, but that was *not* the plan, he reminded himself. The plan was to take care of his horse. Miss Thomasia had made it clear that she was not impressed by him. But that only made him want to change her mind… to prove to her that he was not like other men. He smiled to himself for the first time in hours.

He smiled again when the housekeeper, Mrs Newsome, led him to the front parlour and informed him that only Miss Thomasia was at home. It was the best luck he'd had all day.

'That's fine, Mrs Newsome. That's exactly who I wanted to see.'

It was true, he realised. He wanted to talk—wanted to exchange ideas with someone who would speak her mind, who wouldn't hold back. He could rely on Thomasia Peverett to do just that.

She had not counted on this. There were supposed to be no visitors today—not when everyone was out and only she was at home to receive.

Thomasia pasted on a smile as she came down the stairs, shaking out her skirts, which were wrinkled from playing on the nursery floor with Effie-Claire. She was hardly dressed to receive anyone. They were expecting no one—least of all Mr Rawdon. Her mother was out on her rounds, visiting tenants, her father as well, and Becca was off hiding in her workshop somewhere on the property. She stopped to check her hair in the small hall mirror and smoothed back a few errant strands Effie-Claire had pulled loose. To be fair, Mr Rawdon hadn't expected his horse to become lame either. They were both victims of the unexpected, it seemed.

She had no choice but to go down and greet him, even if he didn't need a horse. Otherwise he would think she was avoiding him—or, worse, that he had routed her…that her abrupt departure a few nights ago had indeed been caused by him. No man drove her from any room. With luck, this would be a short interaction—just long enough to set him up with a horse and see that his lame one was taken care of.

But she was to have no such luck. Mrs Newsome's tea tray preceded her into the front parlour. Tea meant twenty minutes.

She shot Mrs Newsome a quelling look as the housekeeper passed her.

'The gentleman's been out riding in the cold, miss.' Mrs Newsome had no remorse. 'And, let me remind you, you hardly ate anything for lunch *or* breakfast,' she added with a scold. 'Tea will do you both good. You need to keep your strength up for the little one.'

In answer, Thomasia's stomach growled, and she pressed a hand to it as if to silence it. She had indeed eaten very little, her thoughts still distracted over the previous evening, and now the source of that distraction was sitting in the front parlour.

At the doorway, she stopped to study Rawdon, hoping he would somehow be less attractive in the afternoon. He stood with his back to her, looking out over the front drive. He was dressed for riding and making calls. He'd been somewhere, then, not merely out for exercise. His broad shoulders filled out the dark frock coat he wore, and the low-seamed waist of the garment emphasised the athletic tapered shape of him. That tapered torso met long legs showcased in tight-fitting buckskins and rolled tall boots.

Her earlier observations had been right. He was a true outdoorsman. Town men were eschewing boots altogether these days, except for hunting and specific activities, although countrymen like her father—and apparently Rawdon—still rode a horse everywhere. She rather liked a man in tall boots. There was something undeniably virile about them.

Thomasia pushed the thought away—she couldn't think of men in those terms any more, and she shouldn't notice them in those terms either. She cleared her throat. 'Mr Rawdon, what a surprise.'

He turned, his easy smile at the ready. 'I do hope it's not inconvenient. My horse has picked up a stone in his hoof.'

'Inconveniences are what neighbours are for.' Thomasia moved towards the tea tray set on a low table amid the arrangement of furniture by the fireplace. 'Please, join me for some refreshment, Mr Rawdon, or Mrs Newsome will be upset.'

'I *am* inconveniencing you, then. I can hear it in your tone.' Rawdon laughed, and the sound was as warm as she remembered it. 'I knew I could count on you to tell me the truth.'

He took the chair across from the settee, his big body filling it as she poured. 'There is no one else at home, and as you can see...' she gestured towards her wrinkled skirts '...I wasn't expecting anyone. Milk? Sugar? Mr Rawdon?'

'Milk only—just a splash to cool it.' He took the cup and saucer from her, his blue eyes twinkling. 'I shall endeavour to drink this as fast as possible and be on my way. Perhaps we should make it a contest?'

Thomasia blushed hotly. 'You're making me feel bad for being honest. Take your time with your tea. I won't have your burnt mouth on my conscience.'

She regretted the insinuation behind her words immediately. She'd not meant them to hold any sort of nuance, but the words themselves drew her gaze to the mouth in question, to the perfect bow of his upper lip, the firm line of the lower. It was a strong mouth, not too full nor too thin.

'Heaven forbid my mouth should be on your mind,' he drawled, with a hint of wicked teasing that told her he'd caught her gaze. 'Forgive me, I've put you out of sorts with my unintended arrival.'

He sat back in his chair, one long masculine leg crossed over the knee of the other, his presence potent and at odds with the feminine floral decor of the parlour.

'Tell me, what were you doing that had you so absorbed?'

'Nothing that would be of interest to you.'

Thomasia took a sip of her tea. She wasn't about to tell this man—a near stranger to her, even if he was a friend of the family—that her infant daughter, born out of wedlock, was upstairs in the nursery. There was no point in him knowing, she reasoned silently. No matter how his eyes twinkled, she could not trust him with her secret and there was no reason to take the risk. He spent the better part of the year in London at Parliament. He could easily leave in January none the wiser.

'What of yourself, Mr Rawdon? What errands have you been on today?'

'I have spent the day at Beechmont with Sir Maldon, going over issues for Parliament.'

For the first time since his arrival, she saw some of his ease leave him. There must have been tension in those discussions with Maldon...

'Was it distasteful?' Thomasia enquired, sensing that given the opportunity Rawdon might unbottle whatever was bottled up inside him.

'There is always something distasteful about politics.' He paused, appearing to consider his next words, then, 'I am to study a piece of legislation regarding doing away with a father's requirement to financially support children raised by their mother.'

'Stanton's repeal of the Bastardy Act,' Thomasia said grimly, her tone making her dislike obvious.

'You know it specifically?'

Rawdon's interest appeared to have been snagged by her comment.

'I know *of* it. It was discussed in York rather openly. Stanton is not well liked in certain circles.' In *her* circles. The Coffee Yard group thought the man a bully and a very active, deliberate suppressor of women.

'But others feel the legislation would prevent vice,' he began.

'Then I can see we have a lot to discuss.' Thomasia gave him a cool smile over the rim of her teacup. 'Unless you've already made up your mind?' she challenged, seeing once more an opening for The Cause. Why not dive in? He was already here. 'When you say "others", are you talking about yourself anonymously? Men are for ever doing that: hiding their opinions with vague pronouns. Others…they… You needn't be shy with me, Mr Rawdon.'

'Let me be specific, then. By "others" I mean Maldon,' he replied fiercely.

It was plain he didn't like the idea that she'd thought he wouldn't own his opinion just as he had last night, when his word had been under question.

'And are you permitted to make up your own mind, Mr Rawdon? I was unaware an MP had much say in these matters. Perhaps Maldon expects you to do as he directs and your opinion is of no merit.'

There was no reason to pretend otherwise. She knew how Parliament worked as well as he did. She did wonder, though, which part of it caused the distaste he spoke of. The legislation itself, or the way his vote was for sale, brokered to others by others without his direct approval.

'I am my own man, Miss Thomasia. I make up my own mind.'

'But do you get to *vote* on it?'

She returned to the question she'd posed last night.

Men could make up their minds all they wanted in private. It didn't mean anything in the end. Men did what other men told them to do and couched it in terms of honour and duty. It was what Anthony, the father of her child, had done.

She smiled knowingly into the silence. Perhaps she'd come on too strong in her passion for The Cause and he would leave now. Most gentlemen didn't stick around once they'd been abused with sharp words. But he made no move to depart. He looked at her with those piercing blue eyes, his gaze lost in contemplation, not irritation, until she was the one unnerved.

'Why are you still here, Mr Rawdon? I've endeavoured to insult you at every turn and yet you remain. Is there something you want?'

'Yes, as a matter of fact, there is. I want you to be my secretary while I am here in Haberstock. I think your mind might be just what I need to see my way clear.'

How did he manage to do that? For every gauntlet she threw down, he threw another. How could she not pick this one up? What an opportunity this would be for The Cause—to work in the employ of a man who had influence in Parliament. The Cause was always on the outside, limited to newspapers, poster protests and pamphlets. As visible and wide-reaching as those resources were, they didn't command votes—not directly. And yet she was wary. To lobby him she'd have to be with him, in his very attractive company regularly. It was a temptation she'd promised herself to avoid.

'That makes no sense, Mr Rawdon. I am the opposition, the very antithesis of what your mentors believe in.' And that was in more ways than just intellectual opinion. She, with her illegitimate daughter, was the physical embodiment of the women they looked to strike against with their repeal.

'It makes every sense,' he argued. 'You will keep me honest…remind me of my conscience when the waters get murky.' He leaned forward. 'I am surprised you resist, Miss Peverett. I would think you'd leap at the chance to prove a woman is as capable as a man in such a position. Surely your resistance is not on political grounds?'

No, it wasn't. It was on highly *personal* grounds. The Cause aside, it would be dangerous for her to be in this man's presence. There was an attraction between them and he was willing to pursue it, with his light flirtatious comments about mouths and his long considering gazes, whereas she could not afford to be pursued, no matter how much he made her pulse race, no matter how lonely she was. But he was daring her now to make good on her argument that women deserved equality. He'd hire her over a man. He was calling her bluff. Surely, for The Cause, she could endure taking that dare.

The old arguments chased themselves around her head one more time. What an opportunity this was. If she could convince Rawdon, perhaps Rawdon could convince Maldon and others. There would be other benefits, too. There would be inside information that she could report back to the Coffee Yard ladies.

The same excitement that had started to thrum deep within her last night took up its rhythm, whether it be the thrill of The Cause or the thrill of a ballroom, the excitement of being alive, of dancing too close to the edge. She hadn't felt like this since Effie-Claire was born. Her excitement was different these days...more restrained. A cautious emotion she kept on a short leash lest it get out of control.

She ought to think about that now. This opportunity, grand as it was, was not risk-free. What did this mean for Effie-Claire? How could she spend long periods away from her daughter?

'I would only be available a few days a week, Mr Rawdon, or perhaps just half-days.' That would help with Effie-Claire, and perhaps keep her attraction at bay.

'Mid-morning to mid-afternoon would suit me fine.' Rawdon didn't blink at the request. 'There is a house-keeper at Rosegate, and Susannah will be home so you will be chaperoned. I shall speak about the arrange-ments with your father, to make sure all meets with his approval. And I shall expect you the day after tomor-row.' He set aside his teacup. 'Thank you, Miss Thom-asia. You have done me a great favour.'

Thomasia smiled. He'd done her an even greater one.

Chapter Four

Rosegate, Rawdon's home, was located on the other side of Haberstock Village. It was a tidy piece of acreage, dotted with farms and neat fields, a property that had been thoroughly restored in the four years since he had taken up residence.

The previous owner had been elderly and had let the property decline, but there was no decline evident now. Thomasia turned the pony trap onto the drive leading up to the manor house, admiring the oak trees bearing the last of autumn's flaming foliage. Their vibrant hues brought to mind the colour of Rawdon's hair—a comparison she shoved aside as quickly as it came. She could not afford to dwell on any aspect of his person. This was business.

Thomasia brought the trap to a halt in front of a brick house with an Adam-style pediment and four thick white Ionic columns. The house was as neatly kept as the land. From the outside, she could see the long windows were gracefully draped with lace and curtains, tempting the viewer to speculate on the interior.

Thomasia jumped down, and there was a spring in her step as she approached the front door. The drive over beneath clear, crisp late-autumn skies had been invigorating. With the exception of a few visits to church, she'd not left the boundaries of Haberstock Hall since her return from York. She'd not realised how good it would feel to be out—and on her own, without Effie-Claire.

Guilt twinged. A mother should not be happy about being away from her child. She pushed away the guilt before she knocked. It wasn't as if she was out dancing. This was work. This was for The Cause.

She rapped hard on the door and was answered by the housekeeper, who introduced herself as Mrs Grandy, a tall woman with greying hair and an efficient nature.

'Mr Rawdon has arranged for you to work in the library. Come this way with me, Miss Peverett.'

The woman led her past a polished oak banister and down a corridor lined with doors on either side until they reached the library at the back of the house. The library, like much of the house, highlighted oak woodwork. The casements around the long windows were polished oak and featured heavy wine-coloured velvet floor-length draperies trimmed in gold fringe, pulled back to show the lawn beyond. The fireplace mantel was of more carved oak and a warm fire burned in the grate. The bookshelves and the table that dominated the centre of the room carried through with the theme. A small grouping of furniture was gathered around the fireplace, but it was clear from the writing materials on the long table that she was to work from there—not with Rawdon in his office, which was clearly elsewhere.

'Mr Rawdon has left instructions for you,' Mrs Grandy said. 'I'll bring a tea tray for you at noon, if you'd like, but you can ring if there's anything you need before then.'

Thomasia halted in her perusal of the table, Mrs Grandy's words catching her attention. 'Mr Rawdon is not here?' She'd not expected this, any more than she'd expected to work in a space apart from him. The library was beautifully appointed, but it was not *his* office. How was she to persuade him to her cause if she didn't see him?

Mrs Grandy clicked her tongue. 'Oh, Mr Rawdon is seldom here during the day. He's a busy man, what with the estate and his Parliament duties.' There was pride in her voice, at working for such a sought-after man. 'At the moment he's out visiting constituents.'

'Of course.' Thomasia hid her disappointment with brisk efficiency. 'I'll get to these letters right away.' At least she could get a sense of what other policy matters he was involved with by working through his correspondence.

She took a seat at the long table and read through the list. She scrunched her brow and turned the paper over. Perhaps there was more? But the reverse side of the paper was blank. It wasn't that the list was short— far from it. It was the full length of the paper. It was the topics that left her perplexed. There was an instruction to write to accept dinners, followed by a list of names, to write to decline invitations, update his personal calendar, review the manor ledgers…

These were the tasks of a country gentleman. These were not the tasks of an MP.

She sat back in her chair, disappointment surging again. This was not as she had imagined it, the two of them working together in the same room, she copying letters to other MPs and engaging Mr Rawdon in discussion of relevant political issues. He wasn't at home, and even if he was he would be working in another room, which made the point of his even *being* home moot.

She would have to do something about that. Surely he wouldn't be gone all the time, no matter what Mrs Grandy suggested. The weather would do its part in keeping him indoors eventually, and when it did she would find a way to suggest to Rawdon that it would be more efficient if they worked in the same space.

Having a plan of action made her feel a little better. Thomasia picked up the first invitation and began to draft the response, another rationale coming to her. Perhaps she needed to demonstrate her competence at these tasks before being entrusted with others. It was a lesson her parents had instilled in her and her siblings: the idea that trust was built one increment at a time. Someone who did well with a little was more likely to be entrusted with more over time. If she did well with the tasks appointed to her now, Rawdon would feel more comfortable assigning her more important ones.

Thomasia applied herself to the tasks at hand with newfound diligence. She approached each new day with the belief that tomorrow things would be better. Perhaps tomorrow Rawdon would be at home. Perhaps tomorrow he would recognise how well she'd executed the tasks set before her. But two weeks of tomorrows came and went, the last of the autumn leaves fell, leaving the trees in the drive bare, and still Rawdon wasn't at home.

There *were* benefits to working alone, she told herself. She could manage to express her milk without lurking around, looking for a quiet place. She could come and go as she pleased and set her own hours, relatively speaking, and she enjoyed the wages Rawdon left for her at the end of each week. With Christmas approaching she'd have money of her own for gifts, and some to save against the spring.

But these were not the benefits she'd accepted the position for.

Her frustration was at an all-time high as she surveyed Rawdon's list one afternoon. She'd completed everything on it except for the last task: repair the seam of his hunting jacket. The jacket had even been left over a chair in the library for her and there was no ignoring it. How dare he? Thomasia fumed. Instead of recognising the competence with which she'd done her tasks to date, and given her more meaningful work, he'd assigned her a menial task—a *woman's* task. He assumed she'd sew up his jacket along with writing his personal correspondence and the assumption galled her.

Thomasia grabbed the jacket. She'd sew it, all right, and then she'd give him a piece of her mind, just as soon as she saw him. If she *ever* saw him.

This was exactly the kind of little-minded thinking the Coffee Yard ladies fought against. Had he done this on purpose? She could hardly believe that of him. He hadn't struck her as a deliberately cruel man. Although perhaps it was worse that he'd just done it 'naturally', without a thought for the assumptions he was making.

Then again, she'd known from the start a man's progressiveness was inherently limited by his own assumptions of privilege and power.

Thomasia was so caught up in her irritation and her disappointment over what the jacket signified—the fact that Rawdon had somehow let her down—she nearly missed what would become the *pièce de résistance* of her anger: the gleam of a russet head outside the village pub as she drove home that afternoon.

She looked twice to be sure. It was definitely him. Rawdon looked as if he'd just come in from the hunt. He stood surrounded by other village notables, all with tankards in hand and looking to be having a jolly good time, laughing and toasting one another. Was this what he'd been doing these last weeks? Riding out to the hunt, drinking afternoon ale at the pub, while she wrote his personal correspondence and arranged his appointments? And now she could add sewing his jacket to the list of tasks, all so that he could while away the day.

She had half a mind to park the pony trap, march over there and give him a piece of her temper along with his jacket. The only things preventing her from making that scene were consideration for her family and the lessons she'd learned with the Coffee Yard women.

Her family had supported her through a difficult year and welcomed her home, even begged her to come home, with her new daughter. They would not appreciate her storming about the village, berating the local MP, especially if there was no point to it except venting her spleen. And the Coffee Yard ladies had taught her the merits of channelling her considerable passion, of picking her battles instead of letting that passion run unbridled—often towards disaster. Before engaging, she must always ask the question, What is to be gained? Every encounter for The Cause came with risk.

In this case, there was nothing to be gained from confronting Rawdon publicly and much to lose. He would not thank her for it, and that meant no chance of being part of other work for him. He might dismiss her entirely, and then she would have wasted the opportunity to work subtly for The Cause. Finding her inner restraint, Thomasia clucked to the horse and continued. She would make her point another way.

His jacket lay on the bed, pressed and as good as new. Although it hadn't been new for a while, the green wool was one of his favourites, and seeing it restored brought a smile to his face. He hadn't been able to bring himself to give it away when double-breasted jackets had gone out of fashion. In the country, style didn't matter so much, and the jacket was of good quality. Perhaps he would wear it today and it would lift his flagging spirits.

The morning had got off to a dreary start. The rain had kept him from his early ride, and Susannah had left after breakfast to visit a cousin who needed help with a new baby. He would be at Rosegate by himself throughout the Christmas break. While Susannah would spend a boisterous Christmas surrounded by cousins, aunts and uncles, he would spend it rambling about alone. It was not a prospect he was looking forward to. He had offers to go to London, of course, but he was not ready to return to Town. He preferred to stay in the country as long as he could. He was in Town for half the year as it was.

Enough, Shaw scolded himself as he finished dressing for the day. He had many things to be thankful for. One of which was Thomasia Peverett. She had proved to be an efficient secretary. Her competence had allowed him to focus on Parliament matters. He needed to tell her as much today, when he saw her. It would be the first time they'd both be at Rosegate together since he'd employed her.

His spirits lifted at the thought of seeing her. He'd have a competent secretary to hand and his favourite jacket to wear while he worked through the piles of Parliamentary correspondence that waited on his desk.

Shaw reached for his jacket and slid an arm into the left sleeve and then the right. But his right arm got stuck halfway. Confused, Shaw pushed at the sleeve, trying to force his way through to no avail. What was the matter with the jacket?

He shrugged out of it and turned the jacket inside out, inspecting the lining. It didn't take much inspecting to see the problem. It glared at him in garish pink thread. Someone had sewn the lining closed with amateurish stitching. Surely the tailor Thomasia had taken the jacket to had not done this? Perhaps the man had a new apprentice? But that made no sense. No apprentice would sew a sleeve shut, let alone execute such poor-quality work.

As Shaw studied his mangled sleeve, the idea occurred to him that this was not an accident but a deliberate sabotage. His newly restored good humour faded. Who would do such a thing—and why? The list of 'who' was disappointingly short and led directly to the only person who'd had access to his jacket: Thomasia, whose praises he'd just been singing. Unfortunately, the reasons as to 'why' were less obvious. Why she'd done this was anyone's guess.

Shaw grabbed the jacket and headed downstairs, determined to have his answers.

He caught his housekeeper at the bottom of the steps. 'Mrs Grandy, has Miss Peverett arrived yet?'

'Yes, a few minutes ago. She's in the library as usual. I was just taking her some tea, since it's such a damp morning.'

Shaw's gaze took in the tea tray for the first time. 'That's thoughtful of you. Permit me to relieve you of it. I'll take it in. She and I have business to discuss.' He moved his jacket over one arm and took the weight of the tray.

In the library, the long reading table had been abandoned for the fireside. Thomasia sat in a chair, the picture of domestic bliss, in a round-necked blue gown, her dark hair in a neat bun that exposed the slim contours of her neck, her expression softly intent on the make-shift writing desk on her lap as her pen scratched. But he knew better. Her gentle countenance hid mischief beneath. Thomasia Peverett was anything but tranquil.

'Mrs Grandy thought you might like some tea.' He kicked the door shut behind him and made his way to the fireplace, setting the tea tray down on the low table amid the cluster of furniture.

'Thank you, that was kind of her.'

Thomasia's whisky gaze drifted to the jacket over his arm, and he was gratified to note his arrival had stirred a little mischief of its own.

'It's also kind of you to bring it in. Are you on your way out?'

The little minx was playing it cool in spite of her surprise. 'No, I'll be staying in today.' He settled in the chair adjacent and crossed one leg over one knee, giving every impression that he was in no rush to depart the library. 'I was originally going to come and thank you for your work. It's been an enormous help to me.' He watched her carefully. 'But then I tried on my jacket.'

He paused and waited—for what, he wasn't sure. A reaction? An admission of guilt? An apology? Or even just for her to squirm?

But Thomasia made no such move. She was as content as he to let the silence stretch between them until finally he said, 'Why did you do it, Thomasia?'

'Because you deserved it,' she answered calmly, reaching for the teapot. 'Will it be just milk?' she asked, as if her response had been adequate to the question.

And dammit if she didn't look lovely doing it, with those tawny eyes and high cheekbones. It would be easy enough for a man to forget his displeasure, even if it was only ten in the morning—far too early for such seductive thoughts. Was it the rainy day and dark skies that had him thinking of curling up with a woman, of spending a day in bed instead of behind a desk? Or perhaps it was those eyes that elicited such a response? Was she doing it on purpose? Perhaps it was a strategy designed to make him forget his anger towards her, forget her transgression.

He might be tempted, but he would not be so easily led. Two could play her game.

'Milk and an explanation, if you please.'

Chapter Five

'I owe *you* an explanation?' Thomasia arched a slim dark brow in an expression he could only construe as sardonic incredulity as she stirred her tea with a particularly stern vigour. 'You've been absent for two weeks, lied to me about the position and then insulted me. If there are explanations to be given, I rather think they're yours, Mr Rawdon.'

That was a neat trick she had of arching her brow and making a man feel like a cad when it was *his* jacket that had been sabotaged. Shaw wondered how many men had fallen for that distraction in the past. How many men had jumped to explain themselves and scrambled to apologise for ills she'd convinced them they'd committed? Even knowing that, Shaw found himself somewhat at sea, trying to divine the source of her displeasure, but he sure as hell wasn't going to assume culpability for it without enquiring first.

'Lied to you? Insulted you? How? When? As you've pointed out, I've been gone from the house. We've had no interaction.'

He took a careful sip of hot tea and racked his mind for any instance that might have been grounds for the things she alleged. He found none, but Thomasia was happy to oblige in cool, succinct tones.

'You led me to believe this secretarial position was to help you with Parliament work…that you might value the chance to consult me on certain matters. So far I've done nothing more than write acceptances to invitations and handle estate work.'

Ah, she was feeling unappreciated. She needed a sop for her efforts, some commendation. At least that would be the case with any other woman.

'You're not giving yourself enough credit,' he said. 'You've done far more than that. You've added up the ledgers and your efforts have freed me immensely to handle Parliament work. I cannot tell you how grateful I've been, and your work has been highly competent.'

Even as he made this sincere overture he knew it was a misstep. It was not what she was looking for.

'It's not what you led me to believe. You've not asked for my opinion once,' Thomasia contended.

He smiled—the kind of smile he might offer to placate a constituent. Another misstep. 'Rest assured, when I am in need of your opinion I will ask for it.'

'When do you think that might be? I expect that was a carrot to dangle in front of me—one you might easily choose not to act upon,' she replied sharply, her gaze clashing with his over teacups.

Sweet heavens, this woman knew how to prick his temper and make him feel defensive.

'I have not consulted you on matters of state, as you wished, so in your wisdom you decided to sew my sleeve shut?' Shaw summed up. 'Very mature.' He would soon remind her that he would not be led about by a girl who was barely twenty. He was no young swain, eager to please.

His scold was met by her taking another sip of her tea. She was not fazed by the reprimand.

'The sleeve is not for the lie, Mr Rawdon. It's for the insult.' She managed a polite smile and helped herself to one of Mrs Grandy's shortbread biscuits.

'The insult?' Just when he thought he had her pinned she manoeuvred him to new ground.

'Yes. You assumed that, since I was a woman, I'd naturally be handy with a needle and that I would naturally sew up your jacket. I doubt you'd assign such a task to a male secretary.'

He took a moment to digest the latest salvo. *She'd thought he'd meant for her to repair the jacket?*

'That was not my intention. I intended only that you drop it at the tailor on your way through the village,' he replied steadily, watching her for a reaction. For penitence? Surely now she would show some contrition.

'*I* could drop it off? Why? Because you were too busy riding to the hunt and drinking the afternoon away with your friends? You complain of not having enough time, and then you while away your days in the pursuit of leisure.'

Leisure? That was outside of enough.

Shaw set down his teacup and rose, pacing the length of the fireplace mantel in his agitation. She'd gone too far this time. He did not hesitate to sharpen his words.

'You know nothing of my life, or of Parliament. If you did, you would know that those drinks, those activities of "leisure" as you label them, *are* work. They are a chance to talk, to listen, to seek input from my constituents so that I may report local feelings back to Maldon and use them to inform our representation when it is time to vote in Parliament.'

How dare she accuse him of eschewing his civic duties? It set his temper on edge that she knew so little of him and yet had set about judging him.

'The Broxbourne Borough is lucky to have its MPs living locally. There are MPs who have never set eyes on the borough they represent.'

'It matters little if you only talk to men.' She gave a shake of her glossy dark head. 'It's rather insular, only talking to people who are likely to agree with your insights.'

'I talk to the people who will vote for my seat on election day,' he ground out. 'They are the people I represent.'

'Doesn't that strike you as wrong? I thought you said you wanted as much change as you could manage.' She met his gaze evenly. 'I see that you've confused change with a desire for power.'

That was the furthest consideration from his political agenda, and his temper was on a short leash. 'You'd best explain yourself.'

'Stanton's repeal.' She said the words almost coyly. 'Do you really believe any man thinks it's a bad idea to cut off financial support for women bringing up their children? Men see it as protection against the consequences of a one-night affair, but how do women see it? Have you asked them? If you had, you would know they see it as unfair. They see that men are protected from those consequences at the expense of women, who bear all the responsibility for that lapse in judgement.'

She paused.

'Stanton's repeal attempt is legislation for men, by men. But it affects more than men. Men's protection comes at the cost of *not* protecting women and children—those who are least able to protect themselves and who have the least rights in this Society we've created. They are reliant on the protection men toss to them like so many breadcrumbs and now that is to be taken from them, too. Their lives are being decided upon without their voice.'

He stopped his pacing and leaned against the mantel, taking in her words. Did she have any idea of how magnificent she was like this? When she was worked up in a passion, her whisky eyes alight with fervour? And she had a point. He hadn't considered Stanton's repeal in those terms. He'd not liked the legislation on the grounds of his own experience, and he believed a man needed to be responsible for his children, but that was still a male perspective. He'd not thought of it in terms of hearing voices—not the way Thomasia had framed it.

He gave her a half-smile as a truce. He'd not expected to quarrel with her when he'd entered the room. Perhaps he should have.

His mind went back to something else she'd said. 'It occurs to me that I am limited as to how I might ask women their opinions. They can't drink in the pub with me,' he joked, and then waited for her to make a remark about how that was something else wrong with the world.

But she fooled him again, waiting patiently and allowing him to continue.

'I cannot talk to women directly—not like I do with the men. But you could.' He speared her with his gaze. 'Why don't you be my eyes and ears among the ladies? After all, they might be influencing their husbands behind the scenes.'

She ought to jump at the chance. Wasn't this what she'd taken him to task for earlier?

He was mystified when she refused.

'Mr Rawdon, I don't socialise,' she replied, so demurely it was hard to reconcile her response with the firebrand she'd been moments before.

'Perhaps you just haven't had the opportunity for socialising. It is limited in these parts,' Shaw encouraged, trying to understand her reticence.

This was the same conundrum she'd presented that first night at dinner: a pretty young woman, primed for the Marriage Mart, who didn't want to go to London.

'You were eager enough earlier to participate in politics. Here is your chance—starting tonight. I'm due at Maldon's for supper and cards. Susannah was supposed to accompany me, but she's been called to a cousin's. She left this morning. I will not endear myself to Maldon's wife if I unbalance her numbers.' He only meant it partly in jest. He had no desire to upset Maldon's wife.

'Tonight? I couldn't possibly go on such short notice,' she began to protest, looking unnerved for someone who was usually so self-contained.

'Yes, you could. You can go home today at noon.

That will give you plenty of time before I call for you at five. It's an hour to Maldon's by carriage.'

He strode to the door, making it clear the decision had been made and the discussion was over. If he'd learned one thing about Thomasia Peverett it was that she liked to have the last word. Not this time. He turned back, his hand on the doorknob, to seal her compliance.

'Lord Stanton will be there.'

That would be a temptation she wouldn't be able to resist, although he would probably have the devil's own time keeping her in check. Well, that was what he'd have an hour in the carriage for—to make sure she knew how to behave and to make sure he didn't come to regret inviting her.

What an opportunity this was! Thomasia almost regretted her harsh words to Rawdon today in light of the supper invitation—*almost.*

She sat impatiently at her dressing table, letting the maid fuss with her hair. Rawdon would be here at any minute. She could hardly wait to write to the Coffee Yard ladies tomorrow about supper with Lord Stanton. It would be something of a private prank. Unbeknownst to him, he would be sitting down to supper with a member of the opposition, who would be sowing delicate seeds of dissent under his very nose. She would make the most of the half hour she'd have with the ladies while the gentlemen were at their brandy...

'You look wonderful, miss. It's good to see you getting out, and Mr Rawdon is a fine gentleman.' She fastened a string of pearls about Thomasia's neck and stepped back to survey her work. 'Mr Rawdon won't be able to take his eyes off you.'

Thomasia fingered the pearls at her throat, uncomfortable with the idea that this outing was being perceived as more than business by others, that they thought she and Rawdon might be going *together*.

'I'm not sure that's his intention. He merely needs someone to fill in for his sister.'

Although she *did* think she was in good looks tonight, dressed in a gown of deep teal. She only wanted to look good for The Cause, she told herself. A pretty woman could hold a man's interest long enough to make her point. She didn't mean to attract attention beyond that—certainly not Rawdon's—and yet there was no denying the little thrill that ran through her at the thought of turning his head, of knowing she might be capable of attracting such a man.

He was handsome, competent and intelligent, qualities rarely combined in any man. Not that it mattered. There was no point in attracting a man's attention—not for her, not ever again. Men were a complication. And there was Effie-Claire to think about.

Even for a night such as this there'd been arranging to do. There'd been milk to express and leave for Effie, instructions to give the maid, and she felt uncomfortable leaving the baby tonight for an extended period of time, especially since she already left Effie every day for a short time to go to Rosegate.

Part of that discomfort was guilt. Despite her words to Rawdon, and her disappointment over the limits of her work, she did enjoy what work he left for her, and she enjoyed the drive across the village to Rosegate, she enjoyed the time on her own.

Perhaps that made her a poor mother. She hoped not. Her own mother had managed to bring up five children and keep up with her duties as the local herbalist. Surely she could manage with one child and a position that was only temporary. When Mr Rawdon went to London she'd go back to being at Effie-Claire's side full-time. That knowledge assuaged some of her guilt, as did knowing that tonight was not a pleasure outing. Tonight was for The Cause, to strike a blow against Stanton.

There was a scratch at the door, followed by the quiet announcement that Rawdon was here. Her pulse ratcheted up a notch—because of what the evening portended, she told herself. It had nothing whatsoever to do with the man.

But that was a poor defence against the man who waited for her at the bottom of the stairs with her parents. Rawdon wore dark evening clothes, cut to the perfection of his form, suggesting this was slightly more than a country supper party. This was men from Town getting together for an evening and taking one another's measure.

'Miss Thomasia, you look lovely.' Rawdon took her gloved hand as she reached him and lifted it to his lips for a kiss. 'We'll not be too late returning, Dr Peverett.' He turned to her father. 'But you know the drive to Maldon's. I'll keep an eye on the clock and hope Maldon doesn't sit too long at cards.'

She hoped so, too. As great an opportunity as tonight offered, her body held limits on how long she could be gone.

Rawdon handed her into the carriage and took the rear-facing seat. 'We have an hour to ourselves,' he said as the carriage swayed into motion. 'There are some things I'd like to go over before we arrive.'

'Is this to be a business meeting?' Thomasia teased, but Rawdon was all seriousness.

'You might consider it that. Tonight is certainly about business—business masquerading as supper and cards. Careers are made and broken on such occasions.'

She saw for the first time the tiniest chink in Mr Rawdon's usual confidence. Tonight meant something to him. He wanted to make a good impression. More than that, he *needed* to make a good impression. She remembered his comment about risking the displeasure of Maldon's wife. He'd not been jesting. She remembered, too, how he'd whispered low at her ear, *All the change I can before I'm unpopular.*

He was in earnest tonight, and if he'd had his way, Susannah would have been beside him—his sister, someone he could trust implicitly to be on her best behaviour. But Susannah was gone. Rather than risk upsetting his hostess, he'd chosen her to take his sister's place. Perhaps he'd asked her out of desperation because he had no other females to hand. He was worried. She saw that now behind his blue eyes. He'd solved the problem of placating his hostess, but now he was wondering if he'd created another.

He could trust Susannah. But could he trust her?

The realisation that Rawdon saw her as untrustworthy humbled her. She liked to consider herself a good friend, loyal and true to those she cared for. But was Rawdon her friend? He was a family friend, but what was he to her and she to him? A secretary and her employer? Or was he counting on the friendship he held with her family tonight? It was humbling to realise that was all he could count on. After all, she'd sewn his jacket sleeve shut. It spoke poorly of her character. And yet she still saw the dilemma it posed for her. What if being loyal to The Cause meant being disloyal to *him*?

Across from her, Rawdon swallowed. 'Let me be succinct. I need you to be a credit to me. I must know that we are in this together, that you will support me. Can you do that?'

Suddenly it shamed her that he had to ask. Her accusations today seemed like a petty tantrum, proof as to why he had to. Their recent encounters did not recommend an implicit assumption of such trust.

'Yes, of course,' she vowed impetuously.

She would behave. She would be the epitome of a decorous young woman who could make her point without making it an attack. She had learned the art of moderation from the Coffee Yard ladies.

Unless, of course, she was provoked. But surely in the span of a few hours it would not come to that.

Chapter Six

Sir Phillip Maldon's home was a majestic manor designed to impress, with its steep many-peaked roof soaring into the night while an enormous chandelier illuminated the dark through the grand window which presided over the double-door entrance. At first glance, the image would steal one's breath, whether one was a Londoner used to fine things or a denizen of the countryside.

'I've heard of Sir Maldon's chandelier, but I've never seen it before,' Thomasia breathed in awe and delight, looking up at the window as Rawdon handed her down from the coach.

'Neither have I,' Rawdon answered in warm, low tones at her ear that suggested he wasn't entirely referring to the chandelier. 'It's spectacular.'

His hand rested gently at the small of her back—a polite gesture as he ushered her up the steps to the front door, nothing more. Certainly nothing to get bothered about. But Thomasia could not ignore the fact that she *was* bothered by it…bothered enough to feel a flush of awareness and a thrill of excitement flood through her…bothered enough to recognise that her body *liked* Shaw Rawdon's touch, even if her mind was quick to prompt that his touch was proprietorial, a means of staking ownership. One must be careful lest they find themselves possessed.

Once, touch had been a simple, uncomplicated pleasure and she'd enjoyed it. She still enjoyed it. She loved hugging her family, loved them hugging her in return. She delighted in holding Effie-Claire and Anne's little boy. Some of the best moments of her life had been built around touch before Anthony had taught her how powerful and dangerous touch could be, how it could be manipulated. Now it was both a danger and a delight—a double-edged sword.

Maldon's butler took them through to the drawing room, a room that glittered in cream and gold and crystal. 'Mr Shaw Rawdon and Miss Thomasia Peverett,' he announced, bringing all the eyes in the room in their direction.

Thomasia squared her shoulders and lifted her chin out of reflex. She remembered how to do this—how to address the room with all her confidence on display, to let everyone see how pleased she was to be there.

No one looking at her tonight would guess that she'd tried to get out of this—that she felt guilty for being here instead of sitting on the nursery floor playing, guilty for revelling in the freedom of being out of the house for a short while, for feeling like her old self even though she knew better because that girl was gone. No one knew she was an opponent in their midst.

Tonight's freedom didn't come without risk if her secrets were discovered.

Their host came forward with his wife. 'Rawdon, it's good to see you. I trust the journey wasn't onerous? Miss Peverett, what a delight. I hope your father is well? Please give him and your mother my regards.'

He smiled broadly, but not broadly enough to hide the speculation in his eyes as his gaze moved between them. What did this mean, she and Shaw Rawdon together? When she'd allowed Rawdon to talk her into this, she'd been focused on how to manage the practicalities of the outing. She'd not stopped to consider more particular implications. Had he? Had he known how this would look to the others? Had he intended to prompt such speculation?

Maldon directed Rawdon towards a group of men at the fireplace. 'Let's get you a drink. You know everyone, of course, Rawdon?'

Lady Maldon performed the same function for her, slipping an arm through Thomasia's with a practised smile. 'Come, let me introduce you. We'll leave the men to their politics.'

Their strategy to divide and conquer was off to a splendid start, ably helped along by their host and hostess. This was what she'd been brought along for—to be Rawdon's eyes and ears. She ought to be glad, but she felt the loss of him by her side keenly—an odd sensation, given that this was business only. They weren't friends and they had no aspirations as lovers.

She accepted a glass of ratafia from Lady Maldon and sipped at it in long, slow intervals. Her father had advised against drinking alcohol while she breastfed

Effie-Claire. Her gaze was less cautious, having developed an exceedingly annoying and unbusinesslike habit of drifting in Rawdon's direction.

He was taller than the other men, broader and brighter, too, his russet hair standing out among heads that were liberally peppered with grey. He was also decidedly younger. No wonder he was eager to impress these men who could act as mentors and patrons, who had the means to advance a burgeoning career for a price. Would he be willing to pay that price?

It occurred to her that she didn't know. In fact, she knew very little about Shaw Rawdon. He was new to Haberstock, having arrived only four years ago in the district to take over Rosegate. Beyond that, she'd not paid much attention. It had not been the sort of news a girl newly turned sixteen with other things on her mind had paid attention to.

Rawdon had kept to himself that first year, busy restoring the estate to its current tidy splendour. Then, his land and house ready, he'd moved fast—she could see that now, in retrospect. Within the next three years he'd been elected to Parliament from a closed community where everyone had known everyone for generations. Somehow he'd managed to fit in, managed to parlay his status as a landowner into a seat in the House. Impressive. Ambitious.

She watched him laugh at something Maldon said. Had his rise been accomplished on charm and charisma alone, or was there something more at play behind the scenes? In her rather painful experience, no one was ever all that they seemed. Anthony hadn't been. His charming golden exterior had hidden a corrupt, selfish soul. Everyone played a part. These days, she could add herself to that list.

Tonight she was the ingénue. She knew what these women gathered about her saw: a pretty young girl, still fresh to the world. They treated her like the virgin she wasn't. They did not see her as a mother, a girl who'd made a poor choice in love, or as a political activist who disagreed with their husbands' positions. They didn't see any of that because she didn't let them—because she *couldn't* let them.

In the gentlemen's corner Lord Stanton leaned forward, intent on something Rawdon was saying.

'Mr Rawdon cuts a very fine figure,' said Lady Stanton. She had caught Thomasia's gaze and followed it to its conclusion. 'My husband is quite taken with him. He could be a promising young man if he plays his cards right.' She opened her fan, inviting confidences, her eyes knowing. 'You could be a lucky young woman, too, if you played *your* cards right.' She smiled behind the fan. 'But you'd do best to snatch him up while his star is still ascending. Don't wait. You can ride his coattails to success alongside him. And what delicious coattails they'd be, too.'

She gave Rawdon a lascivious perusal that shocked Thomasia in its frankness.

'He needs a wife sooner rather than later for advancement. He can't depend on his sister for ever.' She turned her gaze in Thomasia's direction with consideration. 'It would be a well-timed arrangement for you both,' she advised. 'Especially with your sisters so well placed now.'

Thomasia fought back the retort that climbed up her

throat, begging for release. There was much that needed saying, but this was not the place. She'd promised herself and Rawdon that she'd behave. Besides, Lady Stanton was only responding to what she saw—a pretty girl on the arm of an ambitious, eligible local man. It was not a battle worth fighting. The Coffee Yard ladies would be proud of her.

At supper, Thomasia thought perhaps the fates had rewarded her restraint by seating her beside Lord Stanton for the meal. He was a tall, spare man, who gave the impression of being as dry as a stick—an impression that was not hard to believe, given the kind of legislation he supported. What a prime opportunity this was! She could not have planned it better herself and she did not intend to waste it.

Thomasia went straight to work after the first course. 'I am told you plan to propose a repeal of the 1845 Bastardy Act in the coming session...' It was a polite enough conversational enquiry, and it was all it took for Lord Stanton to elaborate.

'Yes, I am. My repeal is an attempt to encourage moral behaviour by keeping childbearing where it belongs—inside a marriage as a *wife's* duty. A little something to keep families together and to emphasise the importance of marriage.'

Was that really how he saw it? Family-focused? She tried to get a polite yet pointed question in but failed as he continued.

'I think, my dear, that the marital knot has been allowed to untie itself too casually these days—or not to be tied at all while people enjoy the benefits of marriage without the vows,' he added delicately. 'It results in children being brought up without a family.' He shook his head sadly. 'I blame women like the Marchesa di Cremona, now the Viscountess Taunton. What a scandal that was…divorcing the Marchese and coming home to marry Taunton, all because she was not accustomed to her husband's lifestyle.'

That was not what Thomasia had learned when she'd been in London. The Italian marchese had been a brute. She struggled with the desire to correct him. 'You would see women forced to stay in unhappy marriages?' she questioned carefully. Marriage reform was another of the Coffee Yard ladies' agenda items and she was well versed.

'The problem, Miss Peverett, is that women don't know what they want.' His tone was positively patronising. 'They want freedom, but they want to be financially supported by the husband they want to be free of—it makes no sense. They cannot have it both ways. Marriage is good for them—as are children. It settles them down, keeps them busy and out of trouble. It has worked wonders for your sisters. One of them has a child already, proof that marriage is exactly the right antidote for wayward spirits.'

Thomasia bristled at this slight to her siblings, and this time couldn't resist a bit of clarification. 'Hard work does the same. My sister Thea, the Countess of Wychavon, still works at the gentlewomen's hospital, and Anne goes out with Lord Tresham's mobile health clinics even though she has a child now.'

Stanton furrowed his brow. 'Well, I am surprised at how tolerant their husbands are.'

Thomasia met his gaze evenly. 'Perhaps they are not

intimidated by their wives' ambitions.' She delivered her barb with a smile, and was gratified to see that Stanton wasn't quite sure if he'd been insulted.

'What of your ambitions? Will you be settling down soon? Showing your sisters how it's done, eh? Marrying at a decent age.'

His gaze lingered too long on her bosom for her comfort. Thomasia reached for her wine glass, using the gesture to divert his stare. If not for the promise she'd made to behave, the contents of that goblet would have found their way to Stanton's trousers.

She was aware of Rawdon's gaze on her... Perhaps he was wondering what was being said and worrying. 'I assure you, Lord Stanton, I know my place and my duty,' she answered tightly.

Her place was with the Coffee Yard ladies, and her duty was to remove the scales from the eyes of the public so that they could see repealing laws like this wasn't about preserving families but about keeping women down.

She'd never felt her calling as keenly as she did at that moment.

'I think everyone was quite taken with you.' Shaw stretched his legs out across the coach. 'How did you like your first taste of politics?'

The evening had gone well and he was in good spirits. Lord Stanton had asked questions about his plans for foundling schools. He'd taken the man's interest as a good sign, and Thomasia had managed to be charming. More than charming. She'd been captivating in her teal gown and pearls, with that wondrous combination of youthful freshness and womanly lushness on display once more. He'd not liked the way Stanton had looked at her at dinner, though. It had raised his protective instincts.

'It's all so dishonest…everyone posturing, everyone saying the right thing but not the truth.'

Thomasia's answer surprised him with its critical sharpness, and he felt as if her comment was a critique of him instead of the evening.

'It makes me wonder why you asked me to come. Perhaps you had other motives? Stanton and his wife are under the impression you intend to wed soon. Do you?' Her sharp eyes pierced him. 'Were you trying me out tonight? Seeing how I would perform, like a well-trained horse? Has all my work acting as your secretary been a covert audition for a different role?'

'Absolutely not. I think you've leapt to rather wild conclusions. You know Susannah left suddenly today. That was not planned, and nor was the Stantons' speculation tonight. That was an unlooked-for consequence, and I am sorry for it.'

Only partially sorry, though. He'd not intended to 'try her out', as she put it, but he *had* noticed her tonight, from the moment she'd come downstairs to the way she'd sparkled at the supper table, and it was indeed difficult to dislodge the image the Stantons had conjured with their speculation. It was not an unpalatable image. He could do worse than Thomasia Peverett. She was a lovely, intelligent and well-connected woman. She was also prickly and ever-changing, her temper a quicksilver thing. She'd keep a man on his toes—just as she was doing now.

'Lady Stanton believes you should wed soon in order to advance your career. More specifically, she made it perfectly clear that she thinks it would be acceptable for me to trade riding your up-and-coming coattails for my family connections.'

Thomasia's matter-of-fact recitation held a sharp edge. He knew she was challenging him.

'Is it true?'

Shaw chuckled. 'Factually speaking, she's not wrong. I *should* marry. Married men advance. They're seen as stable and trustworthy. Should I marry *you*, though? That's the question. Of course, the idea would appeal to Lady Stanton. She is the sort of woman who would see it as a good exchange.' This was becoming a dangerous conversation.

'Do you disagree? Is it not a good exchange or is it the person you object to?'

He could feel Thomasia bristling across from him. She'd not liked the undertones of his response. He should not have baited her, but he'd been intrigued by how she might respond. In spite of her politics, what did she personally believe about marriage?

'Perhaps I would make such a trade if an alliance was all I was looking for in a marriage.'

Shaw folded his hands behind his head and prepared himself for the question he knew was coming—the question he should have avoided at all costs. Because it would lead down a perilous road when he was in a carriage late at night with a beautiful, tempting woman, and yet he couldn't seem to help himself.

'What *are* you looking for?'

Thomasia wasn't even subtle about it, but he sensed

no flirtation beneath her words—just genuine curiosity. It should have eased his sense of concern in broaching such a topic with a woman, and it did, but in exchange it ratcheted up his desire for this woman with whom he could discuss such things, who was interested in his opinion on such topics. He needed to tread carefully here for both their sakes.

'I'm looking for a partner, for passion, and I am willing to wait for it. So you needn't fear I have any designs on your person, Thomasia. Lady Stanton may speculate all she likes.'

His attempt at humour did not smooth her hackles.

'Are you saying you wouldn't marry me?' She sounded offended.

He laughed out of self-defence. 'What a little hypocrite you are! One minute you're accusing me of harbouring covert marital designs and the next you're upset that I am not.' He threw his hands up in mock surrender. 'All I am saying is that I wouldn't marry you because I don't *know* you. I thought we'd both agreed that a wife should be more than a placeholder.'

He offered her a smile and she smiled back, but something sharp lurked in her eyes that said, *Beware*.

He didn't have to wait long. She sat back in her seat, her gaze on him as she fired her next salvo. 'It's all right. I wouldn't marry you either.'

Not in a million years had he thought she'd say *that*.

'Why? I'm landed… I have income and influence,' he spluttered, entirely caught off guard while the sparkle of her laughter filled the coach.

Chapter Seven

'Who's the hypocrite now?' Thomasia smiled, not unkindly, after she'd had her laugh. 'It's a little different when the shoe's on the other foot, isn't it? And yet my answer is like yours. Just as you prefer not to marry a stranger, I prefer not to marry at all.' She gave another laugh. 'Does that shock you?'

'Nothing you say shocks me. I'm getting used to it.'

Rawdon smiled back, seeming entirely at ease with poking fun at himself. It was a rare man who admitted his own fallibilities. She could appreciate that about him, although she shouldn't. It only added to the list of things that made him so likeable—and likeable was dangerous. Men and women could *not* be friends, and she could not offer him more than that.

'Truly, though, you never mean to marry?' His voice was beguilingly soft in the dim interior of the coach. 'I think that would be a shame. You would miss...so much...'

But they both knew that wasn't what he meant. *Passion.* The word hovered unspoken between them.

'Why?' She dropped her own voice to a low husk, ready to say the unspoken word, in part to goad him and in part to play with fire and see where the conversation led. 'Passion can be had outside of marriage. If I desire it, I needn't sell my soul or my freedom to get it.'

She watched him for a reaction but he gave away nothing, only a nod.

'I am sure your sisters don't feel that way.'

His voice sent a slow trill of awareness down her spine as her mind contemplated the idea of passion with Rawdon.

'They have their happiness and I'll have mine.' She refused to give in to the temptation of his voice, to the notion that perhaps here in the coach, with no one to see, she might endeavour to taste that passion.

'Perhaps you have not met the right man?' He whispered the temptation. 'Have you ever been in love?'

She could have handled the first part of his question. Men were so egotistical, believing that they'd be the right man. It would have been easy to throw that back in his face. But the second part was more difficult. It could not be ignored. Perhaps she could put an end to his probing with some blunt honesty.

'Once. It was very painful, Mr Rawdon. I wouldn't recommend it. Stick to your passion. Have *you* ever been in love?' If he was going to probe, she would do the same.

'I've played at it, I suspect. But I've never been in real love. I'd like to be, though. I'd like to fall in love with my wife.' The low timbre of his voice was seductive in the late hour.

'You have higher aspirations for marriage than most men, Mr Rawdon.'

His gaze lingered on her mouth. She knew that look. It was the look a man gave in a prelude for a kiss. For a moment she thought he might act on it, and then he blinked, his gaze moving to a point beyond her shoulder.

'Call me Shaw. After all, we've bared our souls to one another.' He laughed and tugged at the lapels of his jacket, the moment past.

'Is that short for something? Bradshaw, perhaps?' She fiddled with her skirts, recovering herself from the misguided headiness of the last few seconds. This was far safer ground.

He made a face—an expression that resembled a cringe. 'Crenshaw.' He laughed. 'I know, it's awful. It's a family name on my mother's side. What about Thomasia?'

'It's also a family name, in a way.' She blushed, as if this was as personal as their prior discussion. 'All of us are named for famous doctors. I'm named for a fifteenth-century Italian healer.'

'Do you have medical aspirations like your siblings?' he asked, as if the thought had just occurred to him and he'd somehow overlooked the obvious.

She shook her head. 'I have no desire to practise medicine like Thea and Anne. I want to practise in a different way, through advocacy. I want medicine *for* women, by women.'

This was her passion… This was a critical part of the fight for equality.

He furrowed his brow, not quite understanding. 'But there are doctors who provide care specifically designed for women.'

She knew it wasn't meant as an argument.

'But they are men. It is not the same.' She leaned forward in her excitement to explain. 'Men have male physicians to consult—physicians who know inherently what it is like to live in male skin. Shouldn't women have the same privilege in their healthcare?' She rushed on. 'That privilege did exist once. In Salerno, near Naples, for one golden moment, there were the Ladies of Salerno. They attended medical school, they contributed to a textbook that was used all across Europe, they treated other women, and they treated men. But the point is women had a choice. They don't have that today. They must accept a male physician's perspective, whether they want it or not.'

'What happened to them, your Ladies of Salerno?' Shaw asked when she paused, his voice full of raw inquisitiveness.

'The same thing that always happens to women who have too much power or too much education. They were simply edited out of history. Slowly, over five hundred years, they were gradually phased out of the manuscripts they'd helped write.' Old anger rose. The ending of the story had upset her from the first time her mother had told it to her, when she was six. 'Men are fearful, covetous creatures. They destroy what they do not understand and make conquests of the rest, marking our bodies with their names like flags on a map. Fallopian tubes…pouch of Douglas…hymen…Bartholin's gland.'

She gave an insistent wave of her hand and paused. She'd lost him in her tirade and now she must backtrack to explain.

'Those parts are all named for the men who claimed to have discovered them through years of medical study, as if they were Christopher Columbus in the New World.'

'I see,' he replied solemnly, and she thought he might indeed see, that perhaps she'd made an inroad.

'Now you know why I won't marry you or anyone. Enough of me has already been claimed. I would keep this last piece.'

Although once she'd nearly given it away to Anthony and his false promises, not understanding what she was giving up or what she was helping perpetuate by buying into the Season and the belief that her life ought to be parties and swains and pretty dresses.

'Yes, I do know now.'

His blue eyes glittered in the coach as he held her gaze, serious and sincere, and she felt he saw more than she'd meant to show him—not only that she wouldn't marry because she didn't want to be owned, governed by a system that made her little more than a slave, but also that she would not set herself up to be hurt. Again.

They were nearly home. The hour between Haberstock Hall and Beechmont had sped by. They spent the last mile in silence, perhaps each of them reliving the evening and regrouping. She was glad now that he hadn't given in to the impulse of the moment and kissed her. She was glad, too, that she hadn't encouraged it. It would have been easy to have leaned forward, tilted her head, parted her lips just an inviting fraction. She'd stolen kisses before—quick secret kisses in a garden. She knew how to do it, and she knew how meaningless they were in the end.

Such kisses held little value. She did not want to *steal* a kiss from Shaw Rawdon, to coax from him that which he might not have freely given otherwise. When he kissed a woman he'd mean it. It would be a token of his passion and that passion would be exquisite—much like the man himself.

Sweet heavens, she was no better than Lady Stanton with such imaginings. She roused herself as the coach turned down the drive to Haberstock Hall. Such imaginings were best set aside. Tonight was the product of close confines, the late hour and good wine, all of which had spurred on a provocative conversation. It was and could be nothing more. She was a mother with a child.

Effie-Claire woke crying and fretful the next morning. Thomasia lifted the baby from the crib beside her bed, only half-awake as she fed her. The late night had left her with less sleep than usual and she was feeling the effects. She was regretting that conversation in the coach as well. How would she face Rawdon after such a frank discussion? Rawdon. Not Shaw. She could not permit the familiarity. He was her employer—nothing more. That balance needed to be restored today. There was no sense in perpetuating the fantasy. He'd been right last night—he barely knew her, and if he ever did he would thank her for keeping her distance. Unwed mothers weren't good for a man's career.

Effie-Claire finished feeding, but she didn't settle like she usually did. Instead, she remained fretful. Nothing eased her. Not walking the corridors, not looking out of the windows, not a nice rocking session in the chair beside the fire in her room. By half past nine Thomasia was convinced something was wrong with the baby. She took the child to find her mother in the herbarium.

'I think it might be colic,' she suggested to her mother, tickling Effie's nose with a frond of lavender.

Her mother looked up from her work table. 'Run your finger along her gums and see if there's a bump. My guess is that she might be teething.'

Thomasia found the telltale bump immediately and sighed, disappointed. It was going to be a long day. There was nothing to do for a teething baby but help the child get through it and minimise the discomfort.

'I'll get a carrot from Mrs Newsome for her to chew on and I'll send a note to Rosegate telling them I won't be coming.'

It was an unfortunate day to miss. She didn't want Rawdon thinking she was a coward. But how could she leave Effie when Effie needed her?

Her mother came to her, taking Effie from her arms. 'Go to Rosegate, dear. I'll look after her. I've managed more than one teething child in my day.'

Thomasia was underway in fifteen minutes. Thank heavens for mothers, she thought as she chirped to the horse. What would she have done without her mother's assistance that morning? Still, she wouldn't abuse her mother's offer. She would gather up her work at Rosegate and bring it home, under some plausible excuse that she was needed here.

What did mothers who couldn't bring their work home do? Mothers who didn't have mothers of their own able to step into the breach? What happened to mothers who had no one to take care of their children? Who had to choose between their wages and their family? It was all the more reason to see Stanton's repeal defeated. Mothers shouldn't be put in such a position to start with.

Thomasia had her excuses prepared by the time she arrived at Rosegate, only to discover she didn't need them. Mrs Grandy met her in the hall with the news that Rawdon had left this morning on unexpected business for Maldon that had arrived at dawn and he wouldn't return until the end of the week.

'He's left you instructions,' Mrs Grandy said.

'Very good. I'll take the work with me and do it from the Hall, so that you needn't worry about me being underfoot this week,' Thomasia improvised.

This would do both her and Mrs Grandy a favour, she reasoned. She could be at home with Effie, and Mrs Grandy needn't worry about tea trays and luncheons for one. There was the added bonus of not needing to face Shaw immediately after their rather intimate conversation. All tallied, it was a most fortuitous week for him to be gone.

It had been one hell of a week and he had deuced little to show for it other than accumulating miles on Stanton's behalf, lobbying for a cause he didn't believe in. He went to bed each night disgusted with himself and the flimsy rationales he created to justify his efforts. But he was home now.

Shaw set his valise down in the Rosegate foyer with a grateful sigh. He pulled out his pocket watch and smiled. He'd made good speed home from the train station, and would be in time for tea with Thomasia before she left.

He'd not seen her since their outing to Beechmont,

and the conversation in the coach had lingered in his mind all week, growing ever more tempting, ever more tantalising the more he ruminated on it. His mind had replayed every word, every nuance, every glance countless times.

That had been a magical hour. Had he ever talked to a woman like that? Or had a woman talk to him straight from the truth of her heart? He found he wanted more of it, more of her. He'd spent a large part of the week wondering what Thomasia was doing, imagining her *here* at Rosegate, in the library, sitting at the table or in the chair before the fire, writing letters, her dark head bent to her work.

It was an infatuation only, born of midnight hours and loneliness. He'd parlayed an hour's conversation into a domestic fantasy. It could be nothing more by their own definitions and boundaries. He hardly knew her well enough at this point for it to be more than fantasy and infatuation, and she had no intention to open her heart at present. These were hardly the ingredients needed for a relationship to blossom.

'Mr Rawdon, sir, you're home!' Mrs Grandy bustled forward. 'Welcome back. You've been missed.'

'And I've missed Rosegate, Mrs Grandy, along with your tea trays. Might I have one sent to the library? I'll take tea with Miss Thomasia before she leaves.'

He watched Mrs Grandy's smile disappear.

'Miss Thomasia isn't here. She hasn't been here all week.' The housekeeper reached for his bag to take upstairs.

Shaw grimaced, his good mood fleeing. 'No, Mrs

Grandy, leave it. Send word to the stable to have Chiron saddled. I'll just need a moment to change.'

Part of him felt betrayed. All week he'd been imagining her here in his home, doing the work he'd hired her to do, and she'd never been here. Never once had his mind-pictures of her been real.

That sense of betrayal had morphed into righteous anger by the time he'd galloped to Haberstock Hall. Not all of his anger was for Thomasia. He'd saved some for himself. He'd convinced himself Thomasia Peverett was special—a one-of-a-kind woman who'd been hurt by love, perhaps a woman who was waiting for love to be redeemed. He didn't like discovering his impressions were incorrect. He was seldom wrong about people and he didn't like it.

He threw Chiron's reins to a groom and stormed up the front steps. He must have looked as thunderous as the grey skies overhead, because Mrs Newsome took a step backwards when he entered the hall.

'I'm here to see Miss Thomasia.'

The words were polite but the edge on them was unmistakable.

'She's indisposed, Mr Rawdon,' the housekeeper replied firmly, but the nervous clasp of her hands at her waist gave away her concern. She had all the airs of a servant who'd been instructed to turn away callers to protect her mistress.

'She *is* here, and she *will* see me, Mrs Newsome. This is a matter of business.'

He pushed past the housekeeper and headed up the stairs. He would apologise later, once he had answers as to why she'd taken a week off work without permission.

The sound of laughter met him on the landing. Thomasia's laughter. He'd know the clear bell sound of it anywhere, and he followed it down the corridor to a door that stood ajar. He could hear her talking, could hear a baby's gurgle as he approached.

Shaw stopped at the door to gather himself, his anger receding at the sound of a baby. Perhaps Anne had come to visit and brought her child. That would explain the week off. He could understand that, and would have given her time off to be with her sister if he'd been here. He could hardly be angry over something he would have granted.

He made use of his vantage point to peer into the room without being seen, letting a smile chase away the remnants of his anger. Thomasia sat in a rocker, the picture of placid domesticity, with an infant on her lap, a book in her hand. She hadn't been talking... She'd been reading. Shaw's heart thumped in approval, in want. For a woman who claimed she would never marry she looked incredibly natural with the baby. How could she not want that?

He gently pushed the door open and announced himself in friendly tones, so as not to startle the infant. 'Hello, Thomasia, this looks cosy—who is this fine child?' He offered a broad smile to put her at ease, to assure her he'd not come to berate her. Only he needed to know that had been his original motive.

At the sight of him Thomasia gasped and clutched the child to her. It seemed a very protective, very defensive gesture. 'Mr Rawdon, what are you doing here?'

'Shaw, remember?'

There was guilt in her eyes, and fear, too—something

he'd not anticipated ever seeing in Thomasia Peverett's gaze. This was not guilt over missing work… This guilt went deeper—as if a dire secret had been revealed. But in a moment she'd mastered it.

'I have just returned and wanted to make sure all was well,' he lied—just a little. She needn't know his visit had been prompted by thinking the worst of her. 'Mrs Grandy said you hadn't been over to Rosegate all week. I was…concerned.' He smiled again. 'But I see the reason for it now.'

'What is that reason, Mr Rawdon?' Thomasia's voice was cool, her gaze wary.

'A family visit from your sister. I wouldn't stand in the way of that. Did Tresham come with her? I wouldn't mind a good chat with him.'

Thomasia's gaze narrowed. 'My sister and Tresham have not come for a visit.'

Something was wrong—no, not wrong…just not what he'd thought. His interpretation of the facts had somehow led to an incorrect conclusion. He furrowed his brow, trying to realign the information, but Thomasia was faster.

'This is Effie-Claire, my daughter.'

All hell broke loose in his head.

Chapter Eight

Shaw could only stare. He felt rooted to the ground as the chaos of her words chased themselves around in his head. How could that be? This was the one question that managed to force itself to the fore amid the disarray of his mind.

There were explanations, of course, and his logical mind latched on to one. She was a widow—a young, tragic widow—with a child whose father had died before her birth. His conclusion made sense. Love for her had been painful, she'd said. It most certainly had been if it had led her to a marriage cut short and a child to raise alone.

And yet this rationale was already full of flaws. She'd allowed herself to be introduced at Maldon's as Miss Peverett. Where there was one flaw, others surged, too. She did not dress in mourning, she wore no ring— although those things were more easily explained away. Surely there was an explanation for the name as well. For it to be otherwise was to cast aspersions and scandal on Thomasia. For it to be otherwise was…unthinkable.

Shaw found the power to move. He knelt before the

baby with a smile. 'She's a beautiful child,' he complimented, chuckling as the baby grabbed his finger.

'Today she's an angel.' Thomasia smiled down at the infant with unmistakable fondness. 'She's been teething this week.' She lifted her gaze to watch him with wary eyes. 'I couldn't leave her.'

'You could have brought her. Mrs Grandy would have doted on the darling—although your tea trays would have likely suffered,' Shaw joked. He was feeling like a cad for having been so quick to anger over her absence. He should have known she'd have a good reason.

'No, I couldn't have,' she corrected. It was not a demur. 'This—Effie and I—is not what you think,' she said solemnly, holding his gaze with her own.

'And what is it that I think?' he prompted, not liking being gainsaid, nor the pit that was forming in his stomach as his earlier justifications withered away.

Her tawny port eyes didn't blink. 'You're thinking there must be a reasonable explanation for this—that perhaps I am a widow—and you're already spinning a tragic tale.' She gave a hard laugh. 'I can see from your expression that's exactly what you thought…what you *wanted* to think. Should I let you think that? It would be easier than the truth. Although I can see already that you can't quite make your interpretation work.'

Something turned in his gut and an invisible stone weight settled there. In one short sentence she'd decimated his logical answer and forced him towards the unthinkable. His mind scrabbled for purchase, grabbing for answers as a man sliding downhill might grab for roots and vines, anything with which to break his fall.

'I would have the truth, Thomasia.'

The bottom of the hill was fast approaching, and he was rushing towards it at a crashing speed.

Thomasia rose, the child in her arms, and paced before the window, unable to meet his eyes. 'You are confused because I am beyond your honour, Shaw. Your honour won't allow you to conceive of the truth, so I will say it for you. I am not a widow. I am not married now and nor have I ever been. I am a mother with a child born out of wedlock.'

She gazed out the window and he thought perhaps she looked away not only for herself, but for him as well, to give him time to organise his thoughts, his expression, his response, or perhaps to give him time to slink away without having to face her.

'Why didn't you tell me?' he asked quietly, feeling the past and the present roaring in his ears.

But he knew the answer before the words left his mouth. This was not something a woman advertised about herself. It was a scandal of the highest order. It put a woman beyond both honour and Society. He'd seen it first-hand with his own mother—how hard she'd worked to present the façade of a decent widow to the world so that no one would guess what she'd done.

His mind tried to right itself. It was full of questions, all of them centred on Thomasia. His immediate concern was for her. He'd seen the fear that had flashed in her eyes when he came upon them. What did she fear from him? That he would be angry? That he would take that anger out on her? Or was it a more emotional fear that he would expose her? His mother had known all those fears…

'Did you think to keep the child a secret?' Another inane question. He seemed to be the master of them today.

'I thought I had until spring.'

She turned to face him, to let him see the hint of accusation in her eyes, a reminder that she'd had it all planned out until he'd come along with his offer of work, then dragging her to Beechmont and drawing attention to her.

'I'm sorry.'

The words were entirely inadequate. His mother must be turning in her grave at her son's behaviour. She'd brought him up better than that, taught him to give a woman both respect and privacy. He felt like an utter cad.

Thomasia gave a wry half-smile that mocked him. 'Sorry for what? For running roughshod over Mrs Newsome? You must have to have got this far. Or sorry for barging in here uninvited? Sorry you met me? Sorry you gave me work? Sorry you took me to Beechmont? There's a lot to be sorry for.'

'No, I'm not sorry I've met you.' Far from it. She livened up his days with her sharp intellect and her sharper tongue. And at night remembrances of the day, of their exchanges, lingered in his mind as he drifted off to sleep. 'I *am* sorry that you feel you have to hide away—sorry that you feel you are defined by this.'

Because she was defined by it. She was not wrong about that, nor about her choices to shield herself and her child from Society's discrimination. Now that the initial tidal wave of shock had ebbed, his mind was able to see beyond to the implications represented by the sweet baby in her arms, and something in his heart began to break.

A little voice whispered the beginnings of the old saying that had shaped his childhood. *It wasn't fair... It wasn't right.*

The baby began to fuss, and after a few failed attempts from Thomasia to soothe her it became apparent the child was hungry. Thomasia threw him a pleading look he was slow to catch. *Oh, she needs to feed her.* What an idiot he was.

'Perhaps I should go? Yes, of course I should go.' He stumbled over his words. 'I'll take my leave now.'

He made her a bow in the hopes of making up for his awkward words. He didn't want to go. He wanted to stay. He wanted her to invite him to wait until the child was fed so that they might talk. But Thomasia issued no invitation. All her attention was on the baby, and he wondered if she even noticed him leaving.

His unanswered questions kept him company all night. He'd tried to settle when he arrived home. He'd been unable to distract himself by looking over his correspondence and immersing himself in the latest government reports. He'd finally given up and opted for an evening of contemplation, sitting before the fire in the library, a glass of brandy at his elbow, letting his thoughts have free rein.

The most obvious questions were, who was the father of Thomasia's child and why hadn't they married? Thomasia was from a good family with a sound background. She'd have been courted by gentry, minor peers, second sons of more major peers, and men of established professions with upward mobility—officers, established vicars, doctors… These were men who knew their duty if they trifled with a woman of good breeding. Anticipating wedding vows and a coming child were both reasons to accelerate a trip to the altar in their world, not to walk away from it. Surely there'd been an expectation that they would marry beforehand or they would not have dallied?

Shaw swirled his brandy in the glass, watching the firelight play across the facets of the crystal. What if that expectation could not be met? What if the young man had been killed before they could wed? That was a likely possibility with the war on. What if the father had jilted her and she hadn't told him about the child? Shaw could imagine Thomasia in a temper, doing such a thing. But a calmer Thomasia would not do something so rash—something that would put her in an unthinkable predicament for life. Unless that predicament had been a marriage she didn't want. Then why would she have slept with the man in the first place if she despised him?

Every answer he manufactured spawned more questions, more dead ends. He finished off his drink. Damn, but he wanted answers.

His conscience dug at him. *She doesn't owe you any. Who are you to her that you are entitled to such intimate information?*

Indeed, who was he to her but the employer who'd dragged her to a supper she'd asked not to attend? The man who'd invaded her sanctuary? Those were hardly the acts of someone qualified to be privy to her innermost thoughts. They were reserved for someone who was her friend.

Why does it matter if you know or not? his conscience nudged again.

That answer he did have. *Because I need to make this right. I have ruined her plans, or at the least put a crimp in them. I owe her,* Shaw thought. *I will survive any scandal that might emerge, but she will not. For me, scandal would be short-lived, but she will never outrun it.*

Although it sounded as if she was determined to try. *I thought I had until spring,* she'd said.

To do what? To decide how to stay? How to leave? Where to go?

More questions, and few answers to go with them.

Maybe tomorrow, when she came to work, he would find a way to speak of these things, to assure her that he was her friend, her ally, that he had no wish to bring her sadness, that she was safe with him.

But she didn't come to work the next day. Or the one after that.

He was going to have to try a different tactic than waiting for her to come to him. If she wouldn't come to work for her employer, perhaps she'd come to tea to speak with her friend.

The note was signed *Your friend, Shaw Rawdon.* Thomasia looked down at the piece of paper in her hand and then looked up once more to the front door of Rosegate.

Was he her friend? The notion struck against her understanding of men and women. Men and women were not friends. She wasn't entirely sure she was here because of friendship. She was here because she felt she owed him something—perhaps a sanitised explanation of her situation—and she was here because she wanted to inveigle from him his promise that he would not expose her. She was here to 'stop the bleeding', as her father would say.

Thomasia brushed at the skirts of her dark blue driving costume and adjusted her hat one last time. They were stalling fidgets. She was still uncertain that coming was the best idea. She'd favoured a clean break, but apparently he had not. Perhaps he needed assurances, too—although she didn't know what those might be. Perhaps it had occurred to him after he'd had time to think that being seen associating with her was dangerous for his political career.

She laughed a bit to herself at the irony as she climbed the shallow front steps. Here she was, worried that he might expose her, while he was stewing over the very same thing—that she might blackmail him by threatening to tell people he'd been keeping company with a fallen woman.

Shaw answered the door himself, favouring her with his warm smile. 'Thank you so much for coming.' He bowed over her hand and then abruptly looked over her shoulder. 'You didn't bring Effie? You could have...' His voice was low and private. 'You are both safe here with me and with my people. No one would dare utter a word without your permission.'

The sincerity of his words brought a strange thickness to her throat out of nowhere. How different his reaction was compared to Anthony's. Anthony had been furious when she'd told him. But that didn't mean she could trust Shaw's word any more than she could have trusted Anthony's.

'The fewer who know the better—for all of us.'

She let him usher her into the hall and then down a short corridor to a sitting room she'd never been in—a reminder that this was not a business visit. The room had pale yellow wallpaper and was filled with blue-chintz-covered furniture. It was not a room for work, but a room where people might sit comfortably and talk easily.

Mrs Grandy bustled in with a tea tray and deposited it on a low table. 'We've missed you, my dear.' She flashed Thomasia a quick smile.

'I've missed everyone as well,' Thomasia replied, feeling the thickness in her throat return.

She had missed coming to Rosegate, missed sitting in the library writing Shaw's letters, missed feeling accomplished at the end of the day when she looked at the stack of correspondence ready to be sent out.

'I've missed you, too,' Shaw said as she poured the tea. 'I hope you'll resume working here once Effie-Claire is feeling better.'

Thomasia looked up from the tea. She'd not expected that. She'd thought to save him the difficulty of having to directly ask her to discontinue her work, or the effort of coming up with an excuse for not needing her. 'I don't think that's a good idea.'

He took his teacup from her, their fingertips accidentally brushing. The warm charge of his touch travelled up her arm. 'I don't know why anything has to change. Your having a child has no bearing on the quality of your penmanship.'

'Don't be obtuse, Shaw.' His name came too easily

to her lips. 'You know it changes everything. If people were to find out, it would tarnish your reputation.'

'That's ridiculous.' Shaw's jaw tightened.

'It's reality. For now.' Thomasia reached for a small triangle of ham sandwich. 'Someday perhaps we'll live in a world where women alone with a child won't bear the consequences for a relationship that went sour.' She met his gaze evenly. 'Is that why you invited me here? To offer me my job back? That could have been done in a note.'

She knew what he wanted but she would make him ask for it.

He leaned forward with easy grace to retrieve a biscuit. 'No, not entirely. I wanted to speak with you—to tell you that you have nothing to fear from me, and that I stand as your friend.'

His blue eyes held hers, warming her. How she'd like to believe those words, but that was a dangerous risk to take. She'd believed Anthony, and now he was the stick by which she measured all other men. Men betrayed. Men were loyal to themselves first and foremost.

'But you have something to fear from me,' Thomasia replied. 'You wouldn't want me to tell anyone about the child—especially not the Stantons.'

'You would not do that. It makes no sense, not when you're desperate to remain hidden.'

Shaw had dismissed the threat. Thomasia could not. Did he realise what kind of peril he was in? All it would take would be for the Stantons to make a mention of the supper at Beechmont in London and for that to reach the wrong ears—Anthony's ears and his father's ears. If they wanted to, they could make Shaw's life uncomfortable, embarrassing, because of her association with him.

She should not have gone to Beechmont, and she should not have let herself be lured by the thought of a night out, of a chance to work against Lord Stanton's bill. But she'd convinced herself that the chances of word reaching Anthony were minuscule, that a chain of events that would result in Anthony knowing was unlikely. But the fear remained. There would always be fear where Anthony was concerned.

Shaw sighed. 'Will you tell me who it was that broke your heart and taught you to distrust men?'

'Can't you guess?' She was on the defensive now, protecting the very things she'd come here to say, to share.

'I'd rather hear it from you. I have spent most of the night guessing.' Shaw refilled their teacups, giving every impression of settling in for a long talk. 'I can't help you if I don't know what I'm up against.'

'You can't help anyway,' Thomasia said briskly.

It was becoming harder and harder to resist laying her burdens on his broad, willing shoulders, but she knew they were only willing because he didn't *know*, didn't understand. Once he did, he'd be glad she insisted they end their nascent friendship.

'Try me,' Shaw challenged.

Thomasia eyed him and assessed her choices. Telling him might be the best weapon she had in her arsenal. There was nothing like a little honesty to drive a good man away. She didn't have to tell him everything… Just enough to protect them both.

Chapter Nine

Despite her reluctance to tell her story, it was a very short tale if she removed all the emotion. Boiled down to the facts, it was straightforward and hardly original. A recitation of facts she could do. It would allow her to skirt the hurt and the self-castigation—at least that was her intention when she started talking.

'Ferris's mother, the Duchess, invited Becca and me to stay on in London after the wedding...'

But even those simple words couldn't protect her against the memory of those days. Instead, they conjured images in her mind as she talked of that heady time: the romance surrounding Anne's wedding, the excitement of being allowed to attend the honeymoon ball, the thrill of wearing new clothes made by a real London modiste, being on her own for the first time without her parents.

'Those days were everything a girl like me had dreamed about...' She sighed and gave a little smile, feeling her stomach flip at the way Shaw looked at her, all blue-eyed thoughtfulness.

'What was a girl like you?'

Shaw gave her an easy smile. Another of those and she'd be spilling all her secrets.

'Innocent, naïve… Only I didn't think so. I thought I had it all handled, that I knew what I was doing.' Thomasia gave a toss of her head. 'I was the daughter of a doctor who believed in bringing up women who were in control of themselves in both mind and body. I'd seen Anne struggle through a broken heart before she met Ferris. I'd seen Thea fight for respect as a healer, even though Society has decreed a woman can't practise medicine. I knew that men weren't chivalrous. But that didn't stop me from wanting to fall in love, from thinking I'd found a man who was different from the rest.'

What a little fool she'd been.

'There *are* men of honour in this world, Thomasia,' Shaw put in quietly, but she met him with a doubtful raised eyebrow.

'I think I was in love with being in love, of having my own fairy tale like Anne or Thea. It made it easy to overlook what should have been obvious. After all, don't all the stories teach us that love must be fought for? That lovers stand up for one another against those who oppose them? I don't think romances have done women any favours in that regard, beyond creating false expectations.'

She shook her head. It would be too easy to digress here, and she wasn't finished with her tale.

'But before his faults were obvious he was thrilling.'

She'd be honest about the experience. Whatever Anthony had been offering her, she'd been swept up in it.

'It was exciting to belong somewhere, with someone…'

'You did belong, though—to your family,' Shaw said.

'Yes and no. My family loves me, and I love them, but I'm not *like* them. At my core, I'm different.'

How could she explain that to him without telling him the reason why? She'd not meant to share so much, and yet now it seemed she had to fill in the edges of the story in order to make it complete.

'My sisters and my brother have always known who they are and what they want to do with their lives. Anne wanted to be a herbalist and Thea a doctor. Becca has always wanted to build things that make people's lives better. But not me. For a long time I didn't know what my calling was. I didn't have their direction. They were always found while I always felt a bit lost…a bit left behind. But in London I shone.'

The Duchess had seen to that. There'd been invitations to the best parties and outings. There had been ball after ball and new gowns galore and everyone had watched her. She'd been popular, her dance card full—at first because the Duchess had arranged it, but later her card had filled of its own volition. Her court had grown from a group of young men encouraged by the Duchess to include her to young men who came of their own accord.

Oh, how she'd revelled in that—in knowing they came because *she* drew them. She hadn't had the dowry to truly be a Diamond of the First Water, but she'd made the Society pages and hostesses had known she was good for business. If she came to a party the young men were sure to follow, and that benefited everyone. And the following morning the mantel of Cowden House had always been bedecked with bouquets for her.

'How superficial it sounds now.' She felt an embarrassed blush heat her cheeks. 'Such dangerous silliness.'

There had been so much glamour and sparkle to distract her that she hadn't seen the peril until it was too late.

'By late June one man in particular had devoted himself to me. He was charming, gallant, well dressed… but they all were. However, he was more daring than the rest, more audacious in his flirting. He offered the most extravagant compliments and the most interesting outings: viewing the Pleasure Garden fireworks from a barge on the Thames, a box at the theatre, a prime viewing spot for the races at Ascot, picnics in Richmond… I was caught up in all of it. I'd never had such access to fun before. Haberstock was quite dull for a girl who wanted to see the world.'

She'd been thoroughly enchanted.

'The Duchess was sceptical about him. She warned me. And the Duke warned him.'

But Anthony had made a joke of the Duke's warning, telling her that they had to fight such old traditionalists. What did they know about love? About this new world where people married for it?

'He said all the right things: that he loved me, that we would wed at the end of the Season. And I believed him. So when our passions took a deeper turn there was no reason to deny them.'

Those kisses, those caresses, had turned her to jelly—including her mind. She hadn't been able to think straight around him.

'Why didn't you marry, then?'

Thomasia drew a deep breath. She didn't want to remember the hurt. She had loved him even if he hadn't loved her. 'It turned out love was just a word to him—a word that unlocked doors and allowed him to get what he wanted.'

'But surely the baby superseded such considerations—' Shaw began, but she waved off his protest.

'There are some things that trump even a child—like an inheritance contingent on marrying the right sort of woman. His parents had a suitable bride chosen for him and the keys to a grand estate dangling from a chain. All he had to do was walk away from me—which he did.'

Eventually. It had not been a clean break.

She could see Shaw bristling. 'I don't need your indignation or your pity. It's better this way. If he hadn't left us then, he would have left us later. That would have been worse—to be married to a man who was out carousing, keeping mistresses, ignoring his wife and child.' It had taken a while for her to accept that. 'Married, I would have been entirely powerless, completely trapped.'

'And what are you now?'

His tone suggested he didn't think she was any better off. Of course he'd want to argue that point. A man wouldn't see it as she did. In a man's mind a woman ruined by a man could only be redeemed by another man.

'Now I am free.'

Although she knew that freedom wasn't entirely complete, and nor did it come without a cost. She was free of a man who'd proved not worthy of her, but she wasn't free of the stigma Society marked women like her with. If she lived honestly, under her own name, that stigma would follow her. It would only be through creating a lie—a false name, a false story—that she would be free of it. But that would mean living a lie, always looking over her shoulder to be sure the lie was safe.

Neither seemed like good choices to her, which was why she was living quietly at Haberstock Hall, trying to decide what to do next, which price she was willing to pay.

Shaw was quiet, his eyes resting on her, not condemning, not judging, but assessing. Perhaps he would realise that she'd only told him what he might have guessed on his own about her story: a girl taken advantage of by a gentleman who refused to honour his commitments and that girl having a child. It was an old story, unfortunately oft repeated.

'Who is the father?' Shaw asked, but she was ready for that question. That information was not part of the story.

She shook her head. 'It doesn't matter what his name is. My life has moved on and so has his. He married this past summer, to the bride his parents had chosen for him, and thankfully so. I am beyond him now and glad of it.' She spoke the words with a hard-won conviction earned over the last year and a half. But Shaw still noticed the old fear beneath them.

'Weren't you beyond him the moment he walked away from you?'

'It was complicated,' she offered, hoping that would be enough.

'Complicated? How? I'm beginning to think you are not really as free as you believe, and that concerns me, Thomasia.' Outside, it had begun to rain. Shaw chuckled. 'You might as well tell me. The weather will keep you here for a while.'

'The conditions of his inheritance made things ambiguous, as if there might be a chance for us, at a time when I thought I might still want that.'

But she'd seen quickly that Anthony was an opportunist. He'd only come back to her, feigning new interest in the child she carried, when he'd believed the baby had the potential to be useful. It was almost more difficult for her to talk about this part of their relationship than it was the other.

'To claim the estate he had to marry. To claim the inheritance he needed to produce a legitimate child within a year and a half of his wedding. It was a posthumous attempt by his great-aunt to keep him faithful—at least early in the marriage.' She paused, waiting for Shaw to connect the pieces.

'He came back?' Shaw arched an incredulous brow.

'He came back and proposed, thinking he would claim it all in one fell swoop.'

He'd begged her so prettily to forgive him. He'd claimed to have been overwhelmed by her announcement, that surely she knew he'd intended to marry her all along.

'If not for the Duke of Cowden's interference I might have believed him. I was heartbroken and desperate. But the Duke discovered the terms of his inheritance and it became obvious he was using our situation to satisfy them. Two days after proposing he showed his true colours again, when his father and their solicitors confirmed that the marriage had to be to a woman who met his parents' approval. By then, I knew I needed to be as far from him as possible for my own sanity. I couldn't put myself through the highs and lows of being near him, of hearing about him, of watching him court his bride. It was making me ill and it wasn't good for the baby.'

'So you went to York,' Shaw supplied, 'and waited for him to marry.'

'After what he'd tried to do in winning me back I didn't trust him not to try again, not to try and manipulate the will. As long as there was an estate and an inheritance dangling just out of reach for him, his child was his key to half of it, and I was potentially his key to the other half. I didn't feel safe. He was—*is*—a man without morals or ethics, as his behaviour at the end avowed. He is also a man with some influence. I feared if he could find a way to manipulate the will he would also find a way to force me to marry him. You cannot imagine the relief I felt when I heard he'd married. I am nothing to him now but a dalliance from his past.'

She would carry the scars and her gratitude for that knowledge for the rest of her life. It had been a hard-learned lesson.

Shaw's face was stormy. 'He walked away with an estate and an inheritance, while you walked away with—'

'Effie-Claire. I think I got the better end of it,' Thomasia cut in quickly, unwilling to let Shaw finish that sentence.

'Does he support her financially?' Shaw asked carefully.

'He doesn't even know of her other than that I carried his child. I made no overture to him when she was born.'

Thomasia had been thrilled when her baby was a girl. She remembered thinking at the time that surely a girl would be of no use to Anthony in his inheritance hunt—that this would be another way to keep her and the baby safe should he care to make enquiries.

'I have my family. I don't need financial support.'

She held his gaze for a long moment, reminding him that she fought for those who did.

It was a noble fight, Shaw thought, to stand up for those who couldn't stand up for themselves, and to embrace a cause that didn't directly affect or benefit her. He understood her politics better now…understood where her motivation came from. She knew she'd had a lucky escape. Her family was the one thing that set her apart from other women in her situation—women who *had* to count on financial support from the fathers of their children.

He understood, too, that Stanton's repeal attempt didn't seek to uphold Society's moral fabric as much as it sought to protect men like the roué who'd taken advantage of Thomasia and the man who'd taken advantage of his mother, men who should not be protected. What did *that* encourage? Certainly not the family values Stanton purported to uphold.

'What happens in the spring, Thomasia?' This was the other question that had formed in his mind as she talked. 'You and Effie can't hide at the Hall for ever.'

Shaw understood better, too, why she had eschewed the invitation to London. She didn't want to encounter *him*, the father of her child. For all her protests that she was beyond him, Shaw sensed she still possessed a latent fear of encountering him, of reminding that man of her presence.

'I haven't decided yet. I will either stay and face the disappointment of the village, or I will go away and make a new life. I have time.'

She sounded composed as she laid out the options. But Shaw knew what the latter meant: to live as he'd lived his early life, for her to assume a false name, live a false life, and bring up a child under that aegis. It was quite a house of cards—one that could be toppled by a simple enquiry, a curious stranger or a neighbour. It meant living alone. She could not risk marrying. Ever. There were few men in the world like Alan Rawdon, who'd married his mother and never blinked at raising another man's child.

Not that she wanted to marry. She'd made her opinion of men plain. He'd like to change that opinion if he could. He'd like to show her that not all men were self-serving cads. But he'd got off to a miserable start there. He'd been the one to drag her to Beechmont, into country Society, because he'd needed a partner for the evening. He was acutely aware that if word of her situation got out before spring he'd have only himself to blame. However, he still had time to make things right—starting with getting her back to work for him.

'There *is* something we need to settle between us,' he began seriously. 'I was wondering if I could coax you into returning to work. We could work from Haberstock Hall instead of from Rosegate. You could be near Effie.'

He was rewarded with a flash of light in her eyes, her face visibly brightening.

'I would like that very much.'

She looked as if he'd given her the world. Perhaps she heard, as he meant her to, his acceptance. He was not going to repudiate her and he was not going to expose her. Those would be priceless gifts to her, and her relief was palpable.

He grinned in response to her obvious pleasure. 'Good. We'll start tomorrow.'

He would show her what a friend he could be. He sensed she needed one. Despite the support of her family, there were burdens that she alone must carry, and should there ever be a scandal she would fight those battles and bear those scars alone.

She shouldn't have to.

The thought awoke the protector in him once more on her behalf. He didn't like the idea of her fighting alone. Alone, she could not possibly win, could not possibly stare down scandal. She needed a champion.

It should not be you. You have a political career to think about, his conscience reminded him.

But if not him, then who? Her brother was off tending soldiers in the Crimea and her father did not go about in Society much. No, it needed to be him. He was here, nearby, and if there was danger to her in the immediate future it would likely come from cages he'd unwittingly unlocked.

It did not occur to him until much later, after she had gone home and he was settled once more before the fire, that he was not untouched by his discovery of Effie-Claire. And it wasn't just the similarities with his own past that were touching him—it was what this meant for his present.

Shaw sipped his brandy, letting it burn down his throat along with the reality he'd shoved aside in order to focus on Thomasia's needs, to allay *her* fears. But now there was *his* reality, *his* fear to reckon with. The bottom line was that he could not marry her. He could no longer be a potential candidate if she was his bride.

He'd not realised how much he'd relied on those nascent hopes, built his hopes around them in his head...

Lord Stanton was eyeing him for advancement, and Maldon had openly suggested he think of marrying soon. Maldon had even offered his wife as a matchmaker. But there was a certain type of woman they saw him with. *Miss* Thomasia Peverett, virginal and untouched, a girl from a good local family, might have fitted the bill. But associating with an unwed mother, exposing others to her, passing her off as a young woman of good character, were unforgivable sins in Stanton's world. Thomasia had not been wrong when she'd suggested that being seen with her socially would ruin his career if word of Effie-Claire got out.

The irony was not lost on him. He'd gone into politics to make the world better for those less fortunate, and befriending one of those very people he sought to help had put him at the heart of a scandal that would destroy that career. Befriending? That was a rather tame word for it. He'd been halfway to falling for her, and he hated himself for thinking that he had to put a stop to it because his career depended on it.

There was something of the hypocrite in that when he wanted to make her promises he was not certain he could keep, and that uncertainty shamed him. What about what his heart wanted? Which had been to scoop up that precious baby girl in the nursery and draw her mother into his arms and assure her that he would stand between them and anyone who wished them harm, whoever they might be.

Chapter Ten

Anthony Halston, the second son of the Earl of Drake, had burned a very necessary bridge a year and a half ago—or at the least set it on fire. But it was a fire that he was now hoping to put out, given the current circumstances he found himself in.

He took a long swallow of his drink, making the solicitor wait for him to unveil his grand design—just as he'd made the solicitor take the train from London and travel to him. He'd grown used to the luxury of this Suffolk estate and was loath to leave it for something as mundane as business. Nor was he keen on losing this newly acquired luxury through no fault of his own.

'Read the last part of the will again.'

'Of course, milord.' Browning was a small, patient man. He adjusted his spectacles and proceeded to read the same sentences he'd read just minutes earlier. '"The trust, in the sum of fifty thousand pounds, will be released in full to Lord Anthony James Arthur Halston, upon his producing his first legitimate child."'

Fifty thousand pounds. It was hard not to salivate

over those three words. Fifty thousand pounds would solve a lot of problems—primarily the problem of maintaining the luxurious estate that had come to him upon his marriage to one Miss Sarah Jane Osmond, now Lady Halston, plus a London residence and all the needs that went with London living…needs that easily outstripped his current resources. But getting to those fifty thousand pounds was proving to be something of an obstacle.

'Are there any provisions for the instance that my wife cannot bear a child through no fault of mine?'

He'd married her in August, after a year-long courtship, during which he'd been put through arduous paces proving to the future Lady Halston's family that he was worthy of her and her settlement. He'd been happy to dance to their tune, knowing the second son of an earl wasn't likely to do better.

Marriage had also given him an increased allowance from his father, who was pleased to have his wild son settled down with a wife who came with a townhouse and respectable money, the ability to claim an inheritance and the promise of more money once he had a child. It was an ideal set-up, and he'd gone to work at once on the begetting of that child.

'No, milord,' Browning said carefully. 'I am sorry for your recent loss, and I hope you will convey my condolences to your wife.'

Lady Halston had promptly conceived and then promptly miscarried quite tragically three months later. The doctors had informed him there would likely be no future children—not from that quarter.

'So the money will just sit there unclaimed?' He blurted out the question that had burdened him since

the news from the doctors. 'That seems patently unfair—
and wasteful, I might add.'

'You may add all you like, but it won't change the
conditions, milord. I am sure this is disappointing.'

Browning began shuffling his papers as if he were
about to depart. Little did he know his work was nowhere near done.

'I am disappointed, Browning, but not surprised. I
just wanted to verify the situation before moving forward.' Anthony steepled his hands over the flat of his
stomach. 'I have a naturally born child. It would bring
my wife and me comfort to adopt it and have the child
in our home. But children are not cheap. Before adopting, I would need assurances that such an arrangement
would suffice for the conditions of the will.'

In truth, he cared only about the funds. He was not
going through the trouble of adopting a by-blow if he
didn't get anything out of it.

'It would be unusual, milord,' Browning answered
warily. 'It was not your great-aunt's intention that you
should adopt a by-blow to fulfil the conditions of her will.'

Anthony gave a short bark of laughter. 'No, it was
not. That old biddy's intention was to see me lured into
marriage and to be kept faithful until a child was produced. She wanted to see me tamed. But my situation
has become unusual—something she did not foresee
in her attempt to make me a family man.' He lifted
his glass of brandy and swirled it, catching the light.
'Surely you can see the irony in it? In order to become
a family man I must now adopt a by-blow—the one
thing she'd wanted to guard against. It's not a scenario
either of us imagined.'

Browning gave a rueful half-smile. 'What you propose does not satisfy the *spirit* of your great-aunt's will…'

'I am only interested in the letter of the law,' Anthony replied sharply. He might be the family wastrel, but he was not stupid. 'I will ask you again: Will adopting my natural child satisfy the condition of producing a "legitimate" child? To the extent that we could defend such a claim in court if need be?'

Perhaps it wouldn't come to that, but he wanted to be prepared before he set sail on this course. It would take considerable effort on his part and he must be certain. Thomasia Peverett would not let that child go without a fight. It was too bad the will hadn't allowed him to marry *her*. She was a dark-haired spitfire, up for anything.

Well, actually, the will hadn't held him back on that account. He could have married Thomasia and had the money. But he would have sacrificed everything else: the estate that had come with his marriage, his raised esteem in his father's eyes—as indicated by the allowance his father was now willing to give a son married to a woman of rank—and the extravagant wedding gifts. All of that had become his without having to do anything but say 'I do'. He'd wanted it all and he'd never imagined he wouldn't get it. After all, he'd already proven he could sire a child…

'I think we could make a creditable case, milord,' Browning acceded reluctantly. 'Do I need to remind you how displeased your father would be over a scandal that will drag the earldom into the ignominy of a court case?'

'I think for fifty thousand pounds he can tolerate a bit of scandal—or he can come up with the fifty thousand to replace that which will be lost to me by any other means.' Anthony waved a hand. 'I suppose I could divorce Lady Halston...' That would be an even larger scandal for the family, and one that would garner less public support. 'But I would think adopting a child would resonate with the public. Here I am, giving my bereaved wife a child to love, and giving a child born into misfortune a home and all the benefits that come with having an earl for a grandfather.'

He might even come out of this looking like a hero— provided Thomasia didn't look like a martyr. But that would only be if things went public...something neither of them would want.

'That settles it. We need to locate her. I want you to set someone to work when you get back to London. Bow Street, perhaps.'

Browning looked up from his papers. 'That won't be necessary, milord. We can simply ask her brothers-in-law. Tresham is in Town.'

'No, absolutely not.' Anthony was firm on this. 'We must be discreet. Asking her family will alert her. I do not want her to see us coming.'

A flustered Thomasia would be easier to deal with than one who was prepared to stand her ground. He wanted her frightened and taken unawares. He wanted the element of surprise on his side.

Thomasia found it was surprisingly pleasant to work with Shaw. They set up stations in the library at the Hall, each of them taking an end of the long reading table: he to devote himself to annotating reports and keeping notes on the issues he was expected to respond to, and she to do his correspondence. They fell into an easy rhythm, doing their own work, but looking up to ask an occasional question, which sometimes led to longer discussions on issues ranging from taxes to public welfare.

Thomasia relished those discussions. Shaw was a good listener, always considerate, always careful not to interrupt and to hold his own opinions until she'd finished. He didn't dismiss her ideas out of hand. He listened, he asked questions, and he wasn't afraid to challenge her assumptions, to test them. And she wasn't afraid to engage in debate—which usually ended in them laughing together.

It was easy to laugh with him, to talk with him, to simply be in his presence. Too easy—and that ease made her sceptical of her good fortune. Did she dare trust it? She'd not questioned such things with Anthony and she should have. Should she be questioning things now? What did Shaw get from all this, when most men would have run by now?

He hadn't only fitted his work to suit her life, he'd fitted *himself* into that life. They worked together and they played together, if that was an apt word. Each day they seemed to extend their time together. They took lunch together and, weather permitting, took a walk or a gallop across the estate after they'd eaten, or after work was completed for the day. They also took tea at day's end, with Effie-Claire fresh from her nap and playing on the floor at their feet. The baby was crawling everywhere these days, and delighted in pulling herself up with the help of her mama's fingers and low tabletops.

Teatime might be her new favourite part of the day, Thomasia thought, when all three of them were together and the world was quiet and peaceful. Nothing else seemed to matter in those moments. Whatever the day had brought, whatever difficulty or worry, it simply faded away when she was with her daughter. And with Shaw.

She could no longer ignore that last thing. There was simply too much evidence for it. He made her think, made her laugh, made her feel like her old self—a girl who laughed and danced. And he made her embrace her new self: a woman who put her child ahead of all else, who saw injustice in the world and strove to overcome it with her arguments and her passion. It created a heady mix. A new Thomasia who didn't have to choose between the old and the new but who was a combination of both. She liked this emerging person, but it came at a price. She had to recognise Shaw's role in that world, and that scared her a great deal.

She did not want to be close to a man, and yet Shaw had become a friend. Telling him her story had not pushed him away, as she'd anticipated. It had, instead, drawn him closer. And arguing her position had not deterred him. Instead, he'd listened. He was not put off by her opinions and beliefs. He behaved as no man she'd ever met had. That disconcerted her, threw her off her political game. It was fast becoming difficult for her to look at him and see a political adversary—someone who must be swayed to her side, someone to use to her advantage—and far too easy to look at him and see a friend, a confidant.

She didn't trust herself. She feared she was on the brink of another mistake, another disaster.

'Shall we walk in the gallery today?' Shaw looked up from the long table as the last of the mantel clock chimes faded, announcing four o'clock—their self-appointed end of the day and the herald of Effie's arrival.

It had rained most of the afternoon, and raindrops ran in rivulets down the panes of the long library windows, keeping everyone inside.

Within moments, the young maid who looked after Effie while she worked entered with her sweet girl, and Thomasia took her in her arms. 'Oh, my, you're getting heavy.' She laughed. 'Perhaps it's best if you *do* learn to walk soon. You're getting too big for me to carry you.'

The thought broke a little piece of her heart. It was one more thing she'd have to give up too soon.

'Let me take her,' Shaw offered, transferring Effie-Claire to his arms.

She went with a gurgle of delight. Effie quite obviously adored Shaw, and there was something undeniably touching about the sight of the baby carried against the safety of his big body.

He juggled Effie for a moment and then held out his other arm for her. 'Shall we be off to the gallery?'

Effie liked the gallery, because it was wide open and she could crawl there without getting into trouble. Shaw set her down and they strolled, keeping one eye on the baby and one eye on the paintings, while Thomasia regaled him with tales of her Peverett ancestors.

'There's been a healer at Haberstock Hall since the

sixteen hundreds—starting with Richard Peverett, right there.' She nodded towards a man with a long nose, dark curling hair and brown eyes.

'I see the resemblance,' Shaw teased, tapping his own elegant nose. 'Do all of the Peveretts have long noses?'

'No!' She punched him playfully in the arm, only to meet muscle. 'Ow! You're made of iron.' She shook out her hand with a laugh. 'The dark hair and whisky eyes, though, are definitely a family trait.'

'Cognac eyes,' Shaw corrected with a smile. 'Cognac or brandy—either is classier than whisky.'

'Is that a compliment?' she flirted, giving a toss of her head. She was feeling light-hearted today…free, a little bit daring.

Shaw laughed. 'I imagine you're not short on those.'

'These days I'll take what I can get. I've had to alter all of my dresses…'

The words slipped out before she could think better of them. It was too easy not to mind them when she was with him—everything was too easy. Easy. She used that word too often in conjunction with Shaw.

'I shouldn't have said that. A lady doesn't talk about such things with a gentleman.'

Shaw arched a russet brow and chuckled. 'What a contrary creature you are. You have no worries over sharing your political views, but demur to discuss waistlines—yours, by the way, is quite fine.'

'But now it's as if I was fishing for the compliment. It's not the same thing at all as talking politics,' Thomasia explained with a sigh, feeling some of the earlier lightness leaving her. 'Thank you, all the same.

Everything is…well, *different* now, with the baby. I'm still getting used to being myself, and working out who that self is.'

They stopped to watch Effie playing on the floor, content for the moment to sit on a blanket with her stuffed rabbit.

'I love her so much, Shaw. I didn't know someone could be loved that deeply until I had her.'

They took a seat on one of the wide square ottomans that lined the centre of the gallery, close to Effie. Thomasia slid Shaw a sideways glance, her voice quiet.

'You know how people say they would give their life for their children? It's true—but not in the way I thought they meant it. It's not that you would die for your child. You can only do that once. What good is that? Who will be there for them after you're gone? And, in truth, it is an unlikely sacrifice these days. But we do give our lives for them every day. Each choice I make is for her. My life, my body, is at her disposal. If she has a bad night, I have a bad night. If she's hungry, I drop everything to feed her. She has a piece of my soul now, and I will never belong wholly to myself again…'

Thomasia paused.

'Sometimes I'm not sure how I feel about that. I'll never be the old me again. I liked her, but I like the new me, too.' She gave a soft laugh. What a soppy philosopher she was. 'I'm sorry. I spend too much time in my head these days,' she apologised. 'Sometimes all my thoughts just come rushing out.'

Shaw's hand closed over hers and rested on her lap. His hand was large and strong, like the rest of him, and his voice was low, matching hers in the quiet space between them. 'It means you're a good mother, Thomasia, and a human one, too. I believe it's important that we actively think about our lives and what they mean. Otherwise they pass by, unexamined.'

He held her gaze and lifted their hands, measuring his palm against hers, looking at her fingers coming up short against his.

'Is that why you're an MP?' she asked. 'This is your life's calling? To be a politician?'

'Politics are only a *means* to my goals. Being in politics is the best way to get access to achieve them.' He gave her a winsome smile as he talked of his plans. 'I want to see that all children are provided with an education under the laws of England—no child left out, not even orphans. I want to especially focus on foundling schools, so that those children who might need an education the most—children who have no family, no parents to lean on in making their way in the world—can at least have that.' He paused. 'What is it, Thomasia? You're staring at me as if I have something on my face.'

'No, your face is fine.'

More than fine, it was handsome and expressive, and it begged for her fingers to trace its contours—the elegant nose, the sharp cheekbones. Those blue eyes begged her to jump into their depths, but most of all what drew her was the passion she saw in them, his consideration for others, the consideration he'd shown *her*.

She threaded her fingers through his with a smile. 'I was thinking how nice this conversation is…just two people talking, sharing what's in their hearts.'

It was nothing like the conversations she'd had in London, where one was expected to be witty and glib, and where one definitely did not share anything real. She'd never had a conversation like this with Anthony, and yet she'd gone to bed with him. What a fool she'd been.

'Thank you for this conversation. It's not just me that's different—it's the house. It's so empty without all my siblings here. When I was growing up there was always someone to talk to. Now there's just Becca. And she's always in her workshop...' She sighed. 'I miss Anne. She has a child, too, so she would understand these things, but she's in London and she has Ferris, so maybe it's different for her.'

Maybe Anne didn't feel so alone.

'You have me, Thomasia,' Shaw offered. 'You have my shoulder to cry on, my ear to listen.'

The overture nearly undid her. Tears pricked at her eyes. Perhaps it was the surprise that did it. He'd offered those things so readily, so willingly, as if he were a friend of long standing and not a new friend of only a month. Of course, he'd known her family longer, but not her, and this was an offer uniquely for her. It was an offer Society didn't feel she deserved.

She smiled. 'You really are splendid, you know, and I'm sure I'll make use of them.'

She gave a laugh to cover the emotion that welled in her eyes and in her throat. It had been a long time since she'd had a friend. She'd had support, and she had her sisters, but having a friend was different. Yet the thought of friendship with Shaw was edged with sadness. What if she'd met him before, when she could have been more than his friend? What if there could have been more talks like this one?

Shaw's eyes were steady on hers, blue flames burning at a low simmer at their centre, and it seemed something unseen crackled in the air between them. His voice was low and gravelly when he spoke. 'I sincerely hope you do.'

Thomasia's smile widened, and before she could think better of it she leaned forward and kissed his cheek, surprising them both.

'What was that for?' Shaw chuckled at her impetuosity.

'For this conversation, for being you...for everything, Shaw.'

She'd never known a man like him and she didn't know what to do about it. Probably she should do nothing. She should take his offer of friendship and let it lie. But she'd never been very good at settling for the status quo.

Chapter Eleven

She did not want him to be her friend. Thomasia pulled the brush through her hair with a tug of finality that punctuated her conclusion as she made ready for bed that night. Effie was asleep in the crib and she was alone with her thoughts. She'd been lost in those thoughts all evening, ever since Shaw had departed and left her to play through their extraordinary conversation in her mind.

Had it been extraordinary for him as well? Or did he speak like that with everyone? A certain jealous part of her hoped not. That same part wanted to believe that the stories they'd shared on the ottoman were unique to them alone. For her, they were. She'd not shared those thoughts with anyone else—not even her family. There was something about Shaw that encouraged her to talk with him. Perhaps it was the sincerity of his gaze, or the comfort he was able to convey in a simple touch. Whatever it was, it was potent enough to get past her defences.

Thomasia set aside the brush and began to plait her hair, her fingers moving through the process automatically, leaving her mind free to continue its exploration. Given her previous experience with a man, it was rather amazing and worrisome that she was so open with Shaw. She still could not shake the fear that she was moving towards yet another disaster with a man. And yet there had been a certain chemistry between them from that first night when he'd sat beside her on the piano bench and they'd argued over Clara Schumann.

He'd unnerved her that night. Once, she would have attributed that feeling to the hot debate between them, but now she understood there was more to it than that. Shaw Rawdon was a handsome man, strongly built and well muscled, but that was not the first thing one noticed about him. One noticed that he was an intelligent man, open to differing views, a compassionate man who'd not shown her pity but genuine empathy, a man who loved children, who had an easy way with them, who didn't begrudge their presence. He didn't hold a woman's past against her. He was a man of integrity.

Careful there, her mind warned. *Don't be fooled by that last. Integrity will only go so far.*

At some point his integrity would run up against practicalities, and practicalities would win. His integrity would not be infinite.

She rose from the dressing table and checked on Effie before crawling into bed. It was a good reminder to fall asleep on—that even Shaw Rawdon was still just a man, a fallible man who would eventually fail. But perhaps he wouldn't fail too soon. That was the best she could hope for.

She turned on her side and readjusted her pillow. That was why she didn't want to be his friend. It was too easy to forget she was on a mission for the Coffee Yard ladies. She was meant to use his access to Parliament to try and turn Stanton's repeal or bury it. But too often these days when she looked down the table in the library she saw a friend, not a tool. And that friendship was dangerous in its own right.

What more might he be? What more might she allow him to be?

Thomasia punched her pillow. It was terribly uncomfortable tonight—or maybe it was her thoughts that were uncomfortable. They were peppered with *what ifs*. What if she'd met Shaw before she'd met Anthony? What if Shaw wanted more than friendship with her? There had been that moment in the carriage on the way home from Beechmont when a kiss had seemed imminent. There were the long glances he stole when he thought she wasn't looking. There'd been…today.

Was he waiting for her to make some indication that she'd be open to more? But what would that look like? He was off to London at the end of January. He had a career to think about and she was a walking scandal. There could be no future for them in the long term. Whatever 'more' might be, it needed to be wrapped in winter's solitude, and she would need to content herself with that.

It was a fanciful notion, born of late-night mental meanderings that included visions of Shaw with Effie in his arms, the remembrance of his spiced wintry scent as they sat close, their hands interlocked. How different this vision of romance was from the vision she'd held a couple years ago—a vision full of dash and daring, of sneaking off for stolen kisses and outwitting chaperones, of racing around London and flying through ballrooms on the arms of ten different young men every night who whispered nothing but insincere flattery.

She'd been prepared to protect herself against the latter. Such strategies would not get past her defences again. But nothing had prepared her for Shaw Rawdon. After spending the day working in his presence she was never eager for him to leave. The evenings felt empty without him, and the days never truly seemed to start until he arrived in the morning. She found him intoxicating, and his brand of romance nearly irresistible.

She yawned, sleep finding her whirling mind at last. Maybe it wasn't so much that she didn't want to be his friend, it was that she *shouldn't* be. She knew better.

And you kissed him anyway.

Her conscience couldn't resist that last sleepy jab. She'd kissed his cheek and had wished it had been his mouth.

Thomasia Peverett had kissed him. Chastely. On the cheek. In a charming, impetuous expression of gratitude. She'd done nothing wrong, only something spontaneous, and she'd been clear about what it meant. They were friends.

Shaw didn't want to be her friend any more than he'd wanted that kiss to be on his cheek. It would have been the work of a moment to turn his head slightly, to have her lips on his. But he'd resisted the urge. Just as he had in the carriage. Just as he'd resisted acknowledging those conclusions, trying to convince himself otherwise, but to no use.

He'd been attracted to her from the start. To her

beauty, her mind, her sharp debate. Now, sitting at Beechmont with Sir Maldon, all he could think about was that kiss, the soft, brief feel of her lips against the raspy bristle of his cheek, and the spontaneity of the woman who'd delivered it.

It was entirely possible that no cheek kiss in the history of the world had ever had the scrutiny this one was getting now. This one had kept him up half the night and had followed him to his meeting with Maldon today—a meeting that was going poorly. It would be the last meeting they'd have together before Parliament sat in January. Maldon and his wife would spend Christmas in London, as many politicians did. Shaw would exchange letters with him, but they would not see each other face to face until he joined Maldon in London. It was his last chance to make a case against Stanton's repeal.

'Sir, the repeal of this Act is repugnant when one digs into it. It's protecting the wrong people and exposing those who ought to be protected to the worst the world has to offer, and it's doing so by using morality as a smokescreen to hide behind. If we really want to help the institution of "the English Family", or women who find themselves bringing up children alone, we need to find other ways to do it.'

He'd made the case as objectively as he could, laying it out plainly, without embellishment. But Maldon sighed.

'Those ways need to not offend Lord Stanton. If you stand against him you endanger his patronage and favours for both you and me, as well as his support on local issues that benefit Broxbourne. You and I want to

see the railway expanded here. He's on the railway commission. We need him. He and his friends decide where
the new lines will go. You want support on foundling
schools. You need his connections with the education
committees. Those are issues we can affect and see successful immediate results. We can have a branch line
within five years. You could have foundling schools set
up in that same time. But the women's issue is like a
hydra, Rawdon. There's no getting on top of it—it has
too many heads. It won't be resolved in our lifetime,
and it won't do you any favours at the ballot box. Even
if you could achieve something it wouldn't be visible…
It wouldn't be tangible to our voters.'

'So we don't try? We do nothing?' Shaw pressed.

He imagined Thomasia sitting beside him, listening to Maldon and bristling with righteous indignation.
He did not want to report to her that his efforts had not
borne fruit. That Maldon remained as intractable as
he'd always been on the issue.

Maldon nodded. 'It's not that I don't see your points,
Rawdon. It's that it doesn't make a difference. We stay
in office, we do the best we can where we can. That's
all a good man in office can hope for. The sooner you
come to grips with it, Rawdon, the better you'll sleep
at night.' He slid Shaw a knowing glance. 'And you'll
sleep better with a wife beside you, too. I'm sure my
wife would be glad to help in that area if you need a list
of eligible girls. Unless, of course, you have someone
in mind already?'

He was probing—and not subtly.

Shaw obliged with a vague answer and a smile. 'I'll
be certain to let Lady Maldon know.'

He could imagine the sort of women Maldon's wife would have on her list for his consideration. They wouldn't be women at all, but proper young girls from good families—girls fresh from the schoolroom, blank slates, waiting be coached by a husband into what they ought to believe. He was not interested in that sort of wife.

In contrast, images of Thomasia Peverett floated through his mind. Thomasia in her blue wool work dress with its tiny white lace trim at wrists and neck, her dark head bent over the pages. Thomasia glancing up from her end of the table to challenge his comments, cognac eyes flashing in interest as she voiced her counterarguments. There were softer images, too. Thomasia with Effie-Claire, her sharp gaze tender, her voice quiet. Thomasia with *him*, talking of life, talking of her personal hopes and fears, her face honest and open with her own thoughts, absent of all guile.

She did not flirt with him like other women did—at least not intentionally. He understood her reasons for that. She was cautious. And yet she was not immune to him…

Maldon cleared his throat and Shaw became cognizant of the fact that he'd let his thoughts stray—perhaps obviously. Thomasia had that effect on him, and what could be done about it needed significant consideration.

Maldon eyed him as he rose and went to the sideboard, filling two glasses with brandy for them. It was Maldon's way of signalling that the business portion of their meeting was over, or nearly so.

'As I said, perhaps you have someone in mind already…'

He handed a glass to Shaw with a fatherly smile, but

Shaw didn't warm to it. In his estimation the meeting had gone from bad to worse. He'd failed to convince Maldon to stand up to Stanton's repeal. Thomasia would be disappointed in him and he was disappointed in himself. The lines he'd once drawn for himself—lines designed to preserve his integrity—were quickly being crossed, or perhaps even erased. How far would he go to get what he wanted?

He finished his drink quickly. He needed to get out of Maldon's study and into the fresh winter air on Chiron.

'Sir, I'll wish you a happy Christmas and I'll see you in London in the New Year.' He had to think through how he should best respond to the situation he was being put in. This was exactly the type of compromising scenario he'd wanted to avoid.

Maldon shook his hand. 'The same to you, Rawdon. We have an exciting session to look forward to. I am counting on you to help me bring change to Broxbourne.' He covered Shaw's hand with his other hand and gave him a long, stern look that bordered on the paternal. 'I like you, Rawdon. You have great potential. Take my advice: find a wife and remember what your real goals are. Fight the battles you can win. You'll get used to it.'

Shaw did not think he'd ever get used to it…this utilitarian approach of balancing means and ends against the most and fewest people served by his actions, always with an eye towards ulterior motives.

Outdoors, he mounted Chiron and spurred the big gelding into a hard canter. He let the cold wind act as a purge on his agitated thoughts, but his mind would not settle. He did not want to go home to empty Rosegate and spend the night rambling about with those thoughts and no one to share them with…no one to be a sounding board, no one who'd understand.

Without thinking, he turned Chiron towards Haberstock Hall. There was only one person he wanted to be with tonight—one person with whom he could lay down his burdens. He spurred Chiron into a gallop, as if the thunder of hooves could churn over the warning in his mind.

Be careful what you're inviting with this visit. She kissed you. She is lonely, she is vulnerable and so are you. Don't pretend you're not. It might be the perfect storm.

So be it… Let it break, came the response, such was his mood.

He turned from the road, cutting towards the Hall through the meadow, letting political contretemps give way to other images, more peaceful images, of an evening spent with a glass of red wine, sitting before a fire in the library, making a stuffed bunny hop across his lap and making silly voices while Effie-Claire gurgled with delight and Thomasia's cognac eyes sparkled with laughter…

Chapter Twelve

Thomasia saw instantly that he was troubled. Even from the distance of the staircase his discontent was evident. It was in the windblown chaos of his hair, the set of his jaw and his stormy gaze. He wasn't angry, but tormented. The word might be too dramatic, but the concept was not far wrong. Something had upset him. He'd ridden hard from Beechmont.

She took the last stairs in quick steps. 'What has happened?'

She'd not expected to see him today—further proof that something was amiss. He'd come here instead of going home…come to *her*. She searched his face, looking for the source of his displeasure.

'Nothing yet.' He managed a small smile for her, his eyes finding a hint of their usual twinkle as they rested on her face. 'I simply found that I had to see you. Is it possible? Am I intruding?'

'Of course not—come in.' She helped him with his coat and muffler, laying them over the settle in the hall. 'Shall I call for tea?' But it was too late in the day for tea. She worried at her lip. 'Or would you rather wait for supper? It's nearly time. I must warn you, though, it would just be myself and Effie. Mother and Father are playing cards at the vicarage tonight.'

It seemed as if his whole body relaxed at the offer, and his smile broadened. 'Supper sounds perfect. Perhaps something simple in front of the fire in the library?'

Thomasia rang for Mrs Newsome, giving instructions for supper and asking to have Effie brought to the library. Then she slipped her arm through his and led the way. 'Let's get settled and then we'll talk. You can tell me all about your meeting.'

Within minutes they were ensconced in what had become 'their' chairs, before the fire in the library, Effie content on the carpet with a few of her favourite toys. Shaw sat in his chair, his head back, eyes shut as he took a few deep breaths.

'Was it that bad?' Thomasia ventured the question carefully in the silence.

His eyes opened, slow and deliberate. 'It's that *this* is that good. Us—you and me and Effie—here before the fire at the end of long day.' He gave her a smile that went to her toes. 'This is exactly how I imagined it as I rode over. It was all I wanted—to see you, to talk it over with you. I couldn't go home and be alone.'

That heart-in-his-eyes look, those words—they were dangerous. It would be easy to read too much into them, to think he meant anything more by them than that he simply needed to talk. And yet the fantasy lingered of a little family gathered together at day's end, simply celebrating being in one another's presence.

But such domestic daydreams kept women down. It

made the fantasy doubly dangerous. Thank goodness impossibility kept those dangers at bay. There was only so far the fantasy could go for her, and any damage it did her would just be to her heart.

'We discussed Stanton's repeal again,' Shaw began, and she knew from his sigh that it hadn't gone well. 'I don't know what is worse—a man who blindly supports the repeal of a piece of legislation because he's unaware of the repression he's perpetuating, or a man who *knows* the repeal is flawed and chooses to support it anyway.'

'And expects those around him do the same?' Thomasia surmised. She reached out and placed her hand over Shaw's. 'I'm sorry.'

There was nothing else to say. She could see the moral struggle in his eyes. What he felt for Maldon was frustration, but what he felt for himself, a man who was in very much the same position, was deeper, closer to loathing.

'What are the stakes?' she asked quietly.

It must be something grand if the price was tempting Shaw, or was it something else he feared? Was there a skeleton in his closet that Stanton had threatened to expose? She couldn't believe the latter, but one never knew. It was clear, however, that whatever the reason, the limits of Shaw's integrity were being reached and perhaps redefined. The thought saddened her, although she had to remind herself it was not unexpected. Men failed. Men fell short when their privilege was on the line.

'Advancement, connections to those who can help me with the things I got into politics for...' Her disappointment must have shown for he quickly added,

'More specifically foundling schools, and a branch railway line to improve commerce for Broxbourne. Stanton is willing to support those items in exchange for Maldon's vote.' And by 'Maldon's vote', she assumed that meant not only Maldon's vote but the votes of his boroughs.

'I see,' Thomasia said softly.

How much more tempting such an offer would be for a good man like Shaw, who was not pursuing his goals out of a need for personal gain. He'd gain nothing from foundling schools, nothing directly from the railway branch, while others—a *lot* of others—would benefit. Children would learn to become literate, and by doing so would be able to elevate their status in the world. Farmers would get crops to city markets more quickly, and people would be able to travel to London in the course of little more than an hour, instead of needing to spend days away from home in order to accomplish the journey. These were not selfish plans. It was no wonder he was hesitant to forego Stanton's support.

'It's not just giving up his support, though, is it?' Thomasia said astutely. 'He'll demand retribution.'

Stanton would make life difficult, if not impossible, for a fledgling MP who had openly defied him, and that would not please Maldon, who was hand in glove with Stanton.

Shaw nodded. 'I fear so. Why put up with a disagreeable MP when he could get Maldon to put someone else in the position.' He leaned down to help Effie with her toys. 'A chance to do much good would be lost, at least for the foundlings.' He sighed heavily. 'I don't like the idea of being bought, or the idea that I am just a move-able part, easily replaced when I displease.'

Thomasia gave a rueful smile. 'For women it's marriage. For men it's Parliament.'

Shaw gave a short laugh. 'I fear that is all too apt a comparison.'

Mrs Newsome appeared in the doorway, bearing a heavy tray. Shaw leapt to his feet.

'Mrs Newsome, allow me.' He took the large supper tray from her and brought it to the long table they usually worked at.

Thomasia picked up Effie, unwilling to leave her near the fire unsupervised for even a moment, and joined him. She lifted the lid of the tureen and sniffed appreciatively. 'This smells delicious, Mrs Newsome, thank you. We can handle everything from here, and you can put your feet up for the evening.'

With Mrs Newsome bustling off, looking forward to a quiet evening, Shaw set about serving the beef stew, ladling it into bowls and slicing the loaf of fresh-baked bread into thick pieces for dipping into broth.

'Shall we eat by the fire so Effie can play?' he asked.

It was a perfect solution. She'd been wondering how she might manage eating at the table with Effie on her lap with any amount of dignity. She'd imagined all the ways Effie could put her fingers in the stew and splash it about.

She sat and put Effie back on the floor with her toys, while Shaw brought their bowls and plates to the chairs and made one more trip back for the bottle of wine. He poured and set a glass on the small table beside her elbow.

'Thank you.' She gave her glass a little lift and knocked it against his gently. 'Cheers. This is a far nicer supper than I was expecting.' She'd not been looking forward to eating alone.

'Me, too.'

He smiled, but it didn't quite reach his blue eyes, a reminder that while he had talked about his disappointments today, they had not resolved them.

'What are you going to do?' Thomasia took a sip of wine.

'I don't know. I can try to make sure the repeal never gets to a vote, but I'd have to find other allies to make that happen and do it quietly, in a way that doesn't alert Stanton to my hand in it.'

Or he could give in and give the man what he wanted—that was the unspoken alternative.

'Effie seems happy tonight. I assume her tooth has come through?' The conversational change was abrupt, with no attempt at subtlety. Apparently he was done with talking about work, even if the worries of work weren't done with him.

'Come here, my little dear.' Thomasia picked Effie up and set the baby on her lap. 'Let's show Shaw your new tooth.'

'Oh, well done, little miss.' Shaw beamed at her. 'Will you come and sit with me for a bit?' He reached for her and settled her on his knee.

Thomasia liked the sight of that far too much. He wasn't the only one who had images in his head, fantasies in his heart.

They passed the next half hour companionably, playing with Effie, until Effie began to yawn. That yawn was like Cinderella's clock striking midnight. The magic was about to be lost and she wasn't ready for the evening to end.

'Oh, we haven't even had a slice of Mrs Newsome's pie,' Thomasia lamented, wondering if Effie would last another half hour or even an hour before she needed her bedtime feed and tucking in.

Effie threw down her toys and set up a frustrated howl. Well, that was one way to answer the question. Definitely not. Effie was hungry and tired.

She rose from her chair, scooping up Effie reluctantly. 'I'm sorry, Shaw. Effie needs...'

'I'll wait.' He rose with them, giving her a patient smile. 'Unless you'd rather I didn't?'

The offer was unexpected and it flustered her. 'Yes, your waiting would be fine. I will be about a half an hour, though.'

'I'll read while I wait and help myself to brandy.' He bent his head to kiss Effie on the cheek. 'Goodnight, miss, sleep well.' He tucked her rabbit under her arm and grinned over Effie's head, nestled against Thomasia's shoulder. 'Take your time. I'm in no hurry.'

He should leave immediately. He'd had his talk, his fantasy come to life for a short while, and he'd found some peace. Being with Thomasia had soothed his troubled thoughts even if it hadn't provided any answers. But he hadn't come to her for those. He'd come for the peace. To stay longer invited temptation, and tonight he was in no state to resist. Leaving would be a straightforward matter. It was late. It was a practical excuse they could both concede when he saw her in the morning. She would understand on all levels that his leaving was for the best.

Leaving might be a simple matter, but staying proved easier. It was easier to stay in his chair by the fire, easier to enjoy sipping a brandy and idly flipping through the pages of the children's book Effie-Claire had left on the floor.

He smiled at an illustration of a round, happy puppy on the page and then he laughed at himself. He was indulging the fantasy quite thoroughly tonight. Why not sit here and carry it through to its delicious conclusion? That he was at home, in front of his own fire, waiting patiently for Thomasia to tuck in their children. There'd be more than Effie, of course.

He looked down at the picture book and realised the flaw in the fantasy. It was a nice bit of make-believe but it lacked any edge of realism. If Thomasia was his wife he wouldn't be sitting here waiting for her to finish with the children. They would be *their* children, after all. He'd be upstairs with her, reading stories, tucking stuffed animals into arms, and giving goodnight kisses on sleepy cheeks.

Shaw settled into his chair, satisfied. That was better. He liked that image of them, side by side, caring for their children and taking on the world.

Side by side.

It was what he wanted in a marriage, a partner in all things. It was also what Thomasia would demand of a husband. Her views made it clear she would not play the subordinate in any relationship. She had both philosophical and practical objections to the marital state. But what an amazing helpmate she'd be.

He'd thought it from the first time he saw her, sitting so regally at the Peverett supper table. He'd imagined too easily, even on short acquaintance, how she'd look reigning over her own supper table. With her mind, her looks, she'd be an asset to any man's career. Except that she'd want her own career, he reminded himself with a chuckle. But she would be more than an asset to him. He saw the loving nature of her heart, her kindness, her selflessness. She would be more to him than just a political hostess.

She can be nothing of the sort. We've been over this and you know what she'll cost you.

His conscience kicked at him hard, driving him out of his fireside reverie. If Thomasia sat at his table she'd sit alone. Thomasia Peverett remained a conundrum. She had the skills to be a political hostess, but she would also be anathema to those very ambitions. She'd be her very own paradox.

He didn't make it easy on himself. He wanted to marry, and not only for the reasons Maldon had outlined. But he'd managed an attraction to the most unsuitable candidate in the district.

Well, that was putting the cart before the horse. Now his thoughts were running away with him. Here he was, fantasising about marriage, about fatherhood, with a woman he'd not even kissed, a woman who had made it clear she did not see marriage in her future.

Shaw rose from the chair and busied himself slicing the pie and plopping healthy scoops of cream on top. He needed to get himself under control before Thomasia came back or she'd wish he'd gone. Such thoughts would be bound to send her into retreat.

He heard her steps in the hallway, quick and light, just as he set the pie plates on the little table by the fire. She smiled when she saw the dessert, and the sight of that smile warmed him in ways a fire never could.

'Apple pie is my favourite and Mrs Newsome makes the best.' She resumed her seat and took a bite with relish. 'I see you like cream as much as I do.'

She was nervous, Shaw realised, taking a bite of his own slice. She was smiling a lot and talking too fast.

Because it's just the two of you. There are no letters to write, no work to discuss—you've already done that—and there's no baby to distract her. It's just her, you, and this attraction you both feel but do not act on, not the way you should.

'Are you really so cynical about marriage, Thomasia?' He picked up the thread of their earlier conversation, which had been interrupted when dinner had arrived.

He'd caught her mid-bite and she talked around it, waving her fork and managing to look entirely enchanting. 'Not cynical—honest. It's a trade of goods and services, with an eye towards security. Let's call it what it is instead of burying the truth beneath flowers and bonbons and ridiculous courtship rituals that don't matter in the end.'

Whoever the man was who'd wrecked Thomasia, he'd done a thorough job. Shaw would change that if he could, show her if he could that it didn't have to be that way.

'You don't think that marriage could be for love? For genuine partnership? Surely your parents are a case for that, as are your sisters.'

'They have been very lucky,' Thomasia replied with a ready answer. 'Every experiment has its outliers. History is full of them.'

'Like your Ladies of Salerno?' Shaw baited her quietly. He wanted her to walk into that trap, wanted her to see the flaw in her logic, and she did so with a nod of her head. 'Yet, you still aspire to them, to their purpose. Why should marriage be any different?'

She gave him a small smile. 'Touché.'

'Well? "Touché" is not an answer.'

'You *know* the answer.' She set aside her pie as the conversation turned serious, more battle than debate. 'No decent man would want me. The man who did would hold my transgression over me, use it to his advantage as he would use Effie-Claire. Marriage would condemn both of us. I cannot do that to myself or to my daughter.'

Shaw was silent for a moment, meeting her forthright gaze with his own. 'That's quite dark, Thomasia.'

'It's quite true.'

'It's not untrue. I am sure there are men who would act as you say. But there *are* men who would act contrary to that, who would take Effie as their own, who would love you, Thomasia.'

His heart was breaking for her and the darkness she harboured behind her fire, her passion. Perhaps it was that very darkness that fuelled the fire. It was certainly that darkness which bolstered her defences, making them impossible to get past.

'Forgive me if I find that hard to believe.'

She was retreating, as he'd known she would, but he was ready for it. He would not let her get away so easily.

If ever there was a time to share his own background with her, this was it.

He reached for her hand, forcing her to stay seated. He would not allow her to walk away from him, from them, until he'd told his story. 'Give me a moment more of your time, Thomasia. Let me tell you about my stepfather—a man who didn't walk away from a woman who had a son by another man.'

He gave her time to digest that, to understand each of the players and their roles. He watched her brow knit with questions, and he nodded in confirmation.

'I was a child like Effie-Claire,' he began, 'whose father did not wish to marry my mother. My mother worked in a nobleman's house and was seduced by his son. She had none of the choices you use your voice to advocate for, none of the healthcare resources that might have provided her with a preservative to protect against conception, no ability to resist his advances without fearing for her job, and no family to support her when she discovered she was with child. Of course she had to leave her position without a reference, and of course no one was willing to hire her at another house.'

'What did she do?' Thomasia asked softly, her empathy for a woman she didn't know evident in her gaze. His heart swelled at Thomasia's obvious concern, so easily given and heartfelt for a stranger.

'She was skilled with a needle. She used her meagre savings and rented a cottage in a small village far from the manor where she'd worked. She took in sewing and laundry. Did odd jobs at the big house in the area. Lived under a false name. She gave out that she was a widow and lived very circumspectly with her infant son.'

Shaw shook his head, remembering those early years.

'We lived meanly, with barely enough food and firewood to keep us warm and fed. A young boy is always hungry, always growing out of his clothes. Even as young as I was, I knew we lived close to the edge of starvation and Society. There were people who doubted my mother's story, who saw me for what I was—a bastard. Their children made life hard on me. I spent a significant amount of time defending myself with my fists.'

He felt Thomasia's hand squeeze inside his.

'That's no way to spend a childhood.'

'No, it wasn't. But fortunately there was a visitor to the big house while my mother was working up there, making gowns for the lord's daughters in anticipation of a wedding, who took a shine to her. Alan Rawdon, the third son of a baronet. In terms of a title he had no expectations, but he had a big heart, a decent manor in the country and an open mind. He fell in love with my mother and with her son. He was prepared to take on an instant family. At the age of eight I was rescued. I was given an education and a father figure to look up to as I grew. Everything I am I owe to him. He and my mother went on to have other children—Susannah, and I have a younger brother and sister at home—but they never displaced me in my stepfather's heart. He never looked at me and said, "They are mine, and you are not." I have always been his eldest son.'

He wondered what his stepfather would think of him now, though. His sitting in Parliament pleased Alan Rawdon. But what would he think of his working with men who stood for things that struck against all his stepfather and his mother had taught him to stand for?

'You were very lucky, indeed, Shaw.' Thomasia was quiet, thoughtful. 'It explains why you didn't run when you found out about Effie.' She gave a little smile, but it was not full of hope. 'Thank you for telling me your story.'

She was being obtuse, acting as if there was no reason for his having told her other than to simply share a piece of himself. It was her way of ignoring what he really wanted to discuss. He was going to have to spell it out to her.

'I told you because I mean to prove myself to you. Have I not shown myself to be such a man? A man who will not run from difficulty?' he asked quietly, his tone even, demanding an answer.

She tossed him a look that said the example didn't count. 'You're not courting me, Shaw. You are not looking to marry me. We are friends, nothing more.'

'Nothing more? Are you sure about that?' He was pressing on while he had a chance. There was uncertainty in her eyes, she wasn't sure what to make of his words, or maybe she was and wondered if she dared. He did not want her uncertain, didn't want to use that uncertainty against her. He didn't hold with emotional ambushes.

'*You* can mean well, Shaw, but it won't change others' responses to me and Effie. Neither will it change what others will think of you if you openly associate with us once it becomes known that I have a child.' She rose suddenly and gathered the pie plates. 'It's getting late, Shaw.'

It was only eight o'clock. Still, he had a bit of a ride home in the cold and the dark. He wouldn't mind, the cold would take the edge off him. But that wasn't why she'd interrupted their conversation. He'd made her uncomfortable—with him, with herself, with feelings she was having trouble admitting to? All of it?

He followed her to the table and helped her assemble the tray. 'Why can't you answer the question, Thomasia?'

She whirled on him then, the sharp turn bringing her up hard against his body. He caught her by both arms, the cognac flame crackling in her eyes igniting a primitive spark in his own. 'Because men fail, Shaw,' she snapped even as he steadied her, even as he saw the pulse jump at the base of her neck, even as her breath caught and her body reacted to the nearness of him.

'*That* was spoken like a woman who has never had the love of a good man,' he growled. 'Try me, Thomasia.'

Chapter Thirteen

It was absolutely the last thing she should do. She should not try him, should not test the desire that leapt between them like flames to dry kindling, but it seemed that particular fire had already caught. Denying it would be akin to lying, to pretending that desire wasn't there in the most ridiculous pretence—the kind where truth stared one in the face. Especially when that truth looked like Shaw Rawdon, his beautiful strong face bathed in firelight.

She was going to regret these next moments either way: regret knowing, regret not knowing. She couldn't win.

She'd rather regret the pleasure.

Thomasia reached up on her tiptoes, her arms twining about his neck, and kissed him, her lips moving softly over his mouth in the gentlest of brushings. She felt his mouth open, taking the invitation, felt his body move into hers. And she let hers move into his, the kiss no longer hers but theirs, a slow, joint exploration of one another.

He tasted of cinnamon and apples, of cream and brandy, sweet and sharp all at once—not unlike the man himself. Heat simmered in the kiss, and desire hummed beneath its surface. She wanted this: his mouth on hers, his hands on her. She wanted to get lost in the promise of his strength, his goodness, his passion. Especially the last. Because—oh, yes—there was passion here, too. A passion held in check for fear it would overwhelm them both, lead them to a point of no return.

'I think this is a good note to leave on.' Shaw murmured the words against her ear.

'Not yet,' she whispered back. 'Hold me just a little while longer.'

She smiled up at him in an attempt to mitigate the words, to make them sound playful as opposed to desperate or, worse, wanton. She wanted to regret them as soon as she uttered them, for revealing too much, but in the moment she couldn't. It felt too good to stand there, wrapped in his arms, her head on his chest, listening to the steady beat of his heart. Because above all other things Shaw Rawdon was steadiness personified in a world that, for her, was filled with uncertainty. What would happen in the spring? Would she even be here?

She breathed him in one final time and then stepped back, casting about for something normal to say. 'Will you be all right in the dark?'

'Yes, it's not that far, but thank you for the concern.' He gave her a kind smile. 'I'll see you tomorrow.'

She thought she heard a note of assurance in the last—an assurance that tonight had not changed them, that tomorrow would follow the same routine she'd got used to, that all would be well, that she could trust him.

* * *

Shaw should never have given her those assurances. All was not well.

Thomasia grumpily stared down the length of the library table the next afternoon. How could Shaw sit there, reading through reports? How could he focus when her thoughts were scattered to the four winds, when her gaze couldn't manage to stay fixed on a single page without glancing up to look at him? The sight of him was sending her thoughts whirling back to last night, back to the memory of his mouth on hers, back to the taste of him, the smell of him, and the intimacy of those details, those moments. How wonderful it had felt not to be alone, to *be* with someone else.

There was a price for that, though. As a consequence, things were *not* the same. They were better and worse than before. Better because she'd satisfied her curiosity and kissed that delectable mouth. Better because that kiss had been a slow, sweet, heady elixir, and to be in his arms had been exquisite. Worse because she wanted to kiss him again…wanted to be in his arms again. Worse because in wanting such things, in acting on such curiosity, she'd broken every promise she'd made to herself when Effie was born: no more curiosity, no more spontaneity, no more giving in to passion. She would be the perfect mother to atone for her momentary lapse in judgement. She'd broken those promises last night. The worst of it was, she wasn't sorry she had, and she ought to be. One ought to be sorry when one broke promises. And she was angry. At Shaw. For being so unaffected…for being able to act *normally*.

Her temper boiled over and she threw down her pencil. 'How can you sit there and pretend nothing happened? How can you be so *cavalier*?'

But she knew how. Kisses didn't mean as much to a man—even if that man was the steady, intoxicating Shaw Rawdon.

You knew he wouldn't be different and you let yourself believe otherwise.

'How is it that a man can kiss a woman and not be changed by it?'

For she would desperately like to know. Maybe if she knew she could stop making the same mistake. Maybe then she wouldn't be swept away by her feelings.

Shaw looked up from his papers at the outburst. So she felt it, too, this frisson of tension that underlaid the day. Only in true Thomasia fashion she was willing to act on that tension, while he was doing his best to keep a lid on the slow simmer that kept his blood warm and his body aroused.

He'd had the devil's own time keeping his mind on his work, knowing that she was just feet away at the end of the table, knowing what she tasted like, what she felt like in his arms. But he'd promised her all would be well, that their kiss needn't change them.

'I thought that was what you wanted.'

Shaw set aside his notes and met her gaze in reminder. She'd risen, her hands braced on the table, and fixed him with a fierce stare. What a virago she was—so full of fire she couldn't contain it, no matter how hard she tried, and she *did* try. He saw that restraint daily. What a shame that was…Thomasia on control's leash.

She was not meant for restraint. But the world had little use for such passion, especially for a woman.

His comment startled her—she'd not expected that. For a moment she was without words.

'What *I* wanted?' Her voice rose. 'Why would you think I wanted you to kiss me and act as if it meant nothing?' she railed, and he could see dangerous memories flash in her eyes—memories of other kisses, of another man to whom her passion for living had meant little, a man in whom she'd nonetheless invested that passion.

He'd meant to be empathetic, but his own temper was rising, too. How dare she equate him with that other man? How dare she believe he was capable of delivering such cold-hearted hurt? Especially as nothing could be further from the truth. That kiss had kept him up half the night and uncomfortably so.

'You were clear you wanted nothing to change,' Shaw replied evenly. 'I am aware that you feel unready to entertain a relationship. I would not push you where you don't wish to go, therefore I must wait for you to decide what you want.'

It was not a position he was used to being in, waiting for the woman to take the lead. But he understood that was how it would have to be with Thomasia. She would not allow herself to be courted. It was an easy defence. She could see courtship coming a mile away and turn it aside before it reached her. But perhaps if there was something or someone she wanted badly enough she would do the courting herself. That was how it had been last night. She'd certainly wanted that kiss and now she was struggling to come to terms with that want. As was he.

Something in her gaze crumpled and some of her anger seemed to redirect itself. He almost couldn't bear the sight of her flame diminished in any degree by frustration and condemnation—not for him but for herself. He regretted it on those grounds alone. He'd not meant for it to bring her pain.

'What I want, Shaw, is for *you* to be as undone by that kiss as I was—as I *am*.' She flung the challenge at him with the last of her anger, but it was an anger without rancour.

'I am, Thomasia,' he answered quietly, willing his voice, his words, to carry the sincerity she needed. A man had given her useless words before. 'I was so undone by it I was up most of the night with thoughts of it, with thoughts of you and of what I want in life.'

He saw her in that life, standing beside him. He paused, not wanting to overwhelm her with the truth. She wanted him undone—so be it. But he knew that if he told her all that entailed she would bolt.

He moved from his end of the table and held out a hand to her. 'Come and walk with me.'

The afternoon was grey, but the rain had not arrived yet. The library opened on to the garden and they might take a brief stroll there. Changing their location, moving away from the scene of the kiss, might benefit them both. He'd thought of nothing else all day, and clearly she hadn't either.

She met him halfway and took his hand. The feel of her skin against his, her hand in his hand, brought a sense of peace. Did she feel it, too, this sense of wholeness when they were together?

Outside, the air was crisp with encroaching winter—

a reminder that December was well underway. Shaw welcomed the briskness, letting it clear his mind, letting his thoughts focus on the one thing that mattered in this moment: Thomasia.

'I am not him.'

Shaw let the words settle between them. That was the real issue here. The sooner they dealt with that, the sooner they could move forward.

'Whoever he was, he has taught you some poor lessons: that men fail, that kisses are trite, that a kiss does not undo a man, that love is a phantom, that love is a tool to entrap a woman in eternal servitude.' He shook his head. 'That is not what love is...not what a man is. It is not who I am.'

Thomasia shook her head. 'It's not only that. It's me. I promised myself I would never be so curious again and I broke that promise so easily. I gave in to temptation. I set myself up for hurt knowingly.'

'You're to be a nun for the rest of your life? You're to be alone? All because of one indiscretion?'

He could not imagine a worse fate for Thomasia, who loved to hug her daughter, who loved to touch people when she talked, who'd kissed him so spontaneously. She was made to touch and be touched.

'I feel that the punishment doesn't fit the indiscretion.' He wouldn't use the word *crime*, not in conjunction with sweet Effie-Claire. That darling baby was not a crime, no child was.

'A nun or a wanton are my only choices. My sister Anne likes to say in Society's eyes a woman can only be seven things. Perhaps I am doomed to be wanton.'

Thomasia shivered and he shrugged out of his jacket

and wrapped it around her shoulders. He would have liked to pull her close instead, but she was not ready to welcome his touch. He touched her with his words instead.

'It's no sin to love, Thomasia, to love with your whole heart. It is a risk, though, and I would always want you to be careful with yourself.' Even if the man in question was him.

He was acutely aware, as they stood in the bare, naked winter garden, that there was immense potential between them for both love and hurt. If there were to be other kisses they would need to set down expectations if they were to protect themselves and each other.

Thomasia looked up at him, her gaze clear, her anger spent, her voice soft. 'I know you're not him. It would be easier if you were. But you're not, and that scares me very much.'

A gust of wind blew through the garden and she shivered despite his jacket. Shaw drew her close, whether she wanted it or not, unable to bear her discomfort for a moment when he could do something about it.

He wrapped his arms tight about her, and murmured into her hair. 'You scare me, too.'

Thomasia Peverett could break them both, and yet he knew he wanted no one else in his arms, that he would go to great lengths to keep her there, where she was safe, where the world couldn't harm her, and Effie-Claire, too. In them, he'd found a piece of himself.

'We've found her, milord.' The runner stood before Anthony's desk at rigid attention. 'She's right where you said she'd be. In Haberstock at her family home.'

Anthony gave a brief nod, less impressed by the man's work than he was. Really, the man ought not look so proud of himself. It was hardly a difficult task. It had been more of a verification than a finding. Where else would she have been if she wasn't in London with her family there? There were only so many places a woman in her situation could go.

'And the child?'

That was his greater worry. Perhaps she'd given the child up, or perhaps the child hadn't lived. Perhaps she'd not carried it to term by natural or unnatural means. She'd been furious and heartbroken the last time he'd seen her. Her whole world had unravelled and he'd offered no support. How could he have? He had his own world to contend with.

'The child is with her, milord. She has a baby girl.'

This was going better than he could have hoped. A baby girl was perfect. Adopting a girl would be far less complicated. A girl wouldn't get in the way of any inheritance issues, should the doctors be wrong and his wife miraculously conceived an heir some time in the future. And, since there was no inheritance to quibble over, Society might even forget in time that she was adopted at all. Eighteen years was nearly two decades away, and this child was young.

The future was looking rosy. His fifty thousand pounds inched closer.

'The child's name?'

'I don't know, milord. It was difficult to discover much about the baby. I didn't dare approach the servants. Strangers stand out in a place like Haberstock. No one can come and go without being noticed...a man asking questions even less so. No one in the village knows. She doesn't leave the estate and, with it being winter, she seldom goes outside.'

'No one knows?'

The report was getting interesting now, despite the runner's hyperbole. Someone must know. It wasn't possible for no one to know.

'I find that hard to believe. The servants at the house know.'

Although it did seem unlikely they would be a useful source of information—the runner was right about that. No one could go asking questions without raising suspicion, especially if those questions were about a well-guarded secret.

'Her family knows…her sisters, her parents. Her sisters' husbands and their families know. Servants plus family means at least thirty people know she's keeping a baby at Haberstock Hall.'

Thirty was not an insubstantial sum. In his experience the more people who were tasked with keeping a secret, the easier it was to prise that secret loose. But who might talk? Who might give him something that could act as leverage when the time came? Not the Treshams. The Duke had been livid with him when he had discovered what he'd done with a girl under the Duke's aegis. He did not know Wychavon, Thea Peverett's husband, well or the rest of the family. It was doubtful that side of the family would spill secrets to a stranger.

'She goes nowhere? Sees no one?'

It was hard to imagine the Thomasia he knew living so secluded. But perhaps she had no choice. She could hardly go out in public with a baby on her hip and no husband in sight. Which begged the question: What did she intend to do? How long did she think she could hide from the world? Was her family ready for disgrace? Perhaps if he could use her family's reputation against her she would give up the child more readily.

'There is one fellow who rides to the Hall daily. I was able to enquire about him in the village. He's the MP for the district. Shaw Rawdon. Owns a small estate called Rosegate.'

Anthony lifted his brows in interest. Now, this was something. 'Why does he go every day?'

'I don't know, but he carries a saddlebag and he stays for hours—like a man going to the office.'

Anthony shrugged. It hardly mattered what the man did there. It only mattered that he did it for hours every day. One could not escape the presence of a baby for that long. Rawdon must know. What did Rawdon's visits mean?

Thomasia was a pretty, vivacious girl. She might be angling for a husband, a father for her brat. That would certainly upend his own plans. It would be much harder to take a child from a married woman who had a man to fight for her. Although if that man was an MP, perhaps he would be his ally. That man would see the need to handle the situation expediently, before word could get out and ruin his career.

Of course such a man wouldn't get within a mile of a fallen woman, let alone align himself with her to begin with, not in any matrimonial sense.

Anthony's agile mind leapt to another scenario, in which Thomasia kept illicit company with the man.

That would be leverage enough for him to prise the child from her, privately or publicly.

'Do you think there's an attachment between Miss Peverett and Rawdon?' he asked idly, not wanting to alert the runner to his suspicions.

'Perhaps, milord. I have seen them out on walks about the estate.'

'Anything else?' Walking was hardly enough to prove an inappropriate association.

The runner shook his head. 'No, but there is something about the way they are together…the way she leans towards him, puts her hand on his arm. She looks up at him, and he walks beside her as if he is ready to fight the world for her. It's hard to describe, but they look as if they belong together, the way people in love look. Do you know what I mean? You can just tell they care for one another.'

Sweet heavens, Thomasia had enchanted his hired runner and from a distance. Disgusting. His runner was clearly a hopeless romantic. No, he didn't know how people in love looked. But he did know how it felt to be with Thomasia. He could well imagine her touch on an arm, on a sleeve, the press of her hand, the light in her eyes as she laughed, the innocent who wasn't so innocent.

He roused a bit at the memory and shifted in his seat, dismissing the runner with a curt thank you. The man had done his job. The man had verified the location of his child. Now it was time for the next steps.

His solicitor needed to build an irrefutable case to compel Thomasia into turning over the child—hopefully privately, without the need for a public scene in court. He glanced at the calendar. Christmas was nearing.

His solicitor would not have the case ready before then. He drummed his fingers on the desk. Thomasia had family—powerful family if she chose to engage them. He didn't dare show his hand until he was entirely sure of his ground.

He blew out a breath. He would wait until after Christmas to send the letter. Then all his pieces would be in place. Now that the child was within reach, he could be patient and sure. It even occurred to him that he might just be doing her a favour—playing the hero after all. Thomasia might relinquish the child without a fight. Perhaps she'd welcome the chance to start a new life out of hiding with this new man.

Chapter Fourteen

She would not trade this for the world: Christmastime at Haberstock Hall. How she'd missed it last year! Thomasia looked about her at the candles glowing on the mantel of the fireplace in the great hall, the evergreen boughs draping the oak banister that led upstairs.

But more important than the decorations were the people around her—her parents, her sister and the beautiful baby girl she balanced on her hip. They'd gathered before the fire to wait for the call to supper—the smells of which had been tormenting them all day as Cook worked her magic—and to hear the latest letter from William, on the front in Sevastopol. He was safe, thank God, and that was Christmas gift enough for all of them.

Christmas would be quiet this year. In part because of her, Thomasia knew. They couldn't have the village traipsing through the house and expect to keep the baby a secret. But it was also partly because her beloved family was changing. Anne and Ferris were spending Christmas at Bramble, his family's estate in Sussex. Thea and Wychavon were spending it in London, so that Thea was not away from the women's hospital. William was at war. There was only her and Rebecca at home now.

'I missed this last year.' Thomasia sighed happily, leaning her head against Becca's shoulder. Last year the two of them had been in York. 'Auntie Claire's was nice, but it wasn't home. Maybe next year we'll all be together again.'

Once, she'd taken those big, loud family Christmases filled with activity and liveliness for granted. Just as she'd once taken her family for granted, and at times even resented it because it was big and boisterous. It was easy to get lost in the chaos when one was the youngest of five determined siblings. She never would again.

That family had stood by her. Anne and Thea had helped her through the early months of her pregnancy, her mother had arranged for her to go to Aunt Claire's, Becca had gone with her, insisting she not face the birth alone, and her family had invited her home. They would do more for her if she'd let them. They would let her stay for ever. But she could not ask them to bear the scandal.

She needed a solution by spring. Perhaps going back to York. Aunt Claire and the Coffee Yard ladies would welcome her. Or maybe she should take her dowry funds and find a quiet cottage somewhere, live under an assumed name and devote herself to Effie-Claire. That would be a solitary existence—one that would require constant vigilance to maintain.

Neither of those options would include Shaw Rawdon. She made her thoughts stop there.

A knock sounded at the door just as her father folded William's letter. Thomasia started, her gaze darting from Becca to her mother. Who were they expecting?

The answer should be no one. Perhaps someone had an emergency and needed her father?

Thomasia turned and quickly headed for the stairs, wanting to make Effie invisible.

'Don't go, Thomasia.' Her mother stalled her with a gentle touch as her father went to the door. 'It will be Shaw. I invited him for supper and for the night. I couldn't stand the thought of him spending Christmas alone once I realised Susannah was away,' her mother explained with a smile.

'Shaw is here?'

Surprise caught her off guard. He'd been out of town taking care of business, making some arrangements he'd wanted to put in place for Rosegate before the New Year. She'd not expected him back for Christmas. Nor, she'd reminded herself countless times since his departure, did she have any right to expect him back—not really, not when she could offer him nothing in return.

And yet here she was, her pulse racing at the sight of him walking through the door, as if she did indeed have a right to expect him—as if he was coming home to her.

He stood in the doorway, looking like a younger and much handsomer version of Father Christmas, wearing his greatcoat and bearing gifts, his auburn hair wind-blown and glistening with raindrops, his cheeks ruddy from the cold.

'Happy Christmas, everyone. I am sorry to be late, the train was delayed, and the road from Broxbourne Station is slow tonight on account of the weather,' he explained as a groom brought in his travelling valise and set it down.

'You're just in time.' Her mother swept forward, instructing the groom to take the parcels to the music room and the valise upstairs to the guest chamber.

Shaw shed his greatcoat and shook her father's hand, laughing and making another remark about the roads, but his gaze strayed to where she stood, and a private flame flickered there that was just for her—as if he, too, felt this was more a homecoming than a visit.

He moved to her side by the fire and bent to kiss Effie-Claire's chubby cheek. 'How are you, Thomasia? Have you had a good week?' he asked, straightening up.

'It's good now.' She smiled, unable to stop smiling. 'I had not thought to see you,' she admitted quietly, almost shyly, unsure if it was wise to confess to having spent the week pining for his company. Life was lonelier without him, and certainly much less interesting. There was no one to talk to when he was away.

'Yes, it most certainly is a good week now.' He offered her a private smile. 'Effie looks like she's getting heavy.' He took the baby from her arms.

'Was your work for the estate successful?'

He'd gone to secure the delivery of new farming equipment by spring. She'd written the initial letters of enquiry. He was counting on the equipment to make planting and reaping more efficient.

He nodded, explaining his week to her while Effie played contentedly with his fingers, and Thomasia lost a little more of her battle to resist his charm. This felt right. Right to stand here in the great hall with Shaw beside her, right to talk over mundane matters like farming equipment, right to see her daughter in his arms as if she were his, right even to think such dangerous thoughts. Effie wasn't the only one who was content.

Be careful, contentment leads to complacency and you cannot afford such a luxury.

But maybe she could, just for a night. It would be a small Christmas gift to herself.

And what a gift it was—well worth whatever pain might follow. A night and a day of indulging herself in Shaw's presence, Shaw's company, beginning as they all sat down to Christmas Eve dinner and sang carols around the piano afterwards.

There'd been a tender moment in the hall upstairs as the house retired for the night and they'd stood alone outside her door, Effie sleeping quietly inside. His lips had brushed hers and he'd whispered, 'Happy Christmas, Thomasia,' and she'd wished with all her wanton heart that he didn't have to go to his own bed.

The magic started again the next morning, with Shaw beside her at Christmas breakfast—a veritable feast of eggs and sausage and crispy toast and Christmas jam, little gifts of nuts and candied fruit at each plate. Then they adjourned to the music room, where the Christmas tree stood in pride of place, gifts beneath it waiting to be opened.

Shaw had brought a doll for Effie he'd found in one of the shops on his trip, and it touched her heart in dangerous ways to see him on the floor with Effie, playing.

This was what it might have been like if she'd not made a mistake with Anthony.

Too soon Christmas was over, and Shaw was determined to head back to Rosegate—but not before he whispered quietly, 'We have to talk, Thomasia.'

The words both thrilled her and worried her. What

did they have to talk about? Was it about work? About Stanton's repeal? Was it more personal?

That was the worrying part. They would have to discuss his leaving. January would be upon them and Parliament would be opening. It would be the end of them and their friendship, or whatever it was that lay between them. He would go to London, the one place she dared not go. He would meet women more suitable to be his wife than she. He would forget about the magic between them and the memories made over the winter, and she would need to make her own choices.

He was not the only one leaving. She would be gone by the time he came home—*if* he came home—during the short Easter recess. She would need to decide what her life was to be like from here on out.

She didn't want to decide. She'd prefer that winter last for ever, that she and Shaw stay in this sweet, indeterminate limbo. If they talked, that would change.

But there was no chance to talk. The days following Christmas were hectic at Haberstock Hall, with her parents and Becca packing for a visit to London to see her sisters: Thea and Wychavon first, and then Ferris and Anne when they returned to Town. She and Effie would have the house to themselves for a few weeks.

'You'll have time to think, my dear,' her mother said, hugging her farewell on the Hall steps, 'and we'll talk it all through when I get back,' she added fondly. 'Whatever you decide, we'll support you.'

If only it were that easy, Thomasia thought as she waved them off. To simply decide. But the future was a multifaceted beast and facing it would be difficult.

It had been easier eight weeks ago, before she'd met

Shaw. Life had been lonelier then, too—proof that no decision came without consequences. Even with the restraint that it had taken all her will to exert when it came to Shaw Rawdon, she was not protected from hurt. She would miss him when winter was over, and winter would end for her much sooner than it would end for others.

How had this happened? How had she let Shaw behind her defences? How had she managed to fall for him when she'd promised herself she wouldn't fall for any man?

Because he isn't just any man, came the answer.

He was right. They had to talk. The sooner the better.

Shaw came to the house late in the evening, obviously having been conscious of not being underfoot while the Hall got its people off for their visit. She knew there'd been no reason or excuse for him to come any earlier. Work had been slow since Christmas and there was less to do…less that required them to work together at the long table in the library.

It seemed to Thomasia, as they sat together not in the library but in the music room, that more than the venue was changing between them—that perhaps the knots that had tied them together in November and December were coming undone now in the New Year, unravelling strand by strand. The need for them to be in one another's company was slowly diminishing as the day of Shaw's departure closed in on them—or was it only her it was closing in on? Perhaps Shaw was eager to be free of her now that there was no use for her services.

Shaw seemed agitated, his gaze restless as it roamed

about the room, and they struggled to make small talk. Not even Effie-Claire's latest attempts to walk filled the gap. Thomasia gave up. Her thoughts and worries were distraction enough, let alone doing battle with his.

She rose and moved to the window, staring outside as she steeled herself against the possibility that he'd come to say goodbye. Perhaps for her winter ended today— although the weather suggested otherwise. Snow had started to fall hard. The dropping temperature was changing the earlier rain to a fast-accumulating blanket of white.

But Shaw continued to surprise her. She could hear him rising, his boots crossing the floor to join her.

'It's not politics I've come to talk about today, although I suppose there's plenty to say. But there is nothing we haven't talked of before. Everyone has to live with their own conscience, even Stanton. I've come to grips with the knowledge that at some point my integrity will be for sale, or my seat will be. All I can do is decide, when that point is reached, how much my moral code can stand before it breaks or before I have to walk away.'

She knew he was thinking of his foundling schools. How much should be traded to get them? Would Stanton's repeal end his career before it even really started?

She felt his approach just before his arms came around her, drawing her close against him as they both stared out into the winter garden. He was all warmth and comfort. Thomasia sighed while temptation whispered. Could she put Shaw in an untenable position? Who would Shaw choose if it came to it? Her? Or Stanton? Why would he choose her? She could be nothing to him. There was no gain there and, since she had no desire to be a martyr just yet, she let the temptation pass.

'Thomasia…'

He whispered her name at her ear, a low, intimate rumble that sent a thrill through her.

'I came here because there is something that has been long on my mind far more than Stanton—since Christmas, in fact.'

The word conjured a host of memories limned in candlelight with evergreen boughs. Christmas: the night he'd kissed her outside her bedroom door. Christmas: when he'd sat at supper with her family as if he'd always belonged there, as if he was meant to be one of them. Christmas: when he'd played with Effie-Claire as if she were his own.

'I have to leave soon for London and I do not want things unsettled between us.'

Damn him. How dare he throw down a velvet glove when she'd been prepared for a gauntlet?

Chapter Fifteen

'What is there to settle?' Thomasia replied with a coolness that was entirely feigned.

Her pulse thrummed and her blood heated. There were so many ways to 'settle' things with Shaw, and none of them all that settling—especially when his arms were about her and every nerve she possessed was aware of him in all his guises, aware of the touch of him, the scent of him, the strength of him.

'Don't play aloof, Thomasia,' Shaw cautioned, his hand closing over her wrist. 'I can feel your pulse. It races like mine. We both know what there is to settle. How should we go on? Stolen kisses and denial? Or shall we embrace what is between us?'

She turned in his arms to face him and stepped back, coming up against the panes of the French doors to buy herself some space, but not much. 'Embrace it? What does that even mean?'

His eyes glistened like twin sapphires this close. 'What would you like it to mean?'

Shaw's gaze never left hers as he reached for her

hand and kissed the tiny piece of skin revealed at her wrist, sending butterflies fluttering in her stomach.

'I want you, Thomasia. In every way possible. Dare I hope you might feel the same?'

She blushed at the frankness of his words even as she revelled in them. They made her feel alive. Her body hummed with their meaning and the intent behind them. But her mind counselled caution. What could come of acting on such fervour but disappointment and hurt?

Joy, pleasure, contentment, even if short-lived, came the reply of her heart.

'Are you asking for one night, Shaw? Shall you come to me just the one time?'

Tonight, perhaps, as snow fell outside, trapping them indoors and no one to know. Temptation whispered with renewed vigour.

Shaw's jaw tightened at the challenge, even as she watched his eyes darken with rampant desire. 'I seriously doubt once would be enough. I am asking you for more than one night.'

He wanted her to be his mistress. It was a logical conclusion, based on their circumstances, but something in Thomasia deflated nonetheless. His behaviour had been nothing but honourable and kind towards her up until now. She'd nearly begun to believe that he was different. Why was she surprised? Disappointed? He *was* like other men after all. All men failed eventually.

She met his gaze evenly and answered before he could ask—before she had to hear him say the words. 'I would not embarrass my family by being a man's mistress openly, and I would not insult them by sneaking around behind their backs, creating lies, so that I could conduct an illicit relationship with their neighbour.'

A neighbour they liked and respected.

'No, not a mistress—that's not what I meant at all.' Shaw was clearly affronted at the notion. 'Is that what you believe I think of you? Of us?'

In her attempt to protect herself she'd hurt him. She was sorry for that. He deserved better.

Her hands pressed against the lapels of his jacket. She could feel the echoes of his heartbeat, hard and fierce beneath her palms. 'It's what I think of our *situation*, Shaw, not of you. We've come to the end of honour.'

She had to be careful or she would have him on one knee, proposing marriage, and that she could not allow. She would not allow his honour to ruin him.

'I will not marry and you must wed. There are only dishonourable choices left to us if we pursue this attraction. You deserve more, Shaw,' she added softly.

Outside, snow coated the garden in the dark. The weather was making the decision for her—or at least allowing her to put off making that decision, saying the words that would commit them either way. Regardless of her decision, she could not send him out in the snow.

'You can't go out in this. I'll have a room made up.'

It was not an answer. It was an excuse not to say yes or no. She was dithering, and things were as unsettled between them as they had been a few minutes ago.

She stepped away from his embrace. 'I need to go up now and check on Effie. It will just take a few minutes to have your room ready. You're welcome to make free of the house. Help yourself to a brandy.'

She offered a smile as she moved past him, thankful that he didn't press his argument. Perhaps he recognised, too, that in her oblique response was another message. Whatever happened, the case was lost and rightly so. Nothing could come of this beyond the walls of Haberstock Hall.

Nothing?

The word haunted her as she made ready for bed, brushing out her hair, slipping a soft white linen nightgown over her head, and then the word stuck in her head.

Nothing.

The word was so extreme, so final, so empty. It was not a word the Coffee Yard ladies liked. There was always *something* that could be done, no matter how small.

She heard his footsteps as he went to his room across the hall. He'd not stayed up. Perhaps she should go to him once, give them both what they wanted. No, neither of them wanted one night. Their discussion downstairs had never been about that, however she'd tried to frame it. It had been about the future and what that could look like, but there were no tolerable honourable options.

Thomasia began to pace, to think. If there were only dishonourable options, were there any that kept the dishonour private, between them? As a moment in time to be kept apart from the world? Where they might exist without consequences? What lay between honour and dishonour? Between mistress and marriage?

Two weeks.

The answer whispered its temptation in the night. Two weeks until Shaw left for London. Two weeks until her family returned. Two weeks of winter and privacy. That would be it. He would leave and there would be every chance she would not see him again. When he left it would be over. If she chose this it would ensure she left, too, before he returned at Easter.

She played with the tie of her nightgown. She could not be here then. There would be the temptation to continue their affair, to want more than two weeks. With that temptation would come risk. If they were discovered it would damage them and their families. If there wasn't temptation there would be heartbreak. The heartbreak of watching him court another, bringing his bride home to Rosegate. She could not stand by and watch that, even knowing that she could never have had him.

She stopped pacing at the window and looked out into the night. So it wasn't that nothing could be done. Something *could* be done. The question was whether or not she would do it. Would she choose two weeks over nothing?

She glanced over at Effie, sleeping peacefully, her rabbit tucked under an arm. Yes, she would. She'd chosen Effie over nothing. There had been a moment when she could have ended the pregnancy, and another when she could have settled Effie with a family in York. But she would always choose love, even if its expression could only be temporary.

Thomasia drew a deep breath and tiptoed quietly across the room. She left the door open, in case Effie cried, and walked across the hall, a journey of ten steps, although it seemed more monumental than that.

She turned the knob and stepped inside. Despite the dimness of the chamber her eyes found him instantly. He stood at the bureau, his back to the door. She heard cufflinks clink into the trinket dish, the first of his accoutrements to be removed as he began to undress. His waistcoat followed, and the lamplight traced the silhouette of his back through the fabric of his shirt.

She really ought to announce her presence before he disrobed further. Instead, she held her breath, watching as he pulled the shirt over his head, revealing in one fluid gesture that beautiful back, with its sculpted shoulders and tapered muscles leading to a lean waist, narrow hips and firm buttocks encased in dark trousers.

But not for long. His hands were already at his waistband. She found her voice. 'Do you have something against buttons, Shaw?'

He turned at the sound of his name, his mind registering only one fact: she was here. Thomasia was here, in his room, an angel in white, her hair streaming down her back in a dark cascade, her tawny eyes aglow with courage and uncertainty—because what was courage without it? He knew in that moment there was only one reason she was here: she was here for him. For them.

'Two weeks, Shaw. It's what I can give you…what I can give myself.'

She was moving towards him with a purposeful stride and he met her halfway across the room, his blood pounding as he took her in his arms, felt her arms about his neck, as his mouth took hers and hers answered, their bodies pressing close, sealing the pact.

Two weeks. It seemed like a blissful eternity. They had time. It was only that reminder that kept him from devouring her. She would not want ravishment, not tonight. Tonight, she would want a deliberate consummation, an intentional awareness of what they were choosing and an intentional celebration.

He smiled against her mouth in understanding. 'What changed your mind?'

'Love. Just because it might be fleeting does not mean it should be tossed aside.'

No, one should not be cavalier with love.

Shaw lifted her in his arms and carried her to the bed and set to the fastenings of his trousers with the fervour of a bridegroom. But she reached out a hand.

'You needn't hurry. In fact, I wish you wouldn't.' Her eyes glittered topaz with desire, with curiosity. 'Might I look at you?'

Any part of him not aroused already went rock-hard at the request. Did Thomasia have any idea how heady he found the idea of being desired by her? How arousing he found it to have her want him? Because he knew what it meant to her to commit to this. Having earned her desire, her trust in this matter, was no small thing.

He slid his trousers off and stood back from the bed, feeling her gaze rove over him, watching her gaze light with...discovery?

She reached for him, drawing him to the bed. 'I want to touch you. I've felt these muscles for weeks now, hiding beneath the layers of your coats.'

She gave him a smile, part seduction, part play, a smile that was completely Thomasia. This was how she was, all honesty and no artifice, and he found it intoxicating.

He lay down beside her, their bodies arranging themselves along the length of each other. Her finger drew a slow line down the length of him, tracing each ridge and plane. 'I've never seen a naked man before,' she admitted with shy boldness. 'Does that surprise you?'

'It disappoints me more than surprises me.'

Shaw fought the urge to take her in his arms and disrupt her exploration, pleasant as it was. Perhaps it secretly pleased him to know he was her first in this regard. The first to be openly and honestly naked with her, and perhaps she with him. It told him volumes about what her prior experience had been like. He would do better, show her better, show her that she deserved better from a man.

Her hand dropped to his phallus, wrapping itself around the hard length of him. 'Does this feel all right?'

Dear Lord, her innocent solicitations would be the death of him before he even had a chance to show her what it could be like.

'It feels good, very good,' he assured her, putting his hand over hers, showing her how to move it up and down. Her eyes glowed wickedly. Perhaps she was sensing how much he enjoyed it. 'But how about you? Might *I* look at *you*?'

The request made her blush. 'It's not necessary. You needn't. You may blow the light out.'

'Why would I do that?' He chuckled, trying to put her at ease and not liking the conclusions he was rapidly drawing. She had never had a lover. She'd had a man who'd put his seed in her—nothing more. If he ever found out who the man was he would hold him accountable.

'Because I'm more attractive with my clothes *on*.' Her blush deepened with her confession. 'I have marks from the baby, and…'

He stopped her recitation with a kiss and levered himself above her. 'Warrior's medals, every last one of them. You brought a new life into the world, Thomasia. You cannot expect that to leave you unchanged, unmarked. Nor would you want it to.'

She laughed up at him. 'You sound like my mother.'

'To be clear, that is *not* a romantic comment at such a moment.'

He liked this love play with her, this talk and banter, this ease of being together. It held an intoxication all its own. As exciting as talk was, though, there were other exciting things, too. He slid a hand beneath her night-gown, pushing it back to reveal a long, slim leg. He bent it and kissed her behind the knee, trailing kisses up her thigh, revelling in the silk of her skin beneath his lips, the scent of her arousal, the catch of her breath as he blew softly against damp curls.

Arousing her was arousing *him*.

He tongued the hidden nub within her folds and felt her body quiver. She gave an audible gasp of surprised delight and he smiled against her skin. 'It's about to get better,' he murmured, just before he made good on his promise, licking and stroking her until she reached the point of frenzied oblivion, bucking hard as her hips rose up to press against him in a begging, wanting, sub-mission to pleasure. She broke with an exhalation that exuded wonderment and awe. This was a new world.

He was sweating and panting as he sat back on his heels, watching her, his own desire rampant and jutting as it waited for its own release.

She reached out her arms for him then, drawing him down to her. He let his arms take his weight, his phal-lus pressing at her entrance and finding a sweet, warm welcome. Her long legs wrapped about his hips, pull-ing him in, sheathing him deep, the thrill of it sending a shudder of joy through him. It was like he was born to be here, with her, the two of them joined in pleasure's pursuit. No other lover, nothing in the past, mattered as he began to move. She was moving with him, instinctively matching him as the pleasure began to build with each thrust, with each answering undulation, until the wave he'd set in motion crested and shattered on the shore of their own private joy.

He buried his head against her shoulder, stifling the cry of completion that shook him at the last as he withdrew, his climax racking him, draining him. All that he was he'd given to her, to these moments.

Shaw felt her hand at the back of his neck, in his hair, drawing him close, heard her breath coming fast as she struggled for words. 'Oh, heavens, Shaw, I'm undone,' she managed between breaths.

'Shh, just let it be, savour it.'

He pressed a soft kiss to her throat, tasting the tang of salt on her skin. He rolled to his side and settled her beside him. This was all he wanted—to lie here with her, to float in this pleasure-soaked, dim-lit darkness. There was such peace, such completion.

He wasn't sure how long they lay there. It didn't matter. Time had lost all meaning. There was only Thomasia and the night, and he knew deep in his bones, in the depths of his soul, where all intuitive truth was buried, that this was meant for him, that *she* was meant for him. Forget two weeks. He needed a lifetime, wanted a lifetime. He just had to figure it out, but later. Right now the present was quite enough for him.

Chapter Sixteen

Thomasia was gone when he awoke, but she'd not gone far. He could hear her across the hall with Effie, her soft tones interspersed with the sweet mewls of a happy infant. Shaw cast an eye towards the window, trying to gauge the time. Winter light came through the slit in the curtains. Morning, then. Not dawn, but full morning. They'd all slept well.

He ought to get up, but he indulged himself a few moments more, listening to the sounds of happiness. All he had to do was convince her and every morning could begin like this. Convince her? he thought with a chuckle. Might as well add a thirteenth labour of Hercules.

He threw back the covers and reached for his discarded clothes, putting on his trousers and his shirt. The rest could wait. It was quiet as he padded across the hall, but the door was ajar. He pushed it open. Serenity greeted him. Morning light lit the pale rose walls, a fire in the grate warmed the room, and beside that fire, in a white-painted rocking chair, sat Thomasia, her hair loose, the baby at her breast, suckling away, enviously content.

When he saw the look on Thomasia's face as she gazed down at the child a swift wave of yearning took him. He was thirty-two—he was ready for this. To be a husband, to be a father, to have a family. To marry Thomasia meant he would acquire both titles simultaneously.

Yes, this is what I want, he thought. *With her...with this woman.*

Thomasia looked up from the rocking chair and spied him, her cheeks flushing as she twisted in the chair, reaching for a blanket.

'No, don't cover yourself for me,' Shaw insisted quietly. 'I didn't mean to interrupt.' He backed away, preparing to leave. He was indeed an interruption, an interloper on this beautiful scene of a modern Madonna and child.

'Stay.' Thomasia adjusted the blanket. 'The blanket is for me—for *my* comfort. I'm afraid I'm somewhat modest when it comes to feeding. Effie's nearly finished. Then she'll doze for a short while.'

Shaw took the chair at her writing desk, careful to keep his voice quiet so as not to disturb Effie. 'The weather looks passably good, if cold. The snow didn't accumulate. I was thinking of bundling Effie up and taking a walk around the estate, or a drive. We won't leave the grounds. We won't be seen. Perhaps we could take a picnic and build a fire.'

He was not sure what he'd expected in response. After all, it was a fairly simple idea. But Thomasia's eyes lit in fervent delight.

'A romp will be perfect. Perhaps we can do both. I know a place we can drive to and then wander from there.' Her excitement was genuine.

She lifted Effie, preparing to burp her. Shaw reached out for the infant. 'Let me, while you plan our outing.'

He hoisted little Effie to his shoulder, taking a towel from Thomasia, and patted the little one's back, watching as Thomasia relaxed. He wondered if she ever had a rest. When was the last time she'd slept the whole night through? Or had a morning to herself when she could ready herself at her leisure?

'You're good with her,' she complimented him.

'You sound surprised.' Shaw grinned, liking that he could surprise her.

'Most men I've met aren't interested in the daily functions of child-rearing,' Thomasia said.

'Most women I've met aren't lovers of the great outdoors, but you are.' Shaw paced before the window, showing Effie the outside world.

'Ah, I've surprised you, then, too.' Thomasia laughed. 'I love walks outdoors, no matter the season. Every season has something special about it. In the winter it's the cold, the way it nips at one's cheeks. I love bundling up in warm knitted mufflers and wool coats and wandering outside. I missed it last year in York. Cities aren't as conducive to winter wanders as the countryside is, and pregnancy certainly isn't.'

She did not often speak of her pregnancy. When she did it was like being allowed a glimpse into the most private parts of her.

'It was icy, and Auntie was afraid I'd slip and hurt myself, and the baby, too. Also, we were trying not to advertise my condition, so I stayed indoors for most of the last three months.' She laughed. 'It was the longest three months of my life. I'm not used to being cooped up.'

No, she wouldn't be. Shaw smiled at the thought. Thomasia was a free spirit, wild and wilful. She sewed jacket sleeves together to make her point. Confinement did not suit her.

Thomasia set the rocking chair in motion with the push of a toe. 'The Coffee Yard ladies kept me sane. I looked forward to those weekly meetings with a fervour. It was my one chance to get out of the house and be with women who didn't care that I was unmarried and expecting.'

'The Coffee Yard ladies?' Shaw queried. This was the most she'd ever talked about anything personal. Usually it was all politics or Effie with her, and he found these personal glimpses intriguing.

'Yes, they gave me my passion—helped me find my calling. They educated me about the realities of the world and how Society works against women. They meet in the coffee yard in the Stonegate, hence their name,' she explained, but then seemed reluctant to say any more. 'I miss them but I'm glad to be out of the city so I can have my wanders.'

She rose and took Effie from him.

'Give me an hour to get ready, and we can set off.' Then she seemed to remember that he'd spent the night unexpectedly. 'If you need anything you can borrow from William.' She bit her lip, considering how useful the offer would be. 'I doubt his clothes will fit, but there's a spare razor and clean neckcloths in his room.'

Shaw smiled. 'If you can forgive a few wrinkles, I think I can manage to look decent enough.'

He kissed her cheek and departed for his chamber, but his thoughts remained back in the rose-and-white room, with the little fire and the woman he cared for. He could have stayed in that room all day, the two of them in dishabille beside the fire, Thomasia in her white nightgown, her hair loose, rocking and talking.

He would carry that picture of her with him for all his days. He knew the most meaningful revelations often came from the quietest, most unassuming of moments, as they had this morning. Thomasia loved the outdoors. Who would have known? He'd certainly not have guessed. Surprising and delightful as the revelation was, there was also an edge of darkness to it—a reminder that he'd not known her long, that there were depths to her that remained hidden from him.

You want to marry her, but you hardly know her, came the caution.

It was time to change that. Starting with their outing today.

Today was a moment out of time, Thomasia told herself as she settled beside Shaw on the bench seat of the pony cart, Effie secure on her lap. Today was just for them. They could bask in the bliss and the fantasy of last night a while longer. They might have two weeks, but she knew those weeks would be interspersed with work. They could not live in one another's pockets without drawing undue comment.

But those were worries for tomorrow. She would not let them cloud today. There were enough clouds overhead as it was, still lingering from last night's snowfall, short-lived as it was. There may be more on the way.

But that was only one of the reasons she'd chosen this particular destination for today's outing.

'Turn here and follow the drive.' She pointed to a track off the road. Soon a well-kept stone cottage with blue shutters came into view. 'This is the old Anderson place. Thea and Wychavon had it renovated last spring, thinking to live here, but things turned out differently for them.'

Just the thought of her sister's story brought a smile to Thomasia's face. Thea's tale was straight out of a children's book in which the princess showed kindness to a wounded animal and was rewarded when that creature turned out to be a prince—or, in Thea's case, an earl.

Shaw set the brake and came around the cart to help her, taking Effie first, before offering her an arm. 'Does someone live here now?'

'No, it's currently empty. Wychavon still holds the lease. We can use it today, though. I thought we could leave the picnic basket inside while we walk. There's acres of fields behind the cottage.' It would be private as well. They would not be seen by anyone else who might be out.

While Shaw put the pony in a stall in the little barn, Thomasia used the key and let herself into the cottage. There was a kitchen to the right, and she set the basket down on the work table. The place looked just as Thea and Wychavon had left it after their honeymoon, as if time had stopped when they'd gone.

Thomasia looked around, adjusting Effie on her hip. It was a cosy place. It would make a good home. She toyed with imagining her and Effie in the place. They could live here on their own. But she immediately discarded the thought. They were sure to be noticed if they did that, and she'd already promised herself she would leave.

'Are you ready?' Shaw stood in the kitchen doorway. 'We should take advantage of the weather while we can.' He reached for Effie. 'I'll carry her—you lead the way.'

They tramped through the empty fields, enjoying the brisk weather, until they reached the river that marked the end of the Anderson farm. Old Man Anderson had built a bench beneath the oaks that hovered between the field and stream, and they sat there, listening to the rush of the winter river.

'Do you hear that?' Thomasia asked quietly beneath the sound of the water. 'It's a wren.'

The twitter came again and Shaw smiled. 'It seems early for birds. Spring is months away.'

'The wren hides away in the winter and practises its song for spring, so that when the spring comes he can stake his territory and sing for a mate. I've always liked that idea. Father thinks these wrens have been here for years, teaching their song to their young, season after season, the old teaching the new. Just like the Peveretts, who have been here for centuries.'

She would miss that when she left. She would no longer be part of that legacy, part of this land. It was one of the many things Anthony had so carelessly taken from her, even before she'd made the decision last night to be with Shaw. She'd never been going to stay indefinitely. It had not been much of a bargain to make last night. Deep down, she'd known staying was never an option.

'I think you're like the wren.' Shaw slid her a smile

as he bounced Effie on his knee. 'Taking refuge in the winter, planning for spring. I think you're very brave, and I will do all I can to help ease your transition back into Haberstock Society, such as it is.'

'I'm not that brave and you should do nothing of the sort. There will be backlash once Maldon realises his MP invited a fallen woman to dinner.'

Of course, it wouldn't come to that. She would be gone before spring—before Maldon or anyone else knew she had a child. It was the least she could do for Shaw. Her course was set now.

She rose and dusted off her skirt. 'We should get back before the rain, or snow, or whatever the weather decides to do, catches us unawares.' She wanted to keep moving—anything to keep her mind off last night, this morning and all she would lose in the future. Giving up Shaw would be harder than she'd anticipated. But there were still thirteen days before she had to come to grips with that.

Back at the cottage, she set out a picnic on a blanket in the parlour while Shaw laid a fire. Outside, the snow had started again. They'd made it just in time. Effie sat on the blanket, playing with the toys Thomasia had brought for her. Thomasia tucked her skirts about her as she sat on the floor, watching Shaw.

His trousers were drawn tight across his buttocks as he squatted before the fire, poking it into life. She knew first-hand how magnificent the body beneath his clothes was. She knew the feel of his muscle, the smoothness of his skin, the scent of his body, the touch of his hand. But it was not those things alone that aroused her. It was his care for others, the very goodness of him, the way he played with Effie and the way he offered help, anticipating what she needed before she even asked. He was quite possibly the most selfless man she'd ever met.

That worried her. If she showed the slightest inclination to being open to a proposal he would make one out of obligation—or, worse, perhaps out of pity for her situation. He would not think of what it meant for himself. She didn't want him to give up anything for her. She could only bring him disappointment, and over time he would regret his decision. What man wanted to raise another man's child? Oh, Shaw thought he wanted to—he had his stepfather's ideals and she was a fantasy in his eyes. He was enchanted by Effie, and by her, too. The passion between them was real, but so was the danger if she allowed his pursuit. Leaving him would save him from that.

'Enjoying the view?' Shaw grinned over his shoulder, catching her perusal.

'Yes—do you mind?'

Shaw came to her and sprawled at her side, stretching out his long legs, his auburn head propped on one big hand. 'You'd not seen a naked man until last night.'

She blushed. There was a lot she'd not done until last night, despite having had a child. His blue eyes were warm as they held her gaze, offering their invitation. To his credit, he'd not asked such questions then.

'Was it that obvious?' She busied herself with the food, assembling a plate of ham and bread. She was unused to such frank conversation. She and Anthony had never talked about sex. They had never talked about anything of consequence—she saw that now.

'Again, only in the best of ways.' Shaw took the plate from her.

Thomasia sighed. 'Last night showed me what a fool I was. It was nothing like it was with Anthony. Everything Anthony and I did was furtive, on the sly. We were always sneaking out.' She looked down at her hands, felt embarrassment riding her hard. 'The way I behaved with him was shameful. We never took our clothes off, we never lay in each other's arms, we never treated each other reverently, as if our bodies were gifts to one another.'

Anthony had never worshipped her as Shaw had worshipped her, never put her pleasure on a par with his. She did not want to make comparisons, but she was unable to avoid them. Last night had been an extraordinary experience, while her experience with Anthony was, if not forgettable, certainly regrettable. He'd been an absolute mistake—except for Effie. She could never regret her daughter.

'The way he behaved with you *was* shameful. He never should have taken advantage of you. He should have been a gentleman and not offered the temptation,' Shaw corrected.

'I didn't have to take the temptation. I could have refused him. I will own my piece in this. You needn't protect me from it or seek to absolve me. I knew what I was doing.'

And she'd been stupid. She'd been caught up in the excitement and the risk. She'd known there were protections she could take. She was the daughter of a doctor and a herbalist. Her mother had seen all her daughters educated in preservatives. She simply hadn't bothered to take them, believing Anthony first when he'd said that a girl couldn't get pregnant the first time, and later when he'd said he'd withdraw in time. He hadn't. It was no surprise, in retrospect. Anthony hadn't the willpower to put someone else's safety ahead of his own pleasure.

Shaw reached for her hand, lacing his fingers through hers. 'I am sorry, Thomasia. Whoever he is, he's a disgrace. He has no idea what he's given up. You and Effie are a treasure beyond price.'

She smiled her gratitude for his words. 'He doesn't matter, Shaw, he is in the past.'

It was true enough for all practical purposes. Anthony was married. He had everything he wanted. He had his estate and soon he'd have his fortune, when his young wife gave him a child. It would be entirely true once she'd left, disappearing into the depths of England with a new name and starting a new life. Anthony would never want to do any work to find her. He hadn't even written to see if she'd had the child. He certainly wasn't going to turn England upside down looking for her just to satisfy his curiosity—assuming he had any curiosity. She'd been far too easy a conquest for him and that was all he'd been interested in.

'He can't hurt me any more.'

Shaw looked down at their twined hands. 'I want you to know that I will never hurt you, Thomasia. That whatever decisions are made between us they will be mutual, I promise you…'

She pressed a slim finger to his lips. 'Stop. No promises, Shaw. You and I cannot see the future.' She wanted to swear she would never hurt him either, but that was a promise she couldn't make. It was already broken.

'Let us have our days and not ruin them with worry over the future.'

She could have thirteen beautiful days with him and that was all. It was the only way she could ensure he would escape unscathed by the scandals that followed her.

She leaned into him, pressing a soft kiss to his mouth. 'Come upstairs,' she whispered. 'We can put Effie down for a nap and I am told Old Mr Anderson's bed is a sight to behold…'

If she could have the fairy tale only for a short time, she was going to make the most of it.

Chapter Seventeen

Shaw let her lead him to the big chamber upstairs, loving the playful spark in her eyes as she tugged him along. Last night she'd been determined, fierce, and then she'd been surprised by what she'd discovered. But today she was owning that discovery, taking the lead in their passion, and he understood how important that was to her. She would be an equal partner in this or there'd be nothing at all.

This was a chance to put the past behind her and perhaps more. This was a chance to move beyond a mistake, to reclaim her trust in herself, in her judgement, perhaps even to reclaim a little of her trust in men. What a conflict that must be for her—to have grown up surrounded by reliable men in her father and her older brother, to see her sisters make matches with like-minded men, only to have her own experience set such expectations on their head.

She pulled him into the room. The space was lit with afternoon light and Shaw stared. 'Oh, my goodness, that is indeed the biggest bed I've ever seen!' he exclaimed. A huge oak four-poster dominated the room, done up cosily with a large hand-sewn counterpane quilt in greens and creams.

'And it's all ours for an afternoon.' Thomasia laughed and sat on the bed with a bounce.

He watched the mattress respond with an enviable amount of give. He was rousing already, just thinking of what he'd like to do in that bed with her, but Thomasia had other ideas about what *she'd* like to do with *him*.

She reached out a hand and drew him to the bed. 'Come and lie down, Shaw. I want to have my way with you.' She straddled him, riding him astride, a wicked gleam in her tawny eyes. 'Like you did with me last night.'

His body went rigid with desire, with anticipation, as he remembered what he'd done to her last night, where his mouth had been. Surely she didn't mean to…? But, oh, surely she did. Her hands were at the waist of his trousers, pulling out his shirt tails. He felt his blood racing. And then she stopped.

'No, I'm doing this all wrong.' She shook her head, and for a moment Shaw believed her.

'You're doing fine,' he encouraged, his voice already hoarse. Dear Lord, she was doing fine. Her touch lit a fire in him at the merest skim of a fingertip.

She flashed him a temptress's smile. 'Boots first, then trousers, and then perhaps my dress.'

He swallowed hard. She was going to make him pay for his pleasure, the little minx, but pleasure delayed came with its own unique sweetness and he was willing to play her game.

She tugged at his boots, and then at the buttons of her gown. As undressing went, it was more playful and practical than it was a seductive dance—right up until she slid a finger beneath the strap of her chemise, a pretty, innocent piece trimmed with a pink ribbon. Then time stopped, eyes locked, and the world slowed as she dragged the cotton garment up over her head and cast it away.

Good Lord, was there anything as stunning as Thomasia Peverett, her dark hair hanging to her waist and gloriously nude in the middle of the afternoon? She stood for his perusal, unabashed and brave. He did not miss the import of it. Last night she'd worried she would not meet his expectations, that her body would somehow fail him. But standing here now, before him, was victory. *Their* victory. The trust they'd earned in one another together.

'My God, you're beautiful.' He could barely make the words. His eyes feasted, and his hands itched to trace the globes of her breasts, to feel her body rise beneath his touch. But all those pleasures would have to wait.

Thomasia returned to the bed and resumed her position over him. Her luscious breasts were close, so close, and yet she would not let him touch. Not yet.

'Me first.'

She licked her lips with a quick flick of her tongue, her eyes dangerous and hot as her hands returned to his trousers. She worked the fastenings open and tugged them down over his hips, showing no tolerance for clothing, for barriers. She had him in her hand, and he felt himself strain against her cupped palm as she worked him.

'Do you like that?' she enquired, tossing her abundance of dark hair over one shoulder.

'What do you think, minx?' His voice had gone from hoarse to rough.

She sent him a coy look and wriggled down the length of his body until she was at eye level with his member. 'I think you might like this better.'

She bent to him and gave him a lick that had him shuddering. Oh, yes, he did like that better. He might like it a bit too much. He didn't want to spend before he'd had his enjoyment. She flashed him one more coy look, as if she guessed that part of the pleasure in this would be the competition of wills. How long could he last against her onslaught? How long could he drink from this particular pleasure's cup before they both capitulated?

Thomasia put her mouth on him fully and everything in him went wild. His pulse raced, blood thrummed, heart pounded, and still desire came, all-consuming— a storm of sensations all at her command with a lick at his tip, a nip along his length. And that was before she employed her nails, gently raking them along the inside of his thigh.

The wildness in him escalated, and then it broke in great pulsing waves as his body embraced the pleasure. A groan escaped him and he bucked hard. Thomasia rocked back on her heels and took him in her hand as release ripped through him. The culmination mesmerised her, a combination of shock and awe in her eyes as she held him.

'See what you do to me, Thomasia?' he said, finding his voice as his body calmed.

She smiled, smug with satisfaction, as she stretched out alongside him. 'That was...fascinating.'

'You're next… Just give me a moment.'

Shaw drew her close and they lay in silence for a while, breathing together, resting together, until he felt himself stir again, his body hungry, this time to be inside her. He rolled her beneath him and held her gaze as he took her in a slow, deliberate joining, their game playing and teasing sated, their bodies ready for something more meaningful. She gave a murmur of satisfaction and stretched against him, her body taking up his rhythm, matching him in this delectable delight of savouring one's lover.

The climax that claimed them rolled in on long, lingering waves, further proof that they were made for one another. When had he ever been so well matched with a woman, in mind and in body?

When had she ever been so well matched? The man beside her understood her. Her needs, her passion, her complexities. Not just her body but her mind. And he accepted her for them.

Thomasia traced a pattern on his chest, savouring this private world they'd built between the two of them, this abstract place where they were safe.

'Tell me something about yourself,' she murmured. 'A story from your childhood.' She wanted to know him, to understand him, to have something of him to take with her when all this was over: a mental souvenir.

He chuckled. 'You know everything. That my mother raised me, that she married when I was eight.'

'You're impossible. I don't know "everything" about you.' Thomasia rolled her eyes. 'I see I shall have to do this the hard way.' She reached beneath the quilt and ran a fingernail up his thigh, watching his face contract with pleasure and then in question.

'Why did you stop? It's not good for a man's health—' he began.

'Tell me a story.' Thomasia drew her fingernail lightly along his thigh once more and he shuddered.

'All right, but you have to keep doing that,' he insisted.

'As long as you're coherent. Tell me about being a big brother. Were you glad to have a baby sister or was she a nuisance?' Thomasia prompted, her hand wrapping around the warm length of his phallus. It was nice just to hold him, to touch him. 'William says Becca and I were nuisances.'

Shaw sighed, his own hand covering hers. Apparently he thought it was nice to be held as well.

'I was nearly twelve when Susannah was born. My mother and my stepfather had been married four years. They'd waited quite a while for her. My mother was understandably reticent about having another child. For a long time she didn't trust her good luck. She couldn't believe such a man existed.'

Shaw sighed.

'I think she believed Alan would leave her, that he wouldn't stay, that at some point he'd tire of being husband to a "fallen woman" and father to a child who wasn't his. But my stepfather was a patient man, and he convinced her he wasn't going anywhere. So they had Susannah, and then a few years later they had two more children—a boy and a girl. They didn't want Susannah to be an only child. I was too old. I'd be leaving home before she was eight. She needed playmates.'

Playmates. Family. Children needed those things. Effie-Claire would not have those things.

Thomasia shifted uncomfortably. When she left in the spring she'd be taking Effie's chances for such a family with her. Effie would never have what she'd had—a messy, noisy, big family to buffer her, to love her, to show her who she could be.

Shaw stilled, as if in tune with the shift in her mood. 'I didn't mean to imply that all children need siblings. I was an only child for quite a while. You are an amazing mother to Effie-Claire. She's lucky to have all your attention.'

'It's all right.' Thomasia rubbed at her eyes. 'It's something I've had to come to terms with. Effie won't have cousins to play with, or siblings—not like I did.'

'But she'll have you.' Shaw smoothed a loose strand of hair back from her face and smiled. 'You're very brave, Thomasia.'

She gave a dry laugh. 'I wasn't always brave. I am brave for her. She makes me brave. I was very scared when I found out I was pregnant. I hadn't wanted to be a mother at barely twenty. I didn't know how to be a mother. I'm the youngest. Anne and Thea were little mothers to me and Becca, but I had no younger siblings. Thea and Anne went out to take care of new mothers and babies, but I didn't. I was suddenly pregnant and I had no idea what to do.' Those early days had been frightening. 'I kept thinking about the Ladies of Salerno, and I'd wished I had a female physician to turn to, someone who would understand.'

'You had your sisters, your mother,' Shaw said softly.

'Yes, and thank goodness for them. They got me

through. It made me realise how lucky I was. What did other young women do? Women who didn't have healers for family?' She sighed. 'I confess that I had only really thought of the Ladies of Salerno in the abstract up until then. But finding myself pregnant I understood very poignantly the need for women to care for women. I think if I'd not had them, I would have tried something…desperate.'

She couldn't bring herself to say it. There'd been a moment when she'd thought of attempting an abortion. But Anne had been there, talking her out of it.

'You made the right choice for you.' Shaw pulled her close. 'So much good has come out of your bravery. Effie has benefited.' He planted a kiss in her hair. 'I am here for you, and for Effie, if you'll let me,' he began. 'You can stay here, give her a family…' His words were coming fast, perhaps because he knew she'd hush him—and she did.

'Shaw, no. We promised ourselves. Two weeks. That's all.'

That promise was only a day old and already it was straining against its bonds. It was tempting to believe him—to believe that all would be well, that she could lay her burdens at his feet and he would magically make them disappear.

But she could not give in to that temptation. It was a façade only. It wasn't that easy. She'd made her bed and eventually she'd have to lie in it. But for now she was happy to lie in Shaw's.

Chapter Eighteen

Whoever said thirteen was an unlucky number had never had thirteen days with Thomasia. Eight days in and Shaw could not recall a time in his adult life that had been filled with so many consecutive days of happiness—nor could he recall a time when such happiness had been tinged with equal amounts of trepidation. Each day spent in her company, each night spent in her arms, underscored what he stood to lose when their two weeks were done, should he fail to convince her otherwise.

Shaw glanced across the breakfast table at Thomasia, dressed in a warm mulberry wool day gown, Effie on her lap gnawing at a carrot, and smiled. 'I thought we could drive over to Rosegate today. I need to collect a few things.'

Thomasia frowned over Effie's head. 'I can't go. There's no one to leave Effie with at present.'

It wasn't so much the issue of leaving Effie as the risk of Effie being seen. Not by his staff—he'd given her his assurances there—but by a random passer-by as they drove through the village. It was a reminder of how small Thomasia's world had become by necessity, in order to protect her child and her reputation and her family. It was a half measure at best, and only a temporary one—despite the enormous sacrifices it demanded of her.

'You go, though, Shaw. We'll be fine here on our own,' Thomasia assured him.

But the issue was larger than that. They would be fine without him today, but what about this spring?

The issue stayed with Shaw on his ride over to Rosegate. Hiding at the Hall was no solution. Thomasia couldn't keep herself and her child cooped up there indefinitely. It would only be a matter of time before someone noticed or a servant let something drop in conversation, even if by accident. Her playing the recluse brought rumours of its own, invited unwelcome attention. Either way, she would not escape notice or censure. Surely she knew that.

Shaw steered Chiron around a pothole in the road, his mind puzzling out Thomasia's situation. They had discussed her options just the one time and those options were limited. Stay and face ridicule or go elsewhere and live under an assumed name. The last option cut at him. It made the most practical sense, in terms of avoiding the disadvantages she'd face here. But it made the least emotional sense. How could she ever come home again unless it was under the aegis of a lie? Perhaps as the widow of a man who had never existed? But how could she not come home? This place was a part of her. He'd seen her eyes light when she spoke of the Hall, when they toured the gallery, when she mentioned her family.

The rake who'd taken her innocence had taken much more than that from her. He'd taken her home and her ability to stay in it.

She's said nothing about leaving. Not out loud, anyway. But she was indeed thinking about it. That bothered him. Did she mean to leave and not discuss it with him? Did she mean to sneak away while he was in London? Or had she decided to stay and face whatever wrath the village turned her way?

He slowed Chiron as he entered the drive to Rosegate. They had four nights and five days left. It was time to talk about it. He wanted an answer from her before he departed for London and he was wise enough to know it was not something Thomasia would decide impetuously.

In the hall, Shaw thumbed through the mail that had accumulated. He would take it with him. He and Thomasia could go through it at their leisure. Nothing pressing. He paused towards the bottom of the pile, his hand halting on a letter from Maldon. Now, this looked pressing. Why would Maldon write when they would see one another in a week?

He slipped his thumb beneath the seal and read, his expression growing grim. He was wanted in London. Now. Unfortunately, trains made such haste possible these days. Stanton needed him to rally the troops ahead of Parliament's opening.

Shaw stared at the note, drawing a deep steadying breath, thinking about what the summons meant. It meant leaving Thomasia earlier than expected. They no longer had four nights. Just one. It meant not seeing her until the Easter recess—although his mind was already racing through how he could take the train home at weekends.

More than just leaving Thomasia, though, it meant settling the question of *how* he was leaving things. The situation that had plagued him earlier, on the way over, rose again in his mind. He could give her the respectability she needed to stay and a reason to stay—to stay for him and the future they might build together. He just had to pick his moment and hope it was the right one.

'Do these moments ever change? Does the passion ever lessen?' Thomasia murmured, nestled against his side as they lay in his bed in the Hall's guest room that night. 'I hope they don't, and yet part of me hopes they do.'

She sighed, her fingers tracing patterns on his chest, part playful, part reflective. Lovemaking had taken a pleasurable emotional toll on both of them tonight. There'd certainly been an intensity on his part, brought on by the note from Maldon, but there'd been an answering intensity on her part as well.

She levered herself up on one arm, her dark hair falling over her shoulder. 'When I'm with you, Shaw, I am filled with such a sense of completeness that I feel I'll just burst.' She gave a low, sultry chuckle in the darkness. 'And sometimes I do burst. I didn't know such pleasure, physically or emotionally, was possible.'

That was another crime to lay at her rake's door. He'd not given a whit for a lady's pleasure.

Damn, but Shaw wished he knew the cad's name. A bout at Jackson's would be a discreet, gentlemanly

way to deal with him, or a decent pinking at Angelo's if
the man wasn't inclined to fists. But, all violence aside,
her words *did* give him another kind of thrill—a manly
satisfaction in knowing that she desired him, that she
felt as he did, that this togetherness between them was
more than sexual.

'I shall miss this,' she breathed softly, laying her head
on his chest once more.

He wouldn't get a better opening than that for the
business he'd waited all night to discuss. He ran his
hand up and down her arm in a gentle caress. 'What will
you do in the spring, Thomasia? Have you decided?'

Her hand stilled on his chest. 'I wasn't aware I had
to decide tonight.' Her tone held a slight edge of defen-
siveness. She must have heard it, too. When she spoke
again her voice was softer. 'My decision doesn't affect us. Thirteen days, Shaw. That was our agreement,
whether I go or stay—although I think going would be
the best option, so you can get on with your life.'

He covered her hand with his where it lay on his
chest. He knew what she meant by getting on with his
life. Finding another woman. It wasn't something he
could even fathom, lying here with her in perfect bliss.
He didn't want another woman. He wanted her. And
Effie. And everything that came with them.

'What if getting on with my life includes you? What
if it's possible for you to stay?' He gave words to the
hope, brought it to life.

She made a sound—part sigh, part laugh. 'We've
had this conversation before, Shaw, and I thought we'd
promised ourselves not to have it again.'

He felt her body shift and she sat up.

'Why are we having it again? Why now?' She peered at him in the darkness. 'What has happened, Shaw?'

She was all tense anxiety and he felt guilty for having worried her. He sat up, too.

'Maldon has happened, that's all. He needs me in London tomorrow. I'll go up on the morning train.'

'You should have said something earlier,' Thomasia scolded.

'Why? And ruin the day? I wanted the day just as it was, with you not worried and us enjoying the moment. Can you forgive me for that?'

It had been a quiet day spent indoors when he'd returned, reading books to Effie and helping her to work on her steps by putting her little feet on theirs and waltzing her about the music room.

'I'd hoped Effie would walk today,' he confessed, grinning in the dark. Could she see what happiness Effie brought him? 'Her first steps will be any day now and I'll miss them. There's a sore spot in my heart over that, but I console myself that she'll be practically running by Easter recess and I can chase her over the fields.'

He paused, feeling Thomasia stiffen. It was as he'd feared, then.

'Will you be here at Easter?' he asked softly.

'I don't know, Shaw. It doesn't matter. It only matters that I'm leaving,' she repeated, the phrase having become her mantra.

He reached for her hand, felt his heart in his throat, threatening to choke his words. Everything hung on his next few sentences.

'Stay, Thomasia. Stay and marry me. Let me give you

the respectability you need. Effie can grow up with a father, with her cousins, her grandparents, her aunts and uncles nearby. I can give her a family, a home. She can grow up at Rosegate and visit her grandparents whenever she wishes. Thomasia, I can give you all of this.'

This was exactly what she'd feared—what she'd tried to avoid. She could give him nothing while he laid the world at her feet, took her every dream and made it come true. His earnestness nearly undid her.

Tears stung in her eyes. She swiped at them. 'This was not the arrangement, Shaw,' she protested.

'So? Arrangements can change. Please, let me go to London knowing that you'll wait for me. We can be wed after Easter, either here or in London, as you prefer.'

'Here. Not London.' Thomasia replied sharply, automatically, not thinking of anything else but avoiding London. She had no desire to run into her past.

In the dark, she thought she saw Shaw raise an eyebrow and realised what she'd done.

'Does that mean yes, Thomasia?'

Yes. No. A part of her wanted it to mean yes. In a different world it would be yes. But not in this one.

'It means I'll think about it.' Then she added, before he could be too celebratory, 'And you should think about it, too, Shaw. I have nothing to give you in return except scandal. Everyone will know Effie-Claire is not your daughter. There will be rumours always. Your career—' she began, but Shaw cut her off with a kiss.

'I dare anyone to say anything,' he whispered against her lips. 'About my wife, or about my daughter. I'll adopt her officially once we're wed, and in time no one will remember it wasn't always that way.'

She sighed into him as he rolled her beneath him, leaving no doubt as to how this discussion was going to end. 'Everything is so easy for you, Shaw.'

A man's world was straightforward. Not so hers. Hers was fraught with scandal and consequences.

He kissed her again, his exuberance evident. He'd not heeded her warning about taking time to think— at least not yet.

'Everything *is* easy, Thomasia.' He smiled down at her, flashing her a teasing grin as his phallus nudged at her entrance. 'Except this one thing. And it's hard, very hard.'

And in spite of her misgivings and worries Thomasia laughed. Why not enjoy one last night? When he got to London and had time to think he'd see she was right to counsel caution. He'd realise that while his intentions were well meant they were also impractical, and that would be for the best. No one need know he'd proposed, and she'd find a way to let him out of the hasty arrangement discreetly, so that he need not feel that he was letting her down.

She wrapped her legs about his hips and smiled up at him one last time.

They said their goodbyes privately and quietly early the next morning in her bedchamber, with a sleepy Effie in her arms. Shaw was dressed and impeccable, his coach outside ready to make the one-hour drive to the station, while she was still in her nightgown, her hair tumbling down and tangled.

'You're beautiful in the morning,' Shaw whispered against her ear.

He smelled of cleanly shaven male and she committed the scent of him to memory.

He held Effie for a moment, kissing her head. 'Be good for your mama and I'll see your steps when I come back.' He put the baby down in the crib and turned his attention back to her, his knuckles skimming her cheek. 'I am going to miss you. I'll write and keep you updated on everything that's going on.' He smiled. 'And you can write to me with your advice.'

Dear heavens, her heart was breaking over the impossible. She could not keep him and he would fight that decision every step of the way.

'Goodbye, Shaw. Have a safe journey.'

She kissed his cheek and he drew her close, claiming a kiss of his own, this one full on the mouth and lingering. And then he was gone. She heard his boots on the stairs. She followed him in her mind's eye across the hall to the front door and down the stairs to his coach. She imagined him getting in, stretching out his legs, perhaps giving one last look to the Hall and a wave, even though he would know she could not see him. Only then did she pick up Effie-Claire and settle in the rocking chair to feed her.

So that was that. It was over. She really couldn't marry him—mutual affection and passionate sex aside. There was a hollow ache in her chest.

He would regret marrying her on practicalities once he realised what she could do to his career. That fear was not exaggerated. She would have regrets, too, although hers would be on principle. How could she marry a man for the protection of his name when that was exactly the kind of submission she and the Coffee Yard ladies fought against? She should not need a man's protection in order to move about Society. She should not need to hide behind a man.

Marrying for all the reasons Shaw suggested smacked against the Coffee Yard ladies' crusade. How could she be true to The Cause while married to a man who was being mentored by Lord Stanton and Sir Phillip Maldon? It would be anathema to both her own and Shaw's credibility—assuming Shaw was still allowed to have any sort of political career.

'It looks like nothing much has changed since last night after all,' she said softly to Effie. 'We still have to leave.' She would start planning that, start looking for somewhere to go. It would keep her mind off Shaw. 'It will just be you and me, darling girl, but we'll have a good life, I promise.'

Her parents had said they'd give her her dowry to live on. She would be comfortable. She would play the widow. With the war in the Crimea it wasn't improbable. They would get a cottage, have a garden, keep a horse and a pony in a quiet village somewhere. She would keep Effie-Claire protected from nasty rumours even if she couldn't keep Shaw.

She looked down at Effie-Claire, who was starting to doze. 'I'll always have you, my darling. You are mine and no one can take you from me.'

Chapter Nineteen

Shaw had been gone a week. That was how she counted time now—not how many days until her parents and Becca came home, just how many days it had been since Shaw had left. Her days were full with Effie, but she missed him. There was a place deep in her heart that was simply empty, and at times she found herself just going through the motions of getting through the days.

She'd felt like that in the early days of learning that she was pregnant with Effie and that Anthony had deserted her. Desolate. That was the only way to describe it. She'd best get used to it, though. She couldn't live her life feeling desolate.

Thomasia sorted through the mail that had piled up on the console in the hall. She'd not had the desire to look through it before, knowing it was too soon for a letter from Shaw. But a week wasn't too soon. He might have written.

Effie was upstairs, being supervised by a maid, while Thomasia undertook the chore of sifting through the mail. She put it into piles: a pile for her father, which was the bulk of the mail, a small stack for her mother and a journal that Becca subscribed to.

Her hand stilled on the last piece of mail, an official-looking letter addressed to her. Who would be writing to her? Perhaps one of her friends from York?

She opened the note, her brow furrowing in curiosity. It furrowed deeper with confusion followed by a host of other emotions as she read and reread the letter a second and then a third time.

Her gaze fixed first on the name mentioned in the first line.

I am writing on behalf of Lord Halston...

Anthony. Anthony was Lord Halston. A wave of uneasiness took her. What business did Anthony have with her? He was a married man now.

Her gaze dropped to the signature at the bottom.

Oswald Browning, Esquire

That meant nothing to her except that Anthony had engaged a solicitor to enquire about their child. She would not have worried much about the letter and would simply have ignored it if it hadn't been for the last line.

Please bring her to London by the twenty-third of the month so that the adoption may be finalised.

In a single line the letter had gone from a polite enquiry about the child to a demand that she be turned over. There was no argument as to why, just the assumption that it would be done.

Like hell it would.

The ferocity of her reaction was all that kept Thomasia upright. She read the missive again, searching for details, for a reason. Why would he want such a thing? He didn't even know the baby's name. *Her.* The simple word snared Thomasia's attention. He knew the baby was a girl and she had not told him. Someone had, though. Who knew? Who would have told him? Had he sent someone to find out? There were ways. He could have traced her to York. There was record of Effie's birth there. Or... A chill went down her spine. Perhaps he'd had someone find her here.

The idea of having been followed or spied on smacked of underhandedness to Thomasia. It also made her uncomfortably paranoid. Had someone been watching the house? Were they watching the house now? Would they attempt to take Effie if she didn't go to London?

No, she had to pull herself together. She was making phantoms out of whole cloth. She tried to reason with herself—but logic only went so far when she thought about how isolated and alone she was here. There was only one maid, and Cook was coming in only to prepare food while everyone was gone. Other than that there was just her and Effie. There would be no help... no one to mount a resistance.

He won't take Effie...not until after the deadline, Thomasia reasoned, drawing long, deep breaths.

She made her way to the front parlour and sank onto the sofa, trying to corral her thoughts for long enough to think. She focused on that one positive: he would not take Effie before the deadline. For him to do so would make no sense. If he meant to snatch her he wouldn't have bothered with a letter, thus alerting her. Surely even sons of earls couldn't go around kidnapping babies? But if he wanted Effie there was a reason for it, and likely some desperation behind it. Perhaps linked to that blasted will of his great-aunt's.

Thomasia willed herself to think about the last time she'd seen him. What had he said? That the inheritance was his upon the birth of his first legitimate child. But then his parents had produced the superior bride with settlements, who would allow him to claim his great-aunt's estate. He'd only been married since last summer. Surely he knew having children took time. But then, Anthony was not known for his patience. He'd want that fortune now and not a moment later. So he'd thought to take her child.

No. He could not have Effie. She tamped down the panic that threatened. The law was on her side. Any court would favour her. Tender Years legislation let mothers keep their children. *Until the age of seven.* She pushed the caveat away. Anthony would not want to wait seven years. By then, who knew? He might have a brood of his own and have no need for Effie.

She glanced at the paper in her lap, feeling a new panic taking her. January the twenty-third. That was tomorrow. The letter had been at the bottom of the pile. It had likely arrived days ago, when she had been ignoring the post. She had to decide what to do now.

Did she run? She could pack up her things and Effie and be gone by evening. She could change her name and disappear into thin air. But for how long? Her parents would be frantic, and if she tried to contact them he might trace her through them. She wouldn't be able to access her dowry if she couldn't contact her parents.

What if she simply didn't answer the deadline? Would that give Anthony grounds to be more forcible? Would it make her look irresponsible? Perhaps jeopardise her chances to keep Effie if Anthony took her to court? What a scandal *that* would be, even if she won.

Thomasia gave a little moan. How could this be happening? She'd thought she was beyond the nightmare that had been her life this past year and more—a surprise pregnancy, being deserted by the father of her child, struggling to give birth, to live her life in a way that kept her reputation and her family's intact. She'd made one mistake, and it seemed that mistake was bound to haunt her just when she thought she was beyond it.

She simply didn't know what to do. She needed help, guidance. She needed her family. She needed Shaw. But they were all in London. Her strength was in London.

Then she would go to London. There was a late-afternoon train. She would have to hurry. It was an hour's drive to the station. Some might say that she was walking into the lion's den. Anthony was there. And it was where Anthony wanted her to be, too. Would it make her vulnerable? But it was also where her family was, where Shaw was, where her hope was.

Thomasia rose, feeling steady for the first time since opening the letter. She could not fight this new threat alone. She would go to Shaw. They would sort through this together. He would help her, but his help wouldn't come without a cost. He would see why she had to set him free. She was simply too much scandal for a good man. Today proved it.

Thomasia stepped off the train into the bustle of the station as evening fell on the city. She was exhausted and second-guessing herself. She balanced Effie on her hip and gripped a valise in her other hand. Effie was getting heavy. She hailed a porter and gave him a coin to fetch her trunk. She felt vulnerable and helpless in the station, and she still had to make it to the street.

She'd been highly conscious of how reliant she was on others the moment she'd stepped into the family coach and made the journey to the station. At Broxbourne Station she'd needed help at the ticket counter and a porter to see to her trunk. A conductor had helped her find her seat when she'd had trouble concentrating on Effie and matching the ticket to the seat number. A friendly older woman and her husband had helped her entertain Effie on the train.

She was grateful for all the help, for all those kindnesses she'd needed. But she was shocked, too. She'd never felt so needy in her life. For this short time she was entirely alone in the world, with no one to rely on except strangers.

It was a reminder of how truly blessed her life was. Even in the worst crisis of her life she'd had her family to turn to. Her parents had made the arrangements for her to go to York. Aunt Claire had seen that she'd had the medical care she needed when she'd delivered Effie. Becca had spent nearly a year with her in York, to provide help and company. Now she lived in her family home, surrounded by assistance when it came to looking after Effie. And today, once more facing crisis, her family would rally about her.

How did others without such resources manage? It threw into sharp relief once more how important The Cause was, to advocate for protection for those who could not protect themselves.

The porter returned with her trunk on a cart. 'Is there anything else, ma'am?'

Thomasia produced another coin—one more resource that she was lucky to have. She could pay for assistance. 'Could you help me find a cab?'

She'd be lucky to find her way out of the station, and Effie was starting to cry. The porter was kind and found her a cab. He loaded her trunk as she gave the driver the address Shaw had left with her: number twelve Arlington Street.

It was a fashionable enough street to be met with a respectable bob of the driver's head. 'Yes, ma'am. Arlington Street, right away.'

'Right away' was a relative concept in the evening traffic of London. The streets were jammed around the station, with people coming and going from their trains. Thomasia didn't care. She was relieved to be on the last leg of her journey and alone. There hadn't been any privacy on the train, and Effie was getting hungry. She should feed her here in the cab. There'd be plenty of time before they reached Arlington Street.

She sighed. Perhaps it would be a good thing when Effie was weaned. It would be one less personal demand on her body and one less inconvenience. Feeding her was no trouble at Haberstock. But after leaving the Hall it had become very difficult to be able to do it discreetly.

Leaving the Hall.

She'd not realised what a cocoon the Hall had been for them.

She looked down at Effie in her arms. 'We're out in the open now, little one.'

But not for much longer. There was shelter to be had. When they reached Arlington Street, Shaw would be there. That would be a kind of emotional shelter. There was literal shelter to be had as well, at Anne and Ferris's.

At last the cab stopped at number twelve Arlington Street, and the driver helped her down before getting her trunk. 'Just set it inside the gate, thank you,' Thomasia instructed.

'Very good, missus.'

She knew what the man was thinking as he took in the brick-and-white townhouse: that her husband was inside, a man of influence and, perhaps more importantly, affluence, and that he would send servants out to see to his wife's trunk. She doubted she would have had such service and politeness from him if he'd known the truth—that she wasn't married to the man inside the house or to the man who'd fathered the child in her arms.

Thomasia knocked on the door, hesitancy filling her. Had she done right in coming here? Should she have gone straight to Anne and Ferris? Would Shaw even be at home? Now that she was here, she was starting to doubt herself. How would she explain who she was to whoever answered the door if it wasn't Shaw? And there was no reason to think it would be.

The door opened, revealing a stern man with a receding hairline and dark livery. 'How may I help you, miss?' He looked her up and down, as if ascertaining that she was a stranger, someone he did not recognise nor expect.

'Miss Thomasia Peverett, calling for Mr Shaw Rawdon, if you please.'

She smiled, as if calling unannounced was an everyday occasion of no extraordinary moment, aware that the man was now ascertaining other things, too—like the quality of her travelling ensemble, perhaps the fact that it *was* a travelling ensemble. Only ladies of means had outfits designated for specific occasions. It might account for something with this man at the door.

'Just a moment.'

He closed the door and Thomasia waited. Surely there was nothing to worry about. It was a good sign that he'd asked her to wait, she told herself. It meant Shaw was at home and his servant just needed permission to let her in. She shifted Effie to her other hip.

The door opened. 'Please, come in, Miss Peverett.'

The man ushered her into a bright hall. It was a modest but clean space, with a black-and-white-tiled floor, a polished console and a mirror framed in gilt. The walls were trimmed in white wainscoting, with pale ivory-on-ivory-striped wallpaper running up to bright white crown moulding where the wall met the ceiling. Very sharp, very stylish, very clean. There was no sign of oak anywhere.

Footsteps, urgent and quick, clicked on the tiled floor. She turned and there was Shaw, striding towards her, concern in his eyes, and she felt her troubles lift and her heart sing at the sight of him.

'Thomasia, what's happened? Are you all right? Is Effie all right?'

He lifted Effie from her arms and hugged them both close. She breathed him in, some of the tension seeping from her.

'It's Effie's father—he's written. He wants to adopt Effie,' she began without preamble, so relieved to share at last the horrible news she'd carried since that morning. Her world seemed to right itself just a little by saying the words. 'I didn't know what to do, where to go...' She was babbling now, the trials of the day catching up to her.

'Shh...hush, it will be all right,' Shaw comforted her. 'We'll sort through it—but not in the entrance hall.' He shot a speaking glance towards the corridor behind him. 'I have people here. Maldon's here. Let me finish our meeting and send them home. Then you can tell me everything. Wait for me in the front parlour. Gregory will bring you tea.'

He gestured to a room on the opposite side of the hall from which he'd come.

'Yes, of course. I should have thought...'

Thomasia gathered her wits. She'd been so relieved, she hadn't anticipated the implications of her presence here. She couldn't risk Maldon coming in search of Shaw. How would she explain? It was highly improper—and that didn't even begin to address the question of Effie.

Gregory showed her to a pretty room with ivory wallpaper boasting big red roses and red drapes at a long window overlooking the street. She sat Effie down on a carpet with an abstract design and sank into a chair. She was here. She'd made it. That was all that mattered at the moment. Help was on its way, and so was the tea tray.

The tea tray did quite a lot to restore her. She gave Effie a biscuit to gum with her new tooth and sipped the strong tea in her cup. It wasn't long before she heard voices and she sat up, alert to any sound Effie might make. But Effie was perfectly content with her biscuit. The voices in the hall rose, the words coming to her clearly.

'We need you to secure support from your friends. Talk up the repeal at your clubs, Rawdon. Talk to other MPs in the House—show them this is in their best interests. We will not back down on this because groups of women are organising against us,' Maldon pressed, his words distinct.

'*Especially* because women are organising.' Stanton all but spat the words, his distaste obvious. 'If we back down to a bunch of women, we are sending a very dangerous message about who holds the power in England.'

Thomasia flinched at his vitriol. It was a sobering reminder of Shaw's position…of the reason she'd started their relationship in the first place so long ago in November. She'd taken the position of his secretary in order to get closer to those with influence. Well, she couldn't get much closer than this—just a few feet away. And neither could Shaw.

There were so many ways her presence here could ruin him. A stone weight settled in her stomach, not only on her own behalf but Shaw's as well. How must he feel? Stanton's demands required that he deny his own origins, his own values and upbringing, in addition to hiding his relationship with her.

Doubt surged. Perhaps she should not have come. He had more to worry about than her. How could she burden him with one more thing when he already carried a great weight? How much longer would it be until he came to despise her? To see her as a symbol of his ruin instead of a symbol of all he fought for and all he loved?

Chapter Twenty

It was hard not to run blindly to her. It was hard to focus on ushering his guests out through the door politely and without undue haste, while not letting his eyes drift towards the front parlour and draw their speculation.

Shaw stood in the hall, trying to act as if nothing untoward had happened when he'd left the study, yet all the while his thoughts were far from discussions of Parliament, legislation and the demands Stanton required to be met in exchange for his patronage. All of that had ceased to matter the moment he'd seen Thomasia's face and his thoughts remained fixed on her, on Effie, and on the sheer desperation and fear that had been written in Thomasia's eyes.

She believed the threat to be serious. What else could have forced her from the safety of Haberstock Hall?

The enormity of that struck him with particular strength. Last week Thomasia had been so cautious as to decry even a short journey to Rosegate, on the grounds that she and Effie might be discovered by the odd passer-by. Now here she was in London—a trip that would have required her getting to the station, taking a train and making her way to Arlington Street. It was quite an undertaking for a woman who'd not been off the Hall's property for six months—for a woman whom he'd asked to come to London with him and who had refused on the grounds of protecting her daughter and her reputation.

Now those very reasons had driven her to the one place she didn't want to go because of the one person she didn't want to see: the nameless man who had turned her life upside down and put terror into the heart of the woman he loved. He quite wished she was here for a different reason, because of a different man—because of *him*. He would welcome her in London regardless of the reason—London had been lonely without her—but he wished love, not desperation, had driven her to him. Still, he supposed it was something that she'd come.

He would be thankful for that, and he would take her presence as a sign not only of her trust in him, but also a sign that perhaps thinking about his proposal had moved her closer to a yes. He hoped, too, that if it had the reasons for it were the right ones. He didn't want her to marry him feeling forced, or backed into a corner with no other option.

And yet those are the very reasons you argued for when you proposed, came the reminder.

How could she come here on any other grounds when he'd given her none?

But that should be the least of his concerns at the moment. She had come because she'd felt she was under siege. Her beloved daughter was in danger and she needed a champion. A prick of anger surged through him at the thought. How dare that irresponsible rake of a man continue to threaten her, haunt her?

He shut the door behind Maldon and gathered his wits. Thomasia was counting on him. She needed him to be focused, to know what to do, and he would not fail her.

With rapid steps he crossed to the front parlour and found her within. She turned at his approach, paler than when he'd left her, the tea tray untouched save for a tea-cup half-full of cold tea.

He knelt before her, taking both her hands—*cold hands*—in his. 'They're gone now, Thomasia. Tell me everything.'

'Lord Halston wants to adopt Effie. He wants to take her from me—' Her voice broke and she withdrew her hands to reach for her valise and retrieve the letter. 'He means business. It is no idle threat. His solicitor sent this.'

Shaw took the letter from her, feeling the weight of the paper as he unfolded it. He scanned it, taking in the letter's formality, noting the deadline. Tomorrow. No wonder she was worried.

'It arrived today?' he asked.

She'd not been given much time. Perhaps that was one of the man's underhand strategies—to force imme-diate action by terrorising her into compliance. What mother wouldn't panic?

'Lord Halston is Effie's father?'

He folded the letter and handed it back to her. Lord Anthony James Arthur Halston. Second son of the Earl of Drake. He knew the man by reputation only, and that reputation was of a wild player who had flamboyant affairs in the demi-monde, who raced pell-mell down the Richmond Road at breakneck speeds. Last summer there'd been rumour he'd run a man down during a race. That had been before he married, however.

Perhaps marriage had settled him? He'd only recently come to Town, after an unprecedented six months in the country celebrating his newly married status. It wasn't so much Halston's recklessness that bothered Shaw, but his manipulations. He was always at the heart of some underhanded contretemps and he always got away with it.

Shaw's stomach clenched at the thought of Thomasia with such a man—a man who'd shown her as little regard as he showed the rest of the world. He knew of such men. One such man had been his sire, and he'd lived his young life with the consequences of that man's choices foisted upon his mother.

Shaw had never felt the absence of a title or the power of a title as keenly as he did now. He knew why Halston had got away with it—for the same reasons his own sire had got away with it. The Earl of Drake would protect the family name by protecting his son even if his son was in the wrong. Halston would have many resources if he was serious about acquiring the child. But Shaw had a resource, too. He would marry her and adopt the child before Halston could act. Although such an action came with its own considerations. Would Thomasia accept such a solution? Or would she accept it only to save her child?

'Something must have happened for him to want me brought to his attention.' Thomasia sighed. 'I need to find out. I need to understand his circumstances.'

'Of course. I can do that.' Shaw squeezed her hands. 'I can make the rounds of the clubs, the balls.' He'd prefer to do that with her at his side, but there was no question of taking her with him. 'I can start tonight— as soon as we see you and Effie settled at your sister's. Do they know you're coming?'

Surely she realised she couldn't stay here with him, much as they both would have enjoyed that.

She shook her head. 'There was no time.'

Something in her gaze froze him.

'Today I felt helpless, and I didn't like it,' she said.

Of course she wouldn't. His Thomasia was all fire and a fierce advocate of independence.

'All I did was take the train from Broxbourne to London, little more than an hour, and yet the whole process had me relying on others.' She glanced at Effie, playing on the floor. 'I realised that perhaps I've been relying on others the whole time, only they were so skilled in supporting me I barely realised it. I thought, too, about other women who are alone always, who have no one to support them...'

He felt her grip tighten on his, her eyes intense and pleading.

'Those men who were here today feel that kind of helplessness is appropriate. They want to ensure it continues. They don't want people to see what they're really trying to do.'

'You heard?'

Even amidst the agony of her own situation she'd not lost sight of the fact that her own plight was part of a larger issue that affected not just her but so many other women in myriad ways—single women left to bring up their children alone, women in difficult, even dangerous, marriages, who didn't dare leave for fear of losing the ability to care for their children financially.

'I heard. If they can't reward betrayal, they will punish loyalty. Sometimes I wonder, Shaw, how you can stand to be associated with such men.'

He gave her a half-smile. 'Me, too. It's a very good question.'

He sat back on his heels and released her hands. He reached for Effie, who squealed in delight as he picked her up.

'On a happier note, what a pleasant surprise it is to see my two best girls.' He rose with Effie and held out his hand to Thomasia. 'I'll have the coach readied and go with you to Tresham's. If I'm to change and make the rounds tonight I dare not delay.'

Dropping her at Tresham's would take some time. It would require explanation and planning. The family would need to be told immediately, and Shaw wanted to employ Tresham's connections as well as Wychavon's as soon as possible. He might not have a title, but Thomasia's in-laws did—several of them, in fact.

The meeting at Tresham's house at number thirteen Cheyne Walk, next door to his medical practice, went as Shaw had expected. There was the initial thrill of surprise in seeing Thomasia and Effie, followed by concern over why she was there, and aghast rage at Halston's demand. Shaw considered it a bit of luck that Wychavon and Thea were there, too, taking tea. It saved having to go over it again.

'You may come with us tonight,' Wychavon offered.

'Thea and I are attending the Reddings' reception for the new Russian ambassador. Town is quiet except for politicians and diplomats, as you know.' Wychavon chuckled. 'So anyone who is looking for good food and decent company will be there. The new Lady Halston's father is in with the political set, so there's an excellent chance she'll drag Halston to it. If he's not there, he'll be at one of his clubs. We can make the club rounds later if needed.'

'Wychavon belongs to all of them,' Tresham teased his brother-in-law good-naturedly. 'My father and my brother are in Town for their Prometheus Club ventures and for the opening of the Parliamentary session. If they can help, let me know. Everyone else is still at Bramble.'

Tresham's brother was Frederick, Viscount Brixton, heir to the Duke of Cowden, their father. Another title to add to their arsenal. It made Shaw feel better. Brixton held a seat in the House, unwilling to wait to take up his inherited seat in the Lords. Shaw had had positive interactions with him last year.

As they talked, the group separated into two. The women drifted off to the kitchen with the two infants— Effie, and Anne's little boy, who was the same age. The four men stayed gathered in the drawing room and Ferris offered brandy. But Shaw was not immune to the shift in conversation.

'She came to you first,' Ferris said, putting a glass into Shaw's hand. 'Perhaps we should be apprised of the nature of your relationship before we go further. This is bound to get messy before it's over, and we should all know the parts we play.'

It was a polite way of asking him for his intentions,

and Shaw commended the man for his concern over his sister-in-law. Tresham was acting as a brother in the absence of Thomasia's own brother, William. He was also acting as intermediary between Shaw and Dr Peverett, should that become necessary.

Shaw's estimation of Tresham rose another notch. Tresham was a good man—as was Wychavon, who had offered his connection to Society without reservation. But that didn't mean either of these men or Dr Peverett would appreciate knowing that he and Thomasia had spent nearly two weeks living essentially as man and wife.

How would he explain to these men that those days had been exquisite, a fantasy come to life for him? That they had not been intended to be an act of dishonour against Thomasia or them?

Shaw took a swallow of Tresham's brandy. 'I have great respect and affection for Thomasia and her daughter. I believe that affection is returned. While I am clear on what I'd like our future to be, Thomasia has some uncertainty. I respect that. Her experience with men does not recommend us to her. I would not want to force her into anything. Enough has been taken from her already, I think.'

Wychavon gave his glass a considering look. 'I think she may not have a choice, despite your sentiments. Halston is an amoral cad, and that is putting it mildly.' He nodded to Ferris. 'Any man who shows utter disregard for a young woman's virtue and for the Duke of Cowden's censure is a dangerous sort of devil who will stop at nothing to get what he wants.'

'He doesn't want the child,' Shaw put in. 'Thomasia believes the child is a tool to get the thing he really wants: access to a fortune.'

'The man has a wife,' Wychavon tossed out offhandedly. 'He can get a child the way the rest of us do.'

'Unless he can't,' Ferris offered, and Dr Peverett nodded. 'Forgive my bluntness…' Ferris began to pace the room '…we know the problem isn't with him. The problem may lie with his wife.'

'He's been married a bare half-year—it would be a bit soon to throw in the towel,' Wychavon argued.

'Halston is not a patient sort.' Tresham shook his head. 'That's what you'll have to figure out tonight, Rawdon. It will help confirm what is actually prompting this…' Tresham groped for a word and found none. 'This *act*.'

'The man will not get his hands on my granddaughter,' Dr Peverett vowed, and his words drove home to Shaw the enormity of Halston's demand.

Not only did he seek to take the child from Thomasia after repudiating her, after leaving her to face the birth of a child alone, but he sought to bring Effie up away from her family, to erase the knowledge of their existence. Shaw did not pretend for a moment that Halston would share custody, or even acknowledge that there was any family outside the House of Drake. Effie would grow up knowing a different mother, different grandparents, a different life altogether.

What kind of love would she know in a household that had managed to produce the amoral Anthony Halston? What kind of ethics would she grow up with? How would she understand herself as a woman as she grew older? Based on the way Halston had treated

Thomasia, Shaw doubted Effie would grow up seeking to lead a life that fought for justice for the oppressed, that championed healthcare that empowered women. She would grow up forgotten, or be taught that her only value was in whom she married.

Shaw thought of Effie, laughing up at him when he'd scooped her from the floor that afternoon, her little arms waving in excitement as she recognised him. How she smelled of sweet, soft lavender when he snuggled her against him as he burped her.

He swept the group with his gaze, realising he was looking at his future father-in-law and his future brothers-in-law, if he had his way. 'To be clear: I am fully prepared to marry Thomasia and adopt Effie-Claire as my own.'

He would not turn Effie over to the likes of Anthony Halston any more than he would allow the cad to break Thomasia's heart one more time.

She'd come to London. The child was with her. Brilliant. Anthony Halston sat back in the leather chair behind his desk in the London townhouse—another property his wife had made possible for him to own—and smiled at this latest report. The runner had been with her every step of the way, following the coach to the Broxbourne Station, and he'd sat five rows away on the train to London. He'd followed her to her first destination in Arlington Street, and then waited to follow her to Cheyne Walk.

That was interesting. Thomasia had not gone straight to her family. Anthony had expected her to go to Wychavon House or to Cheyne Walk. He wouldn't have been surprised if she'd gone to Cowden House either, since the Duchess had been her sponsor. He was, however, surprised by the address in Arlington Street. Home of Broxbourne's MP, Crenshaw Rawdon. The very same man who'd called on her at Haberstock Hall with suspicious regularity, and who had continued to call on her once Dr Peverett and his family had come up to London.

He tapped his fingers on the desk and gave a wicked smile to the empty room. Those attentions seemed to go beyond neighbourly, and he knew just how wild Thomasia could be. Was it possible she hadn't learned her lesson and had taken another lover? Did she think he wouldn't use that against her? The law might offer some favour to women keeping their young children, but not when the father was a lord and the mother had shown the bad judgement to sleep with not one man but two out of wedlock.

He couldn't imagine Rawdon would like his role in the affair coming to light either. It wouldn't do the man's career any good to be embroiled in the scandal of the Season—and Anthony would make sure it was *the* scandal if Thomasia did not come quietly. After all, he had fifty thousand pounds on the line.

Anthony rang for a footman. 'Tell my valet to prepare my things. I need to dress for the evening.'

His wife insisted on their putting in an appearance at Redding's, but he'd escape soon enough to his clubs and a night of gaming, before taking himself off to an address in Piccadilly and the talents of a certain lady there.

He rose and paused for a moment, a thought occurring to him. Thomasia had gone to Rawdon. She'd have told Rawdon about him today if she hadn't already.

Rawdon knew his name and vice versa. Would Rawdon come looking for him or should he go looking for Rawdon? Strike first with his threat?

He rather liked the idea of being on the offence instead of the defence, just as much as he liked the power of being able to ruin a man's career. It was always interesting to see what a man might do to protect himself... and if not himself, those he loved.

Chapter Twenty-One

'Rawdon loves you,' Anne pointed out bluntly as she settled Thomasia and Effie into the upstairs guest room. The others had gone. Their parents and Becca had departed with Wychavon and Thea, and Shaw had returned home to dress for the evening that was fast approaching. His simple act of dropping Thomasia off at her sister's had turned into a two-hour visit.

Under happier circumstances it would have been a wondrous thing to have Tresham's Chelsea townhouse bursting with the family and two children under a year old. Even with *these* circumstances Thomasia had taken comfort in being surrounded by her family, sitting in the warm kitchen, talking, while Anne brewed rosemary tinctures on the stove.

'He only thinks he does.' Thomasia put a pile of linens in a lavender-scented bureau drawer. 'He sees a young woman wronged in romance. I think he's in love with the tragedy of me—and he adores Effie.'

Shaw had been everything she'd needed today: strong, commanding, able to lift the burden from her shoulders for a short while until she could resume it. A week apart had not diminished the contentment she found in his arms, the secret smile in his gaze when he looked at her. He was as handsome and as competent as ever. And her response to him was just as intense.

Thomasia looked up from her unpacking. 'I don't want him to love me, Anne. I can only bring him pain. He wants to save me. He refuses to see how that would ruin him.' She gave a soft sigh and sat on the bed. 'He thinks he's invincible.'

It happened to be one of the things she liked best about him—all that strength. She didn't want to be the one who taught him otherwise.

Anne came to sit beside her. Mrs Green, the house-keeper, was caring for both the children while they unpacked and had a moment's privacy, for which Thomasia was both grateful and ungrateful. She was grateful for a chance to talk plainly with Anne, but knew that chance would come with difficult questions.

'So he's proposed to you, then?' Anne deduced, taking her hand. It wasn't a hard conclusion to draw. There was only one way to save a woman in Thomasia's position. 'Is that the only reason he has proposed? To save you? Or is there another source of his obligation?'

Thomasia pulled her hand away. She could feel her cheeks heating. She could not lie to her sister. 'I have slept with him, but it was made clear there was to be no obligation. It was not supposed to change anything.'

Anne raised a coppery eyebrow in query and Thomasia found herself forced to explain.

'It was to be an affair, and it was to end when he came to Town. Our curiosity, our passion, would be satisfied and no one the wiser. He would go to Town and carry on with his life, and I would leave Haberstock. I was always leaving anyway, in the spring. He wouldn't have to face me when he returned. It seemed like an ironclad solution at the time.'

'But everything changed, didn't it?' Anne smiled softly, her green eyes shining with knowledge. 'Even before the letter from Halston things had changed. With the right man it can never be an issue of a single night. Nor would the right man allow such a thing.'

'It's just that I've already made mistakes in love. You would think I'd be smarter the second time...' Thomasia swallowed hard, trying to find the words. 'He wants to marry me, but I'll bring him nothing but trouble.'

There would always be the question of Effie's parentage and her past if they stayed in Haberstock. People there would know Effie wasn't Shaw's child. The maths simply didn't work. Then there was the issue of what it would do to Shaw's career. Even if the scandal of Effie and Halston's attempt to adopt her didn't go public, simply marrying her would make things difficult for him in Society. What would Shaw do? What would become of his dreams and hopes if he lost his seat because he'd married her? What would become of her own work?

'Besides, Anne, I'd be a hypocrite to argue for women's independence and equality, for a woman's ability to stand on her own two feet in Society without the need to prop herself up on the arm of a man, and then go and marry for those very reasons.'

Anne rose and resumed the task of unpacking. 'But would it be marriage for those reasons, though? Surely those are benefits to marrying Shaw, but they aren't *the* reason, are they? I saw how you looked at him today. You have affection for him. I don't believe for a moment you went to bed with him just for curiosity's sake. After what you've been through, you're too clever for that. You can marry Shaw Rawdon for love without being a hypocrite or a betrayer of your cause. And it might be the only way to keep Effie from Halston.'

'But even if I married him for love it's not fair to him. I would sacrifice whatever was required to protect Effie, but I don't want to require that same level of sacrifice from him. I can't have him laying his life in ruins for me.'

She didn't want to see the passion in Shaw's blue eyes turn to hatred over time.

'To make that sacrifice is not your decision to make,' Anne said. 'Your situation is not unlike my situation when Ferris and I were courting.' Anne tucked a sheet around the mattress of the spare crib that had been set up for Effie in the corner. 'By associating himself with me, Ferris put his reputation, his practice, everything he'd built, on the line. I didn't like it any more than you like the idea of risking Shaw's career. You and I are fiercely independent, dear sister, and we don't like relying on others. But I learned that Ferris knew what he was doing. I am certain Shaw knows what *he's* doing, what he's offering and what the cost is.'

'That's what bothers me most.'

Thomasia shook her head, the sense of her utter reliance on others that had plagued her all day returning. She was keenly aware that she could not resolve this on her own, no matter how desperately she wanted to.

She pulled away from her sister and tried for a smile.

'Perhaps marriage won't be necessary. Perhaps the men will learn something tonight that can be used to spike Halston's guns and this whole episode will be over.'

But even as she said the words she doubted them. How she wished *she* could have gone tonight—that she and Shaw could have gone as a team, like they had that night at Beechmont. But that would have been the absolute worst thing she could do, to directly associate herself with him in the public eye of London. There would have been no chance to protect him then.

The very best thing she could do for Shaw was to stay out of sight, but it was something she was tired of doing. She'd stayed out of sight for well over a year—first in York and then at Haberstock. It was the only tool she had to protect those she loved from the scandal of her. Very soon, she wouldn't even have that.

They finished unpacking her trunk and Anne squeezed her hand. 'Supper should be ready soon. Shall we go down and see how the children are doing with Mrs Green?' She smiled. 'Let it all go, Thomasia. There's nothing more you can do except enjoy your daughter and your nephew. Let the men do their reconnaissance tonight.'

It was good advice, but it was still hard to take.

'You need to behave tonight, Rawdon.'

Viscount Brixton had met them outside the Reddings' drawing room, his blue eyes intent on Shaw, his voice low.

'Halston is indeed here.'

Shaw felt his temper unfurl at the news.

Wychavon put a hand on his chest. 'You're going to leave Halston alone. You may have a glance only.'

Why was it that good advice was so hard to take? He'd have much preferred Wychavon to say, *We're going to jump him in the card room and give him the drubbing he deserves.*

'We'll learn nothing about his purpose if he feels cornered,' Brixton added, ushering the group into the drawing room. 'Besides, there are some others that I want you to meet. Men who think like you do, Rawdon.'

The comment was oddly cryptic, and it served to engage Shaw's attention, forcing him to focus at least part of it on something other than surveying the room and guessing which man was Halston.

The Reddings' drawing room was done in peach and grey tones and populated with several clusters of furniture, allowing guests to sit and talk in small groups as they mingled. A long refreshment table decorated with a carved ice swan in the centre and two champagne fountains, one at either end, and laden with delicacies in between—many of them of Russian origin, out of deference for the new ambassador—had been set up near the French doors that led outdoors.

The reception was well attended, given that Parliament didn't open for a few days yet and those in Town were still sparse. Shaw had hoped for a smaller attendance. It would have made seeking out Halston easier.

Wychavon stood at his shoulder, Thomasia's sister Thea on his arm, looking striking in a plain gown of dark blue silk. Thea and Thomasia shared the dark Peverett hair and cognac eyes, and perhaps even the willowy height, but where Thea's face was all striking angles, Thomasia was stunning. For Shaw, there could be no comparison, and he saw it was the same for Wychavon. The man was besotted with his wife. Besotted enough to be leaving in the fall for Germany, where his wife could attend medical school.

'Excuse me, gentlemen…' Thea spoke softly, her eyes moving about the room. 'I'd best ingratiate myself with the ladies if I'm to learn anything useful tonight.' She gave Wychavon a private glance and took her leave.

Wychavon leaned close. 'I'll put you out of your misery, Rawdon, but you have to promise you won't do anything stupid.'

Shaw nodded, and Wychavon grimaced as if he didn't quite believe him. Smart man, Wychavon. Shaw wasn't sure he believed himself either. Halston had ruined Thomasia and now he was intent on destroying her. It would be difficult to stand by and let the man roam freely about the drawing room.

'Look over by the fireplace, on the left side of the mantel. There's a group of five. He's the tall blond.'

The fireplace was easy to find. It was the centrepiece of the room, with its enormous size and expensive dark grey slate. Two large crystal vases overflowing with creamy hothouse roses stood like sentinels on the mantel.

Shaw's eyes lit on Halston, who looked as if he'd been put there on purpose to complement the décor: creamy blond hair to match the roses, dark evening clothes to go with the slate, and a pale peach waistcoat. Halston was an expensive, elegant man.

An equally expensive and elegant woman preened on his arm in an exquisite peach gown, diamonds sparkling at her long neck. She gave a toss of her blonde head, clearly aware of how wonderful they looked together and how perfectly suited they were to the drawing room.

Shaw watched as she took a flute of champagne and left her husband's side to join a group of women. He saw Thea note the movement. It would be the work of a whole evening for Thea to slowly rotate into a group that held Lady Halston, but he knew Thea would see it done.

'What a pompous, preening prick,' Rawdon swore under his breath to Wychavon.

He moved his gaze away from the fireplace, not wanting to draw attention or to signal that he'd been watching Halston in any way. But he felt distinctly *de trop*—very much the country man compared to a man with the elan Halston had on display.

'Oh, indeed he is,' Wychavon concurred, moving them towards a group gathered in one of Lady Redding's clutches of furniture.

But Shaw could see the appeal Halston must have held for Thomasia, fresh from the country and eager for adventure. The man was handsome by Town standards, well turned out and full of flash. Well connected, too, as the second son of an earl. A young Thomasia would have felt flattered by his attentions. The man looked to be approaching thirty, so he'd have been twenty-eight when she'd known him. He would have stood apart from the young men newly come to Town—the young'uns in their early twenties, just out of university or home from the Grand Tour. His polish would have gleamed twice as brightly.

Shaw hated him for that.

'He's not a happy man, if that's any consolation,'

Wychavon whispered at his ear. 'Now, if you could put him aside for the moment, Brixton wants to introduce you to some people.'

Brixton rose from his seat in the cluster of sofas and chairs. 'Rawdon, there you are. Come and meet my friend Lord Taunton. He's here from Somerset with his wife, Lady Taunton. They're part of my father's investment club. Taunton has an alpaca farm. He started importing them three years ago from South America, and now he's making a fortune in alpaca wool.' Brixton grinned as he clapped Taunton on the back.

Taunton. The name was familiar. Shaw worked hard to place it as he shook Taunton's hand and bowed over his wife's. Ah, yes. Lady Taunton was formerly the Marchesa di Cremona—the Englishwoman who'd divorced an Italian noble under no small scandal. Stanton despised her.

Shaw threw a glance at Brixton, who answered with a quiet nod. Taunton sat in the Lords and he would be no friend of Stanton's repeal. Shaw took a seat with a grin. 'Tell me about alpacas.'

Taunton smiled back, his voice private. 'And after that I'd like to talk about how we're going to bury Stanton's repeal, if you're amenable.'

Over Taunton's shoulder Brixton caught his eye, as if to say, *You're not alone. There are those who will stand against him.* It was a start, but it didn't solve the problem that when this was over he would have to answer to Stanton and Maldon, should his indiscretion become obvious.

Shaw looked about this circle of friends: Taunton and

his wife, Brixton and Wychavon. None of them need worry over their seats. But *he* did.

Taunton leaned back in his chair as the conversation wound down after a period of spirited discussion. 'How do you do it, Rawdon? Walk all those thin lines? Doing this favour and that, all in the hope of getting a little something that means anything? I ask because I admire you for it—not losing sight of your soul, of the reason you're serving.'

'I don't know. It's a question I've been asking myself lately,' Shaw answered honestly. 'As for not losing sight of my soul…I do wonder if I haven't.' Shaw leaned forward. 'This afternoon I hosted a meeting aimed at strong-arming people to support the repeal of the 1845 laws that require a man to support his child, whether married to the mother or not—a repeal I find personally and professionally repugnant. If people do not offer support for rewards, I am to suggest there would be retaliation.'

Lady Taunton spoke up. 'Stanton is a bully and a coward for coercing men into the vote.'

Shaw chuckled at her venom. Lady Taunton and Thomasia would be fast friends. But her words were no laughing matter. The longer he was with Thomasia, the clearer it became to him that he was working in the enemy's camp—working for a man who stood against the things the woman he loved stood for, the things he himself stood for. And he lingered in that camp still, hoping to achieve some good.

It was not the first time he'd had such misgivings about his calling, but the cry was more insistent these days. He knew in his heart that to stay longer would wipe out the last of his own ethics. The time to leave was overdue—and yet leaving, too, came with a cost.

'You know, Rawdon…' Brixton spoke offhandedly, but his keen gaze belied the casualness of his comment. 'The Prometheus Club invests in ventures of all sorts: business, exploration, charities. I hear you have a plan for foundling schools. It's something the club is interested in. You should call on Cowden while you're in Town.'

Shaw nodded his thanks, overwhelmed by what had happened. He was being given an option—a chance to sink Stanton's despicable repeal and then walk away from his connection to that unholy alliance. Not just walk away, he noted. He was being offered a chance to continue with the work that mattered to him through the powerful and exclusive Prometheus Club instead of through the tangle of Parliament.

There would be a cost to it, though. He was not blind. He'd been tested tonight and he'd passed. These men were bringing him into their group because they expected him to marry Thomasia, to protect her from Halston just as they were willing to protect him from Stanton.

In essence, he'd just been welcomed into the family, and it felt good. Now all he had to do was convince Thomasia not only to marry him, but that he wanted to do so for the right reason—that he would want to marry her even if scandal hadn't necessitated it.

Chapter Twenty-Two

The newness of the room had brought Thomasia a difficult night. Effie had not settled in the strange surroundings and had slept only in short bursts, until Thomasia had given up on the crib and taken Effie into bed with her around two. Then it was she who had slept fitfully, careful not to roll on the baby.

Perhaps she would have slept poorly anyway. There was too much to think about.

As the hours drew towards dawn her thoughts drifted away from Shaw and whatever he'd learned tonight towards what the morning might bring. Tomorrow was the deadline Halston had insisted upon. But what next? Would there be instructions? Would there be a meeting with the solicitor? Or, worse, would there be a meeting with Anthony?

Of all the options that was the one she wanted the least. She did not want to see him. How dare he interrupt her life with such an audacious demand? But she knew how he dared. He was a man with influence, a man who was used to getting his way. No one told him no.

But she would. Whatever came next, she would deal

with it alone. Shaw could not go with her without impugning them both. She supposed she might take a family member with her, though. Perhaps Wychavon or Ferris might go. Halston might think twice about bullying her with an earl or a duke's son at her side.

She didn't like the idea of that. She'd rather be taken seriously on her own and not for the man with her. Thomasia yawned and adjusted Effie where she snuggled against her. If she could just sleep an hour or two she might wake up rested enough to face the day and whatever came. Effie was counting on her.

Fear had her sitting up in bed. If she failed she would lose Effie. The impact of that shook her anew, as it had the previous morning. Was it really only that morning she'd been at Haberstock Hall? So much had happened since then.

She shivered. How she wished Shaw was with her. Surely she would be able to sleep if she was in his arms. 'It will be all right, Effie,' she murmured out loud, trying to convince herself as she drifted off to sleep.

Thomasia had overslept.

She awoke to the sound of voices in the kitchen and an empty bed. That panicked her.

Where was Effie?

She flew down the stairs barefoot in her nightgown, calling, 'Anne! Anne!'

She came to an abrupt halt at the foot of the steps, relief and embarrassment flooding her. Effie was in the kitchen, on Shaw's knee. Shaw looked well groomed and well rested. Whereas she was in her nightgown and sporting dark circles under her eyes as if *she'd* been the one who'd spent the evening out on the Town.

Shaw rose with Effie. 'Thomasia, she's fine. We decided to let you sleep.'

He kissed her on the cheek, in front of her sister, and looked far too comfortable with seeing her in her nightgown, never mind that she'd confessed all to Anne yesterday.

'It's just that I feared...' Thomasia couldn't bring herself to finish the sentence. 'I don't know what to expect today.'

She sank into the chair Shaw pulled out for her at the table. Anne put a cup of coffee at her elbow.

'I hate being at his mercy, even in this small way... just waiting. He made the first move and he will make the next.' She put her head in her hands and a moment later felt Shaw's hand at the back of her neck, gently massaging. 'That feels good.' She sighed. 'Did you learn anything last night?'

'It affirms what you thought was happening. According to the gossip that Thea overheard last night, Lady Halston had a dangerous miscarriage in the autumn that has made it unlikely she will have children.' Shaw paused, letting her draw her own conclusions from that.

'He can't access the money without a child.' Thomasia raised her head, fear stabbing at her anew. 'That's why he wants mine.'

Shaw's hand tightened at her shoulders in support. 'He can't have her. We'll meet him together.'

She sat up with an abrupt movement, bumping the cup and sending coffee sloshing onto the table. 'We can't. He'll use that against us. He'll say we're having an affair, that I'm an unsuitable mother...' She was rambling in terror. 'I must see him on my own.'

That cleared her mind. She had to dress, had to do her hair, had to look utterly respectable. She would wear the plum dress, and she'd put her hair up...

Shaw put a gentle hand on her arm but his eyes were intently serious. 'Thomasia, wait. Stop and think. You cannot see him alone. When you see him, you should see him not as Miss Peverett, but as my wife, as Mrs Shaw Rawdon. There would be no talk of an affair then, and he would not be able to bully you.'

'Shaw, we've discussed this. You needn't marry me out of pity.' Thomasia pitched her voice low, looking about the kitchen and finding it miraculously deserted. Anne had taken herself and the two infants off to some other part of the house.

'This isn't about pity. It's about self-preservation— mine, not yours, Thomasia,' he said sternly. 'Have you ever thought that I simply want to marry you? That I would *want* to marry you even if scandal wasn't swirling around our feet?'

'That's only because you don't know any better,' Thomasia shot back. 'Some day you'll resent me for this—for causing you to lose your seat, to lose your career, your dreams.'

'You mean more to me than that. Do I mean more to you? Or was this all a game? A ploy?' His face became blank and formal, his hand withdrawing from her arm. 'Are *we* an illusion, Thomasia? Have you no real feeling for me? No feeling worth fighting for?'

He was skirting the real question: *Had she slept with*

*him in order to get close to him, to influence his vote,
and now that she had was she afraid of claiming it?*

She should say yes. This was her way out—her way
to save him. If she said yes he would have to walk away.
No man would stay with a woman who'd used him,
who'd tried to manipulate him for her own intentions.
But Thomasia Peverett was always honest, even when
honesty didn't serve her.

'No, Shaw. We are real.' So real it hurt to think of
staying with him just as much as it hurt to think of
letting him go. 'I did take the position as secretary
to hopefully influence the direction of your thoughts
on the repeal. But it didn't last.' She sighed. 'I tried
not to like you. I tried to see you as lazy and entitled,
pleasure-seeking...'

'You sewed my coat sleeve shut,' Shaw interjected.

'Oh, yes, I really tried, Shaw. And I thought the day
you discovered Effie and me in the nursery would seal
that. You would react like any other man and be disgusted. More than that, I thought you would run. But
you didn't. You did quite the opposite and that was the
beginning of the end for my plan.'

She moved close to him, placing her hand on his
arm, and held his gaze.

'I went to bed with you because I wanted to, nothing else, but I can't let you sacrifice yourself. You of
all people cannot be married to a woman who aligns
herself with the Coffee Yard ladies, one of those groups
of women Stanton detests, and I don't think I can stop.
I don't want to throw my work away.' She put her hand
against his chest, feeling the beat of his heart. 'You want
to save me, but you have to understand that I want to

save *you.*' She stepped back. 'Now I need to dress. I must be ready whenever the summons comes.'

An hour later Anne knocked on her bedroom door, her expression solemn, her voice quiet. 'He's here, Thomasia. I've put him in the front parlour.'

The morning went instantly from bad to worse. There wasn't going to be any summons, or a meeting on neutral ground under the pretext of a negotiation. His coming here in person was sending a dangerous message: he could find her. He would always find her.

Not that finding her was any great feat at the moment. He'd forced her to come to London under threat of legal repercussions if she did not. It was what it portended for the future that was frightening. He would not give up. He would hunt her openly.

Thomasia rose and smoothed her plum skirts. 'And Shaw? Where is he?'

Had he left? Gone home to assess his options? Lick his wounds? He'd done so much for her and she'd given him so little.

Anne touched her arm. 'He's in the kitchen, pacing like a mad bear because he can't fight this battle for you.'

It was as she'd felt last night, letting him go to the Reddings' without her.

'This will be a short conversation. There's nothing for him to worry over.'

It was true. With every step she took a sense of calm settled over her. She knew what he'd say, what he would threaten. She'd been over it a hundred times in her mind. And she knew her choices. All she had to do was act on them. Shaw was in the kitchen, ready to leap to her defence should it be necessary, ready to block the stairs up to where Effie played with her cousin. For the first time since the letter had arrived, there was nothing to fear. Would Halston realise he had no power here? That she alone held all the power to decide her fate?

She was entirely composed when she entered the front parlour. 'Lord Halston, good morning.' Her head was high, her tones cool, making it clear this appointment was an infringement upon her schedule, that *he* was an imposition.

'Miss Peverett.'

He smiled but he didn't rise. It was a petty attempt to equal the struggle for power between them, this refusal to acknowledge her as a lady.

He was much as she remembered him: well dressed, golden hair gleaming, jaw smoothly shaven, the face of a fallen angel. But what had once been dash and sophistication seemed today to be tinged with hardness and selfishness—portents, perhaps, of the bitterness that would settle on those features with age, which was in fact already settling in early brackets about his mouth.

And what she'd once thought of as his zest for living with wild recklessness was actually discontent. How had she not seen it before? Anthony Halston was an unhappy person. She'd always considered herself the opposite—a happy person, even when she was facing difficulties. What had the appeal of him been? His golden façade paled next to Shaw's russet ruggedness and sincere strength.

He crossed a leg over one knee in an indolent gesture and gave off an air of boredom. 'We need to discuss our daughter. I am told we have one—no thanks to you. How long did you expect to keep news of her from me?'

He was playing the wronged father rather dispassionately. At least he wasn't pretending to be in love with her, offering to set her up as his mistress, as if that was a great gift that would rectify what he'd done in the past.

'You made it clear you wanted nothing to do with us,' Thomasia answered evenly. 'Your wedding proves it. When you had the chance to marry me, to do right by me and by your daughter, you chose not to—not only once, but twice.'

What a lucky escape that had been for her. She would have had respectability, but at the extreme price of her own miserableness. There would have been no cause to fight for. She'd have spent her days fighting for herself, for Effie, for the scraps of a normal life, and she would have lost. Not so with Shaw. Marriage to Shaw would come with the freedom to be herself. How had she not seen that before?

'Am I not entitled to make a mistake? I want to take responsibility for my daughter. It is the least I can do.' He gave her a cool, assessing look that raked her from head to toe. 'You look well, Thomasia. Your new lover seems to agree with you. Wouldn't it be nice to be free to pursue a life with him? I'm sure he's not interested in another man's child clinging to your skirts while he tries to get under them.'

Thomasia stared at him, repulsed by the idea. Did he think he was offering her a *reward* by taking her daughter?

'You are the father of my child. You were *not* a lover,' Thomasia snapped.

What had passed between them had not been love-making. Not in the least. Those brief, furtive encounters did not resemble her passionate nights in Shaw's arms, the long discussions that ended with kisses and caresses, before the passion started all over again.

Anthony tugged at his cuffs, pulling them out from beneath his coat by a fraction of an inch, ignoring the jab. 'Of course, Rawdon seems a little on the rough side for you. You always preferred fine things, as I recall. A country gentleman seems beneath your touch.' He gave a considering shrug. 'There's no accounting for taste.'

He raised a sleek brow and she knew her face had inadvertently given something away.

'You're surprised I know about Rawdon? I know more than his name. I know you went to him first yesterday when you arrived.'

He gave a cruel smile and she braced herself. He was being mean now, deliberately, trying to thaw her cool.

'I had you followed. My man sat five rows behind you on the Broxbourne train and you didn't even know it.'

He chuckled, and Thomasia fought back the fingers of fear that grabbed for her.

'Don't be difficult, Thomasia. I want my child. I want to claim her as my own, bring her up as my own. She'll have every luxury, and far more opportunity than you can give her.' He gave a long-suffering sigh. 'If you truly want what's best for her, you must know I'm right. What kind of opportunity can you give her in Haberstock, where she'll be branded a bastard? What kind of marriage can she make? What kind of life can she hope for? Just hand her over to me and this needn't be messy or public.'

Another woman might be tempted by the offer—a woman who had no resources, no support, no *choice*.

'No, Halston. Now, if you'll excuse me, I have things to see to.'

Shaw. Effie. She wanted nothing more than to wrap her arms about them both.

She got as far as turning her back on him before he drawled, 'I don't think you understand the depth of my commitment on this, or the lack of influence you actually have. I only asked for my daughter to be polite. Now I will simply demand her.'

'You don't even know her name.' Thomasia straightened but did not turn.

'It doesn't matter. I'll probably change it. You likely gave her some absurd family name. I was thinking of Jane. Jane's a nice name—although my wife likes Eurydice… She's fond of the Greeks. Perhaps Eurydice Jane? I think that sounds sophisticated…a name worthy of the granddaughter of two earls.'

He was goading her, and Thomasia knew it, but her temper brewed regardless. 'The law will be on my side. The Tender Years legislation…' She began to speak the litany that had given her mind ease when it had worried over the problem.

He gave a smug laugh. 'Are you a barrister now, Thomasia? How quaint you are, with your ideas of what a woman can accomplish. Do you think any court would give you custody, even for seven years, once I tell them you lived in sin with your local MP?'

She heard him stand up, felt him move across the

room towards her. He came up behind her, his hands on her arms, his mouth at her ear.

'I know everything, Thomasia, and I will ruin him along with you. How would your family feel about that?'

'Take your hands off me.' She stiffened at his touch, not from his threats. She'd anticipated those. Those were the blackmail she'd been expecting.

'I will when I'm ready.' His mouth was at her neck. 'Do you think so little of your family, of your lover, that you would expose them to public ridicule? Do you think so little of your daughter that you'd not send her into the best life possible? This selfishness is not like you, Thomasia. You used to be extraordinarily giving...'

His nuance on the last word made her skin crawl.

'I remember particularly how giving you were in Lady Summerville's grotto that one night...'

That was enough. She was finished with being coolly polite. Thomasia brought her foot down hard on his instep and shoved an elbow into his gut, watching as he doubled over and yelped in pain.

The sound brought Shaw running. 'What is happening here?'

He burst from the kitchen, her knight in shining armour, ready to defend her, and her heart swelled. How had she ever thought being with him was anything like being with Halston?

'Lord Halston is just leaving.'

Thomasia moved to stand beside Shaw. She could take care of herself, but it felt better to be where she belonged, with whom she belonged.

'Just as soon as he catches his breath,' she offered, while Shaw slid her an approving grin.

Halston righted himself and limped towards the door, his elan momentarily spiked. 'This settles nothing. This is not over. I will have that child. I will ruin you both. And I will enjoy doing it if you stand against me.'

Shaw waited until the door had shut behind Halston. 'You punched him in the gut. I trust it was not un-provoked?'

It had taken all his willpower to stay in the kitchen, to let Thomasia deal with this. Only the thought that he would be the last bastion between Halston and Effie should the man try anything drastic had kept him in his place—as had the little reminder in his head that Thomasia would not welcome the interference. She was a pro-tector, just like he was, and she felt the need to protect him as much as he felt the need to protect her. It was what he loved about her—that fierce loyalty—even as it frustrated him. A man protected the woman he loved.

'He was being crass,' Thomasia offered obliquely.

Shaw knew he wouldn't get any more out of her on the subject, but he could surmise well enough on his own. A man had to stand close enough to be hit, to start with, and Halston had been close enough to Thomasia for her to step on his foot *and* reach his gut. The bastard had put his hands on her—or at least tried.

'I would have preferred it be my fist in the man's gut rather than yours.' He gave Thomasia a meaningful look as they walked to the kitchen and sat at the table. 'And I might still get the chance. This is merely round one for him,' Shaw said once they were settled with cups of hot coffee and a plate of Mrs Green's freshly baked lemon scones.

Thomasia took a scone and crumbled it absently. 'I know.'

'What do you want to do?'

He'd tried telling her what to do, tried strongly suggesting alternatives, arguing for options, all to no avail. Thomasia had put him off at every point. Perhaps he'd gone about it all wrong. Instead of telling her what to do, he needed to ask her for her plan.

She held his gaze steady and said, in all seriousness, 'I want to marry you, Shaw. I want you to adopt Effie-Claire and I want us to be a family.'

Shaw stilled. Those were the words he'd waited to hear for weeks now, and yet he held his breath, waiting for the 'but' that was sure to follow. As in *But I can't have that because of your career...because of The Cause...because of my principles that say truly free women don't cave and give in to marriage.*

When none came, he couldn't resist asking. 'But...?' He reached for her hands, desperately wanting to touch her, to feel the truth of her.

'But you have to be sure. You have to want it, too. We will be in this together for ever, and there will be consequences. You have to want this for the right reason.'

Thomasia swallowed hard, and he sensed she was talking to herself as much as she was talking to him.

'You do, too,' he answered solemnly.

He would probably kick himself. He was giving her too much room to back out of this. He should have swept her up in his arms and kissed her senseless two minutes ago instead of inviting a discussion.

'I want to marry you, and I want to be a father to Effie. I would want it regardless of circumstances.

Would you? Would *you* want to marry *me* regardless? Because, as much as I want you, I don't want you dishonestly. I don't want you just because you think you have to trade yourself for Effie's safety. Thomasia, I will find a way to protect you both without marriage, if that's what you want. My friendship is not contingent on anything but my feelings for you.'

Too much of his life these past two years had been lived with contingencies. He was finished with that now.

'I know you would,' Thomasia replied solemnly. 'And I am marrying you regardless. Because I belong with you. I saw that today. Can you accept that I may cost you your career as an MP?'

'It's not you who will cost me my career, if it comes to that. It will be me, and my choices about how I want to live, and it will be for the better.' He smiled as he told her about his meeting with Lord Taunton the night before, and Viscount Brixton's invitation. 'There is a way forward for us. And I think you would like Viscountess Taunton.'

He grinned, and the tension that had surrounded Thomasia since her arrival in London lessened.

'Since you've done the proposing, Thomasia, may I suggest the date?' It was the only decision that mattered to him at the moment. 'Tomorrow morning. I was thinking we could marry at St Luke's.' It was only a few streets away from Anne and Ferris's home—within walking distance. 'I have a special licence. I'd like to put it to good use. And the moment we are wed I will adopt Effie. We can submit the papers tomorrow afternoon, and celebrate our wedding as a family by supper time.'

Thomasia's eyes sparkled with tears and her voice

caught. 'Thank you, Shaw. I will make you happy, I promise.'

He leaned across and stole a kiss. 'You already do. Shall we go tell the family and turn a bad morning into a beautiful afternoon? Your sisters will want to shop, and your mother will want to make a few arrangements.'

'What about you?' Thomasia smiled at him.

'I'll spend the afternoon playing with my daughter. And Brixton thought he might drop by with Taunton to discuss his plans. Taunton's got his toddler with him. The little ones can play together. I can't think of anything better.'

He grinned as the truth washed over him. This time tomorrow he'd be the happiest man in London.

Chapter Twenty-Three

Thomasia thought herself the happiest woman in London…maybe even in all of England. And why stop there? Perhaps even in all the world as she walked to St Luke's the next morning, surrounded by her family—or at least nearly all of it.

The infants had stayed behind with Mrs Green. But Anne, Thea, Becca and her parents, all dressed in their best, made the short trek with her, passing the neat houses of Cheyne Walk on one side, and the rolling Thames swollen with winter rains on the other.

In their enthusiasm, they waved to the people on the street who shouted good wishes in the late January morning, for there was no mistaking they were a bridal party.

The wedding might be rushed, but it was not without its accoutrements. She and her sisters had combed the dressmakers of London until they'd found an unclaimed gown in white that had been easily altered to fit. Becca had spent the evening sewing seed pearls to the bodice and adding lace at the hem, while Thea had created a veil from an exquisite length of lace they'd found at a draper's. Anne had provided her with a lovely bouquet gathered from the Chelsea garden at the end of the street, full of winter herbs and roses from Ferris's mother's conservatory. The end result of her sisters' love and efforts was stunning.

'It's love that makes you beautiful,' Anne said, squeezing her hand.

Perhaps it was. Thomasia felt like the most beautiful bride in the world as they made their way, and not even the grey skies overhead could dim her joy.

The girls and her mother left her outside the doors of St Luke's with her father, to take their places inside. *Inside.* Where Shaw waited. Today she was marrying the man she loved. Today Effie would gain a father, a family of her own. Today she would truly be beyond Halston. But not beyond love.

'Are you ready, my dear?' Her father gave her a fond smile. 'My youngest is getting married today. I can still remember the day you were born.' He grinned.

Thomasia laughed. She'd heard the story so many times growing up. It was a legend in the Peverett family. Hers had been a dangerous birth. There was a reason she was the last.

'Now I am a grandfather twice over, and three of my daughters have found splendid husbands who encourage them to be themselves. What more could a father ask for his girls?'

He pushed the door open and it was time to meet her future.

Thomasia would remember that walk for the rest of her life—especially the happy faces of her rather large family as they smiled at her. Wychavon and Thea, Ferris and Anne, Ferris's parents the Duke and Duchess, along with his older brother Frederick, and his friend Viscount Taunton and his wife. It was a small but distinguished collection of wedding guests, made up of two viscounts, a duke and a duke's second son.

Her mother had managed an arrangement of flowers for the altar and candles. Simple. Beautiful. Like the man who waited for her, russet hair gleaming, eyes solemn and soulful as they held her gaze, reflecting his love for her in their depths.

Her father put her hand in Shaw's and her heart soared. This was not the transfer of a woman from man to man. This was the beginning of togetherness. Her and Shaw, together always, through hardship and triumph, through sickness and health...

The service was over before she knew it. She could recall little of it except the exchange of vows, with Shaw's voice carrying and firm as he pledged in front of all those assembled his love for her. And gave her a kiss which promised passion, protection, pleasure.

For a moment the world stood still, complete in its perfection, because she was complete and Shaw was complete. This happiness coursing through her was not hers alone, but *theirs*.

Then the door to the church burst open, the candles flickering in the draft, as Mrs Green cried out, 'He's taken the baby!' before falling to her knees.

At the words, Thomasia and Shaw raced down the aisle towards the redoubtable Mrs Green, Ferris and her father on their heels. The baby was gone, but from the looks of Mrs Green not without a fight. She sported a blackening eye and other bruises for her efforts, and she was breathless, testament to having come at top speed despite her injuries.

'What happened?' Thomasia knelt beside the house-keeper, panic in her voice.

'That man, Halston, he came back to the house with two other men. He pushed his way in. It was like he knew no one would be there.' Mrs Green gasped out the words, still labouring to catch her breath.

Thomasia nodded. Of course Halston would have known. He'd had her followed in Haberstock, and on the train. He'd not have stopped following her after yesterday. He'd promised retribution and here it was.

Her stomach lurched. She felt sick. Effie was in his hands.

'Where are they going? Which direction did they go?'

'I don't know. There was a coach outside.' Mrs Green was on the brink of despair.

Shaw knelt swiftly. 'What kind of coach? A travelling coach?'

'Yes—yes, it was big and black.' Mrs Green rallied.

Shaw looked at the group gathered about Mrs Green. 'He'll be taking her out of Town…to the country. Where's his estate?'

'Suffolk,' Wychavon provided curtly. 'My coach is outside—let's go. They've only got minutes on us, and London is slow.'

'I'm coming with you.' Thomasia struggled to her feet amid her skirts, throwing Shaw a strong look when he protested. 'There's no time to argue. I am going after my daughter.'

'*Our* daughter,' Shaw corrected, offering her a hand as they raced outside.

They made quite a sight—Thomasia and Shaw inside the coach, Wychavon on the box beside his driver, and the Tresham brothers clinging to the back like tigers as the Wychavon carriage turned down Cheyne Walk, making all haste possible.

Inside the carriage, Thomasia struggled not to break down. Effie needed her to be strong. 'We should not have left her. She'll be so frightened, Shaw.'

She was imagining a thousand terrible things. What did Halston know of children? He didn't even know her name.

Shaw had his arm about her, drawing her close. 'We'll get to her,' he vowed.

We. She liked the sound of that—even as she wondered how it was possible to have experienced such raptures of happiness just minutes ago and now such depths of despair.

But even Shaw's optimism had it limits. The coach seemed to have slowed. He stuck his head out of the window and called up to Wychavon. 'Do you see any sign of him? What's the problem?'

Wychavon shook his head. 'Traffic. I think there's an overturned dray up ahead.'

Damn it. Shaw swore. They'd barely left Cheyne Walk and they were stalled.

He craned his neck to see ahead of them. Traffic was at a dead standstill. With the river on one side, and a way to go before the next bridge, there was nowhere for the traffic to go—no way out of the congestion.

'If we're stalled, he's stalled, too,' Wychavon offered. 'This has been stationary for a while—it didn't just happen. He won't have got through it.'

The realisation spurred Shaw into action. 'Then he's in this mess, too. Let's go and find him.' He leapt out and motioned to the Treshams. 'We can't move in the coach, but we can move on foot.' They nodded, understanding exactly what he intended. 'Wychavon, follow with the coach. You'll have the advantage of height from up there.'

'I'll keep Thomasia safe,' Wychavon said—only to be interrupted.

'I'll be fine. I'm going with them. I've come this far.' Thomasia clambered down, wedding skirts gathered in one hand, defiance written on her face.

Shaw's heart soared. This was his bride, his warrior.

'Just keep up,' Shaw said sternly as he set off, weaving in and out of the traffic, stopping at coaches that met Mrs Green's description, asking people as he wove through the crowd, 'Have you seen a man with a baby? Tall? Blond?'

His great fear was that Halston had continued on foot once the traffic had stalled. If he had, he could be down any of these small alleys.

Despite the cold weather, he began to sweat. But up ahead a large black coach stood in the traffic. He gestured to the Treshams and pushed towards it, aware that Thomasia was behind him.

He hadn't reached the coach before a cry went up from Thomasia. 'He's on the move! I see him, Shaw, he's got Effie!'

Like them, Halston had given up on the traffic and

taken to his feet. The cry had alerted him, though, and now Halston began to run. Shaw found him amid the crowd and darted after him. He was running along the river's edge towards Battersea Bridge, still somewhat in the distance, and he was hampered by eighteen pounds of Effie.

He *would* catch the bastard, Shaw assured himself. It was simple. Halston couldn't outrun him—he could only lose him. And Shaw would not let that happen.

But as he closed in on Halston the unthinkable happened. Halston slipped, losing his footing on the slippery rocks and uneven terrain, one foot flirting with the river.

Fear gathered in Shaw's throat as he imagined the worst: Halston falling into the river and taking Effie with him. The Thames would finish off an infant with its filth alone.

Halston slipped again, and Shaw heard Thomasia scream in horror as Halston lost his footing for a final time, falling into the river.

'No!' Shaw yelled, as if his voice could stop the scene before him from unfolding, and he scrambled after the man, stumbling and righting himself over the muddy terrain of the riverbank. He was nearly there…nearly to Effie.

Hold on, Effie, I'm coming.

In his panic, Halston became selfish, and that was a stroke of luck for Shaw. Halston needed both his hands to battle the swift current and so he dropped the baby in the soft mud of the riverbank, even as the current pulled him towards the middle of the swollen river.

Shaw sank to his knees beside Effie in the mud, gath-

ering the squalling infant in one arm, his gaze searching the shore for a branch long enough to hold out to
Halston and pull him in. There was nothing.

In the middle of the river Halston was beyond help,
beginning to panic. He began to near the bridge and
an additional fear was born: that Halston would be
smashed against its pilings.

There was nothing for it. Shaw had to go in for
Halston. He couldn't stand there and let the man drown.

Thomasia was next to him now, and he handed the
baby to her so he could pull off his boots.

'What are you doing?' Thomasia grabbed at his arm.

'Going in—someone's got to save him,' Shaw answered tersely, struggling out of his coat.

He dived in at a diagonal angle, cutting down the
distance between them and began battling the current.
It took all his strength not to let the current sweep him
forward, as it had done Halston. Within eight strokes
he was alongside him.

'Let me tow you in!' he instructed firmly, but Halston
tried to struggle with him, in a drowning man's panicked fight. Halston pushed him under. That was when
Shaw knew he couldn't save him—not alone.

Shaw gained the surface, vaguely aware that others
were in the water with him. Someone was trying to
help Halston. Tresham, perhaps? Someone was trying
to help him, too, but he shook off the effort.

'Don't worry about me. We have to help!'

He swam against the current, trying to reach Ferris, who was still struggling with Halston. If the three
of them could not stabilise Halston soon they'd have to

let him go in order to save themselves. The water was cold and churning. His muscles were tiring.

They managed to reach Ferris. Wychavon was shouting something. 'It's no good, Tresham. Let him go or he'll take us with him. There's an eddy around the bridge—it will suck us under!'

'Don't let me go! I can't swim!' Halston spluttered, irrationally pushing Ferris underwater.

Ferris lost his grip on the man and the current spirited him away, driving him towards the pillars of the bridge.

'I can get to him!' Shaw cried. 'Halston, take my hand!'

He struck out for the man, and for a moment Halston's fingertips brushed his own, but his fingers were cold and clumsy. He couldn't grab Halston and in another moment Halston was gone, sucked beneath the water. Instinct took over, and Shaw prepared to dive, but Wychavon's hand stalled him.

'Get yourself to land while you have the strength. You can't help him,' Wychavon instructed, half towing him away. 'You're not going to widow your wife on her wedding day!' he shouted over the noise of the river.

A crowd had gathered along the shore and Shaw staggered to the riverbank, falling to his knees in the mud. Thomasia was beside him, Effie in her arms, her wedding gown muddied and torn in her haste.

'You're all right… Effie's all right!' she gasped. 'Oh, God, Shaw, I saw him push you under. I saw the river sweep you away and I thought I was going to lose you, you stubborn man. Don't you ever do anything like that again.'

She was sobbing openly now, the shock of the afternoon taking her. He held her to him, wrapped his arms about his family, feeling his own shock setting in. They were all shaking from the cold, from fear. He needed to get his family to warmth, to safety.

Wychavon's driver came with blankets from the coach and Shaw draped one over Thomasia's shoulders. He wrapped the other around Effie. Thomasia was still crying against him and rocking Effie.

'I need to get them home.' His own strength was ebbing, but he would make it last until his family was secure.

Wychavon, wet and soaking, helped them to the coach.

'I should stay.' Shaw glanced back to the riverbank once he had seen Thomasia and Effie safely inside. There would be questions and legalities to settle.

'No, you shouldn't, man,' Wychavon assured him with a clap on the shoulder. 'Go with your family. We'll all report later.' Wychavon gave a wry smile. 'It's quite a wedding day you're having.'

In the coach, Thomasia had recovered herself. 'You saved her, Shaw. I thought we'd lost her. When he fell in the river I thought he'd take Effie, too.' Her cognac eyes filled with emotion. 'You were so brave today.'

'I was so scared today.' He embraced his wife and daughter as Wychavon's coach began to move. 'I didn't want to lose the most important people in my life just when I'd found them. I never want to feel again the way I felt down on the riverbank...so afraid I wouldn't reach Effie in time.'

Thomasia nodded sombrely. 'I don't think it works

that way, Shaw. We probably will. We'll feel that way when Effie's brothers and sisters are born…when they grow up, when they marry, when their children are born—because I think that's how love works. If love doesn't scare you, it's not big enough.'

Shaw chuckled. 'I suspect you're right.'

She gave a soft smile. 'You'll find that I usually am.'

He kissed his wife for the second time that day. She smelled of damp and river, and he did, too. They were going to need a bath. That would be an excellent way to start their life together.

Four hours later they were all gathered in the Treshams' kitchen, clean and warm, but most of all *together*. The crowded space was something of a marvel to Shaw as he took in the scene that contained his new family. There were three titles in the room and it didn't seem to matter. In this moment, they were all ordinary men, interested only in their wives, their children, and quite possibly whatever was for supper.

Wychavon lounged in a chair while Ferris and Dr Peverett double-checked that Effie was none the worse for her escapade. Thomasia hovered anxiously over their shoulders. Shaw knew it would be a long time before Thomasia would be comfortable letting Effie out of her sight, but he would help her. He would be there for her and he would make sure that she was safe.

The thought thrilled him no end…to look across a room and see her, knowing that they belonged to each other.

Thea and his mother-in-law bustled in and out of the kitchen and dining room, laying the table for supper.

The prospect of a family supper brought with it a sense of normality on this most abnormal day: a wedding, an occasion of great joy, followed by a kidnapping and, in essence, a funeral.

The thought of what the Earl of Drake's family must be feeling was dampening. While his family was rejoicing, Halston's family was mourning. Wastrel or not, grown man or not, a child was a child.

Wychavon came to stand beside him. 'Don't do that,' he said in low tones. He gave a quick jerk of his head, motioning for Shaw to follow him into the hall, away from the warmth and noise of the kitchen.

'I can't help but relive those last moments,' Shaw confessed when they were alone. 'I felt his fingertips brush mine. I had him,' he insisted. 'He was *right there*, but I couldn't hang on…'

He paused, trying to find words for the thought that had haunted him since coming out of the river. Perhaps Wychavon would understand. He'd been an officer in the Crimea. He'd seen men fight and die.

'He pulled away… He wouldn't *let* me hang on. He knew the eddy was coming and it was almost like he wanted it to take him—as if he didn't want to be saved.' Shaw shook his head against the memory. 'But perhaps that's just me, trying to find a way to forgive myself for letting go.'

Wychavon nodded thoughtfully. 'Perhaps you're right… He *didn't* want to be rescued. Scandal waited on shore for him. Kidnapping a bastard child… His wife's miscarriage would likely have become public… perhaps even the conditions of his great-aunt's will. The motives for his actions would have become clear and they wouldn't have shown him in a good light.'

'So there's no chance he survived?' Shaw felt deflated.

When Wychavon and Tresham had returned they'd shared the fact that there'd been no body found but their report had been grim. There was no hope in it.

Wychavon shook his head. 'No. It is likely the body will wash up in a few days and be quietly retrieved by Drake.' He knitted his brows. 'From what I know of Drake, he was a very strict parent. I think life in that household was complicated for Halston. He was not a happy person. I've seen such recklessness in soldiers who have nothing to lose.' He clapped a hand on Shaw's shoulder. 'We did all we could. Now it's time to celebrate the original intention of today. You're a husband and a father all at once. Are you ready for it, man?'

Shaw smiled. 'Absolutely.'

It *was* time to celebrate. The family was filing from the kitchen to the dining room.

Thomasia approached, Effie in her arms. She smiled at him as she glanced between the two men. 'Is everything all right?'

Shaw placed a kiss on her cheek. 'It will be, my darling.' He lifted Effie from her arms. 'Let's go celebrate our wedding. And the future.'

Thomasia cast him a coy smile. 'I thought we already had? I rather liked the way we celebrated it in the bath…'

Shaw chuckled. 'I did, too. Maybe we can celebrate like that again later tonight, and tomorrow we'll celebrate again, once Effie's adoption papers are submitted.'

Thomasia nodded, her smile deepening, becoming more serious, less playful. 'We'll take it one day and one night at a time, Shaw, and we'll take those days together.'

There was much that would remain unsettled: the status of his Parliamentary seat, the status of Stanton's repeal attempt, Society's reception of him and his new wife and child. He could not hurry those things, he knew, but they would work themselves out in time. The things that mattered most were already settled. Thomasia was his wife, Effie was his daughter and his heart was full.

His dreams would find other avenues—avenues that he would uncover with Thomasia beside him, as a partner in life and in politics, whatever form that might take.

Life would never be dull, and nothing would ever be impossible—not when the two of them stood together.

Epilogue

London, spring, a few months later

Thomasia Rawdon was perhaps the only person in London looking forward to going home. Spring had sprung in a glorious profusion of colour: pink flowers, blue skies and an abundance of lavish entertainments after a grey winter of isolation. But Rosegate and married life awaited on the other side of the Parliamentary session currently in progress. She had August the twelfth circled in her datebook as Homecoming. Until then she would persevere and do her best to enjoy the Season. She would certainly enjoy today, despite her nerves over leaving Effie with the nurse they'd hired.

Thomasia fanned herself against the heat of the ladies' gallery. Stanton's effort to repeal the 1845 Bastardy Act had made it to the floor for vote, despite Shaw's best efforts to bury it. But, as she'd told Shaw, perhaps it was best to address Stanton's repeal publicly, in order to put it to bed decisively. At least that was how she hoped it would go today.

She fanned herself a little faster, her nerves rising as the MPs filed in and took their seats at the benches. She caught sight of Shaw immediately, his russet head standing out among blond and brunette. Beside him was Brixton, Ferris's brother.

Was Shaw nervous, too? Today was a big day for him in other ways. Today he would vote with his conscience. He would stand up to his mentors and it might cost him his seat in the upcoming election. A lot would change for him today, regardless of how the vote went.

Thomasia smiled to herself, remembering their conversation in bed that morning. 'The things that matter won't change,' he'd told her.

Her smile widened as she thought about her secret. Things *might* change…just a little.

Stanton's repeal was up first. Thomasia moved a little closer to the edge of her seat, holding her breath as voting commenced. She did *not* want this repeal to pass. Men like Halston and Shaw's sire needed to be held accountable for their actions.

The vote was close, the lead going back and forth between the ayes and the nays.

'How does the gentleman from Broxbourne say?'

'Nay,' came Shaw's firm and unequivocal answer.

Her heart swelled with pride as he glanced up into the gallery, searching for her. The Season had been difficult for them, and his vote today would ensure it became even more so. People had not been in a hurry to befriend them, although nudges from her sisters, Lady Wychavon and Lady Tresham, had certainly made their path smoother than it might have been otherwise.

The last of the votes were called and numbers tallied. It would be close.

The outcome was announced.

'Stanton's repeal of the 1845 Bastardy Act has failed by two votes.'

Failed. Thomasia felt relief flood her. Two votes. Brixton and Shaw. They'd done it. She could hardly wait to write to the Coffee Yard ladies and celebrate with them.

The rest of the short session seemed interminable as she waited for it to let out. When it did, she pushed her way downstairs through the crowd, finding Shaw at the door to the chamber.

Stanton was with him, the man's face florid. She probably should wait until their conversation concluded, but she'd promised to stand beside Shaw and she would do so now—quite literally. She made her way towards him, slipping her arm through his as Stanton glared.

'You will regret this, Rawdon. You've had your fun at my expense, parading this hussy of a wife around, passing her off as decent company, being entangled in the Halston scandal—and now this, voting directly against my repeal. There was much I overlooked about you, Rawdon. Because you had potential. I cannot countenance this. What will people think if I can't even control my own MPs?'

'Are you ready to go, dear?' Thomasia asked sweetly, flashing Shaw a conspiratorial smile.

He looked down at her with those mesmerising blue eyes. 'Yes, I do believe I am.' To Stanton he said, 'You may think what you like about me, and say what you like about me, but be clear: I will not countenance ill words against my wife. Good day.'

His words sent a thrill through Thomasia. Love—real love—was a wonder, and marriage a new revelation every day.

Outside in the bright sunshine Shaw swung her around in a circle, crying, 'We won, Thomasia!' Although they both knew they'd already won, long before the vote. His eyes twinkled. 'Do I get a prize?'

She laughed up at him. This was the perfect opportunity to tell him.

'You most certainly do. But you'll have to wait a few months—about seven of them.'

It took Shaw a moment, and she would remember for ever watching recognition dawn across his face like a sunrise.

'Really? A child? For us? A sibling for Effie?'

She nodded. 'In December…a Christmas baby, I think.'

She was in his arms again, hugging and laughing and crying all at once, not caring what people might think. How could she ever have dreaded spring when it was full of new beginnings?

* * * * *

If you enjoyed this story,
be sure to read the other books in Bronwyn Scott's
The Peveretts of Haberstock Hall miniseries

Lord Tresham's Tempting Rival
Saving Her Mysterious Soldier

And why not check out her other miniseries,
Rebellious Sisterhood?

Portrait of a Forbidden Love
Revealing the True Miss Stansfield
A Wager to Tempt the Runaway